Morse Meets the Media

The death of Sylvia Kaye had figured dramatically in Thursday afternoon's edition of *The Oxford Mail*, and prominently in the national press on Friday morning. On Friday evening the news bulletins on both B.B.C. and I.T.V. carried an interview with Chief Inspector Morse, who appealed for help from anyone who had been on the Woodstock Road between 6:40 p.m. and 7:15 p.m. on the evening of Wednesday, 29th September. Morse informed the nation that the police were looking for a very dangerous man who might attack again at any time; for the killer of Sylvia Kaye, when brought to justice, would face not only the charge of wilful murder, but also the charge of sexual assault and rape.

Lewis had stood in the background as Morse faced the camera crews and joined him after his performance was over.

'That damned wind!' said Morse, his hair blown into a tufted wilderness.

'Do you really think he might kill someone else, sir?'

'Doubt it very much,' said Morse.

Bantam offers the finest in classic and modern British murder mysteries.
Ask your bookseller for the books you have missed.

Agatha Christie
Death on the Nile
A Holiday for Murder
The Mousetrap and Other Plays
The Mysterious Affair at Styles
Poirot Investigates
Postern of Fate
The Secret Adversary
The Seven Dials Mystery
Sleeping Murder

Dorothy Simpson
Last Seen Alive
The Night She Died
Puppet for a Corpse
Six Feet Under
Close Her Eyes
Coming Soon: Element of Doubt

Sheila Radley
The Chief Inspector's Daughter
Death in the Morning
Fate Worse Than Death
Who Saw Him Die?

Elizabeth George
A Great Deliverance

Colin Dexter
Last Bus to Woodstock
The Riddle of the Third Mile
The Silent World of Nicholas Quinn
Service of All the Dead
The Dead of Jericho
The Secret of Annexe 3
Coming Soon: Last Seen Wearing

John Greenwood
The Mind of Mr. Mosley
The Missing Mr. Mosley
Mosley By Moonlight
Murder, Mr. Mosley
Mists Over Mosley
Coming Soon: What, Me,
     Mr. Mosley

Ruth Rendell
A Dark-Adapted Eye
   (writing as Barbara Vine)
A Fatal Inversion
   (writing as Barbara Vine)

Marian Babson
Death in Fashion
Reel Murder
Murder, Murder Little Star
Murder on a Mystery Tour

Christianna Brand
Suddenly at His Residence
Heads You Lose

Dorothy Cannell
The Widows Club
Coming Soon: Down the Garden
   Path

Michael Dibdin
Coming Soon: Ratking

LAST BUS TO WOODSTOCK

Colin Dexter

BANTAM BOOKS
TORONTO · NEW YORK · LONDON · SYDNEY · AUCKLAND

The characters in this novel and their actions
are imaginary. Their names and experiences
have no relation to those of actual people,
living or dead, except by coincidence.

*This edition contains the complete text
of the original hardcover edition.*
NOT ONE WORD HAS BEEN OMITTED.

LAST BUS TO WOODSTOCK

*A Bantam Book / published by arrangement with
St. Martin's Press*

PRINTING HISTORY

*St. Martin's edition published 1975
Bantam edition / January 1989*

ISBN 0-553-27777-4

Bantam Books are published by Bantam Books, a division of Bantam Doubleday Dell Publishing Group, Inc. Its trademark, consisting of the words "Bantam Books" and the portrayal of a rooster, is Registered in U.S. Patent and Trademark Office and in other countries. Marca Registrada, Bantam Books, 666 Fifth Avenue, New York, New York 10103

PRINTED IN THE UNITED STATES OF AMERICA

O   0 9 8 7 6 5 4 3 2 1

Prelude

"Let's wait just a *bit* longer, please," said the girl in dark-blue trousers and the light summer coat. "I'm sure there's one due pretty soon."

She wasn't quite sure though, and for the third time she turned to study the time-table affixed in its rectangular frame to Fare Stage 5. But her mind had never journeyed with any confidence in the world of columns and figures, and the finger tracing its tentatively horizontal course from the left of the frame had little chance of meeting, at the correct co-ordinate, the finger descending in a vaguely vertical line from the top. The girl standing beside her transferred her weight impatiently from one foot to the other and said, "I don' know abou' you."

"Just a minute. *Just a minute.*" She focused yet again on the relevant columns: 4, 4A (not after 18:00 hours), 4E, 4X (Saturdays only). Today was Wednesday. That meant . . . If 2 o'clock was 14:00 hours, that meant . . .

"Look, sweethear,' you please yourself bu' I'm going to hitch i'." Sylvia's habit of omitting all final "t"s seemed irritatingly slack. "It" in Sylvia's diction was little more than the most indeterminate of vowel sounds, articulated without the slightest hint of a consonantal finale. If they ever became better friends, it was something that ought to be mentioned.

What time was it now? 6:45 p.m. That would be 18:45. Yes. She was getting somewhere at last.

"Come on. We'll get a lif' in no time, you see. Tha's wha' half these fellas are looking for—a bi' of skir'."

And, in truth, there appeared no reason whatsoever to question Sylvia's brisk optimism. No accommodating motorist could fail to be impressed by her minimal skirting and the lovely invitation of the legs below.

For a brief while the two girls stood silently, in uneasy, static truce.

A middle-aged woman was strolling towards them, occasionally stopping and turning her head to gaze down the darkening length of the road that led to the heart of Oxford. She came to a halt a few yards away from the girls and put down her shopping bag.

"Excuse me," said the first girl. "Do you know when the next bus is?"

"There should be one in a few minutes, love." She peered again into the grey distance.

"Does it go to Woodstock?"

"No, I don't think so—it's just for Yarnton. It goes to the village, and then turns round and comes back."

"Oh." She stepped out towards the middle of the road, craned her neck, and stepped back as a little convoy of cars approached. Already, as the evening shaded into dusk, a few drivers had switched on their side-lights. No bus was in sight, and she felt anxious.

"We'll be all *righ'*," said Sylvia, a note of impatience in her voice. "You see. We'll be 'avin' a giggle abou' i' in the morning."

Another car. And another. Then again the stillness of the warm autumn evening.

"Well, you can stay if you like—I'm off." Her companion watched as Sylvia made her way towards the Woodstock roundabout, some two hundred yards up the road. It wasn't a bad spot for the hitch-hiker, for there the cars slowed down before negotiating the busy ring-road junction.

And then she decided. "Sylvia, wait!"; and holding one gloved hand to the collar of her lightweight summer coat, she ran with awkward, splay-footed gait in pursuit.

The middle-aged woman kept her watch at Fare Stage 5. She thought how many things had changed since she was young.

But Mrs. Mabel Jarman was not to wait for long. Vaguely her mind toyed with a few idle, random thoughts—nothing of any moment. Soon she would be home. As she was to remember later on, she could describe Sylvia fairly well: her long, blonde hair, her careless and provocative sensuality. Of the other girl she could recall little: a light coat, dark slacks—what colour, though? Hair—lightish brown? "Please try as hard as you can, Mrs. Jarman. It's absolutely vital for us that you remember as much as you can . . ." She noticed a few cars, and a heavy, bouncing articulated lorry, burdened with an improbably large number of wheel-less car-bodies. Men? Men with no other passengers? She would try so hard to recall. Yes, there had been men, she was sure of that. Several had passed her by.

At ten minutes to seven an oblong pinkish blur gradually assumed its firmer delineation. She picked up her bag as the red Corporation bus slowly threaded its way along the stops in the grey mid-distance. Soon she could almost read the bold white lettering above the driver's cab. What was it? She squinted to see it more clearly: WOODSTOCK. Oh dear! She had been wrong then, when that nicely-spoken young girl had asked about the next bus. Still, never mind! They hadn't gone far. They would either get a lift or see the bus and manage to get to the next stop, or even the stop after that. "How long had they been gone, Mrs. Jarman?"

She stood back a little from the bus-stop, and the Woodstock driver gratefully passed her by. Almost as soon as the bus was out of sight, she saw another, only a few hundred yards behind. This must be hers. The double-decker drew into the stop as Mrs. Jarman raised her hand. At two minutes past seven she was home.

Though a widow now, with her two children grown up and married, her pride-and-poverty semi-detached was still her real home, and her loneliness was not without its compensations. She cooked herself a generous supper, washed up, and turned on the television. She could never understand why there was so much criticism of the programmes. She herself enjoyed virtually everything and often wished she could view two channels simultaneously. At 10 o'clock she watched the main items on the News, switched off, and went to bed. At 10:30 she was sound asleep.

It was at 10:30 p.m., too, that a young girl was found lying in a Woodstock courtyard. She had been brutally murdered.

1
Search for a Girl

1
Wednesday, 29 September

From St. Giles in the centre of Oxford two parallel roads run due north, like the prongs of a tuning fork. On the northern perimeter of Oxford, each must first cross the busy northern ring-road, along which streams of frenetic motorists speed by, gladly avoiding the delights of the old university city. The eastern branch eventually leads to the town of Banbury, and thence continues its rather unremarkable course towards the heart of the industrial midlands; the western branch soon brings the motorist to the small town of Woodstock, some eight miles north of Oxford, and thence to Stratford-upon-Avon.

The journey from Oxford to Woodstock is quietly attractive. Broad grass verges afford a pleasing sense of spaciousness, and at the village of Yarnton, after only a couple of miles, a dual carriageway, with a tree-lined central reservation, finally sweeps the accelerating traffic past the airport and away from its earlier paralysis. For half a mile immediately before Woodstock, on the left-hand side, a grey stone wall marks the eastern boundary of the extensive and beautiful grounds of Blenheim Palace, the mighty mansion built by good Queen Anne for her brilliant general, John Churchill, First Duke of Marlborough. High and imposing wrought-iron gates mark the main entrance to the Palace drive, and hither flock the tourists in the summer season to walk amidst the dignified splendour of the great rooms, to stand before the vast Flemish tapestries of Malplaquet and Oudenarde, and to see the room in which was born that later scion of the Churchill line, the great Sir Winston himself, now lying in the once-peaceful churchyard of nearby Bladon village.

Today Blenheim dominates the old town. Yet it was not always so. The strong grey houses which line the main street have witnessed older times and could tell their older tales, though now the majority are sprucely converted into gift, antique and souvenir shops—and inns. There was always, it appears, a goodly choice of hostelries, and several of the hotels and inns now clustered snugly along the streets can boast not only an ancient lineage but also a cluster of black AA stars on their bright-yellow signs.

The Black Prince is situated halfway down a broad side-street to the left as one is journeying north. Amidst the Woodstock peerage it can claim no ancient pedigree, and it seems highly improbable, alas, that the warrior son of King Edward III had ever laughed or cried or tippled or wenched in any of its precincts. Truth to tell, a director of the London company which bought the old house, stable-yards and all, some ten years since, had noticed in some dubiously-authenticated guidebook that somewhere thereabouts the Prince was born. The director had been warmly congratulated by his Board for this felicitous piece of research, and not less for his subsequent discovery that the noble Prince did not as yet figure in the Woodstock telephone directory. *The Black Prince* it was then. The gifted daughter of the first manager had copied out from a children's encyclopaedia, in suitably antique script, a brief, if somewhat romantic, biography of the warrior Prince, and put the finished opus into her mother's oven for half an hour at 450°. The resultant manuscript, reverently brown with age, was neatly, if cheaply, framed and now occupied a suitable position of honour on the wall of the cocktail lounge. Together with the shields of the Oxford colleges nailed neatly along the low stained beams, it added tone and class.

For the last two and a half years Gaye had been the resident "hostess" of *The Black Prince*—"barmaid," thought the manager, was a trifle *infra dignitatem*. And he had a point. "A pint of your best bitter, luv," was a request Gaye seldom had to meet and she now associated it with the proletariat; here it was more often vodka and lime for the bright young things, Manhattan cocktails for the American tourists, and gin and French—with a splash of Italian—for the Oxford dons. Such admixtures she dispensed with practiced confidence from the silvery glitter and sparkle of bottles ranged invitingly behind the bar.

The lounge itself, deeply carpeted, with chairs and wall-seats covered in a pleasing orange shade, was gently bathed in half light, giving a chiaroscuro effect reminiscent, it was hoped, of a Rembrandt nativity scene. Gaye herself was an attractive, auburn-haired girl and tonight, Wednesday, she was immaculately dressed in a black trouser-suit and white-frilled blouse. A flash of gems on the second and third fingers of her left hand betokened gentle warning to the mawkish amateur playboy, and perhaps—as some maintained—a calculated invitation to the wealthy professional philanderer. She was, in fact, married and divorced, and now lived with one young son and a mother who was not unduly chagrined at the mildly promiscuous habits of a precious daughter who had been unfortunate enough to marry such "a lousy swine." Gaye enjoyed her divorced status as much as she enjoyed her job, and she meant to keep them both.

Wednesday, as usual, had been a fairly busy evening, and it was with some relief when, at 10:25 p.m., she politely, but firmly, called for last drinks. A young man, seated on a high stool at the inner corner of the bar, pushed his whisky glass forward.

"Same again."

Gaye glanced quizzically into unsteady eyes, but said nothing. She pushed her customer's glass under a priority whisky bottle and placed it on the counter, holding out her right hand and mechanically registering the tariff with her left.The young man was obviously drunk. He fumbled slowly and ineffectually through his pockets before finding the correct money, and after one mouthful of his drink he eased himself gingerly off his seat, measured the door with an uncertain eye, and made a line as decently straight as could in the circumstances be expected.

The old courtyard where once the horses had clattered over the cobbled stones had access from the street through a narrow archway, and had proved an invaluable asset to *The Black Prince*. A rash of fines for trespassing on the single and double yellow lines which bordered even the most inhospitable and inaccessible stretches of road was breeding a reluctant respect for the law; and any establishment offering "PATRONS ONLY, cars left at owners risk" was quite definitely in business. Tonight, as usual, the courtyard was tightly packed with the inevitable Volvos and Rovers. A light over the archway threw a patch of inadequate illumination over the entrance to the yard; the rest lay in dark shadow. It was to the far corner of this courtyard that the young man stumbled his way; and almost there he dimly saw something behind the furthest car. He looked and groped silently. Then horror crept up to the nape of his neck and against a padlocked stable door he was suddenly and violently sick.

2
Wednesday, 29 September

The manager of *The Black Prince*, Mr. Stephen Westbrook, contacted the police immediately after the body was found, and his call was acted upon with commendable promptitude. Sergeant Lewis of the Thames Valley Police gave him quick and clear instructions. A police car would be at *The Black Prince* within ten minutes; Westbrook was to ensure that no-one left the premises and that no-one entered the courtyard; if anyone insisted on leaving, he was to take the full name and address of the person concerned; he should be honest if asked what all the trouble was about.

The evening's merriness wilted like a sad balloon and voices gradually hushed as the whispered rumour spread: there had been a murder. None seemed anxious to leave; two or three asked if they could 'phone. All felt suddenly sober, including a pale-faced young man who stood in the manager's office and whose scarcely-touched whisky still stood on the counter of the cocktail lounge.

With the arrival of Sergeant Lewis and two uniformed constables, a small knot of people gathered curiously on the pavement opposite. It did not escape their notice that the police car had parked immediately across the access to the courtyard, effectively sealing the exit. Five minutes later a second police car arrived, and eyes turned to the lightly-built, dark-haired man who alighted. He conversed briefly with the constable who stood guard outside, nodded his head approvingly several times and walked into *The Black Prince*.

He knew Sergeant Lewis only slightly, but soon found himself pleasurably impressed by the man's level-headed competence. The two men conferred in brisk tones and very quickly a preliminary procedure was agreed. Lewis, with the help of the second constable, was to list the names, home addresses and car registrations of all persons on the premises, and to take brief statements of their evening's whereabouts, and immediate destinations. There were over fifty people to see, and Morse realised that it would take some time.

"Shall I try to get you some more help, sergeant?"

"I think the two of us can manage, sir."

"Good. Let's get started."

A door, forming the side entrance to *The Black Prince*, led out into the courtyard and from here Morse stepped gingerly out and looked around. He counted thirteen cars jammed tight into the limited space, but he could have missed one or two, for the cars furthest away were little more than dark hulks against the high back wall, and he wondered by what feats of advanced-motoring skill and precision their inebriated owners could ever negotiate the vehicles unscathed through the narrow exit from the yard. Carefully he shone his torch around and slowly perambulated the yard. The driver of the last car parked on the left-hand side of the yard had presciently backed into the narrow lot and left himself a yard or so of room between his nearside and the wall; and stretched along this space was the sprawling figure of a young girl. She lay on her right side, her head almost up against the corner of the walls, her long blonde hair now cruelly streaked with blood. It was immediately clear that she had been killed by a heavy blow across the back of the skull, and behind the body lay a flat heavy tyre-spanner, about one and a half inches across and some eighteen inches in length—the type of spanner with its undulating ends so common in the days before the inauguration of instant tyre repairs. Morse stood for a few minutes, gazing down at the ugly scene at his feet. The murdered girl wore a minimum of clothing—a pair of wedged-heeled shoes, a very brief dark-blue mini-skirt and a white blouse. Nothing else. Morse shone his torch on the upper part of the body. The left-hand side of the blouse was ripped across; the top two buttons were unfastened and the third had been wrenched away, leaving the full breasts almost totally exposed. Morse flashed his torch around and immediately spotted the missing button—a small, white, mother-of-pearl disc winking up at him from the cobbled ground. How he hated sex murders! He shouted to the constable standing at the entrance to the yard.

"Yes, sir?"

"We need some arc-lamps."

"It would help, I suppose, sir."

"Get some."

"Me, sir?"

"Yes, you!"

"Where shall I get. . . ?"

"How the hell do I know," bellowed Morse.

By a quarter to midnight Lewis had finished his task and he reported to Morse, who was sitting with *The Times* in the manager's office, drinking what looked very much like whisky.

"Ah, Lewis." He thrust the paper across. "Have a look at 14 down. Appropriate eh?" Lewis looked at 14 down: *Take in bachelor? It could do* (3). He saw what Morse had written into the completed diagram: BRA. What was he supposed to say? He had never worked with Morse before.

"Good clue, don't you think?"

Lewis, who had occasionally managed the *Daily Mirror* coffee-time crossword, was out of his depth, and felt much puzzled.

"I'm afraid I'm not very hot on crosswords, sir."

" 'Bachelor'—that's B.A. and 'take' is the letter 'r'; *recipe* in Latin. Did you never do any Latin?"

"No, sir."

"Do you think I'm wasting your time, Lewis?"

Lewis was nobody's fool and was a man of some honesty and integrity. "Yes, sir."

An engaging smile crept across Morse's mouth. He thought they would get on well together.

"Lewis, I want you to work with me on this case." The sergeant looked straight at Morse and into the hard, grey eyes. He heard himself say he would be delighted.

"This calls for a celebration," said Morse. "Landlord!" Westbrook had been hovering outside and came in smartly. "A double whisky." Morse pushed his glass forward.

"Would *you* like a drink, sir?" The manager turned hesitantly to Lewis.

"Sergeant Lewis is on duty, Mr. Westbrook."

When the manager returned, Morse asked him to assemble everyone on the premises, including staff, in the largest room available, and drinking his whisky in complete silence, skimmed through the remaining pages of the newspaper.

"Do you read *The Times*, Lewis?"

"No, sir; we take the *Mirror*." It seemed a rather sad admission.

"So do I sometimes," said Morse.

At a quarter past midnight Morse came into the restaurant-room where everyone was now gathered. Gaye's eyes met and held his briefly as he entered, and she felt a strong compulsion about the man. It was not so much that he seemed mentally to be undressing her, as most of the men she knew, but as if he had already done so. She listened to him with interest as he spoke.

He thanked them all for their patience and co-operation. It was getting very late and he didn't intend to keep them there any longer. They would now know why the police were there. There had been a murder in the courtyard—a young girl with blonde hair. They would appreciate that all the cars in the courtyard must stay where they were until the morning. He knew this meant that some of them would have difficulty getting home, but taxis had been ordered. If anyone wished to report to him or to Sergeant Lewis anything at all which might be of interest or value to the inquiry, however unimportant it might seem, would such a person please stay behind. The rest could go.

To Gaye it seemed an uninspired performance. Happening to be on the scene of a murder ought surely to be a bit more exciting than this? She would go home now, where her mother and her young son would be fast asleep. And even if they weren't, she couldn't tell them much, could she? Already the police had been there over an hour and a half. It wasn't exactly what she'd come to expect from her reading of Holmes or Poirot, who by this time would doubtless have interviewed the chief suspects, and made some startling deductions from the most trivial phenomena.

The murmuring which followed the end of Morse's brief address died away as most of the customers collected their coats and moved off. Gaye rose, too. Had she seen anything of interest or value? She thought back on the evening. There was, of course, the young man who had found the girl . . . She had seen him before, but she couldn't quite remember who it was he'd been with, or when. And then she had it— blonde hair! She'd been in the lounge with him only last week. But a lot of girls these days peroxided their hair. Perhaps it was worth mentioning? She decided it was and walked up to Morse.

"You said the girl who has been murdered had blonde hair." Morse looked at her and slowly nodded. "I think she was here last week—she was with the man who found her body tonight. I saw them here. I work in the lounge."

"That's very interesting, Miss—er?"

"Mrs. Mrs. McFee."

"Please forgive me, Mrs. McFee. I thought you might have been wearing all those rings to frighten off the boys who come to drool at you over the counter."

Gaye felt very angry. He was a hateful man. "Look, inspector whatever your name is, I came to tell you something I thought might be helpful. If you're going . . ."

"Mrs. McFee," broke in Morse gently, looking at her with an open nakedness in his eyes, "if I lived anywhere near, I'd come in myself and drool over you every night of the week."

At just after 1:00 a.m. a primitive, if reasonably effective, relay of arc-lamps was fixed around the courtyard. Morse had instructed Lewis to detain the young man who had found the murdered girl until they had taken the opportunity of investigating the courtyard more closely. The two men now surveyed the scene before them. There was a great deal of blood, and as Sergeant Lewis looked down on her, he felt a deep revulsion against the violence and senselessness of murder. Morse appeared more interested in the starry heavens above.

"Do you study the stars, Lewis?"

"I read the horoscopes sometimes, sir."

Morse appeared not to hear. "I once heard of a group of schoolchildren, Lewis, who tried to collect a million matchsticks. After they'd filled the whole of the school premises, they decided they'd have to pack it up." Lewis thought it his duty to say something, but all appropriate comment eluded him.

After a while, Morse reverted his attention to more terrestrial things, and the two of them looked down again at the murdered girl. The spanner and the solitary white button lay where Morse had seen them earlier. There was nothing much else to see but for the trail of dried blood that led almost from one end of the back wall to the other.

The young man sat in the manager's office. His mother, though expecting him to be late, would be getting worried; and so was he. Morse finally came in at 1:30 a.m. whilst the police surgeon, the photographers and the fingerprint men busied themselves about the courtyard.

"Name?" he asked.

"Sanders, John Sanders."

"You found the body?"

"Yes, sir."

"Tell me about it."

"There's not much to tell really."

Morse smiled. "Then we needn't keep you long, need we, Mr. Sanders?"

The young man fidgeted. Morse sat opposite him, looked him hard in the eye and waited.

"Well, I just walked into the courtyard and there she was. I didn't touch her, but I knew she was dead. I came straight back in to tell the manager."

Morse nodded. "Anything else?"

"Don't think so."

"When were you sick, Mr. Sanders?"

"Oh yes. I was sick."

"Was it after or before you saw the girl?"

"After. It must have upset me seeing her there—sort of shock, I suppose."

"Why don't you tell me the truth?"

"What do you mean?"

Morse sighed. "You haven't got your car here have you?"

"I haven't got a car."

"Do you usually have a stroll round the courtyard before you go home?" Sanders said nothing. "How much drink did you have tonight?"

"A few whiskies—I wasn't drunk."

"Mr. Sanders, do you want me to find out from someone else?" It was clear from Sanders's manner that he hardly welcomed an inquiry along such lines. "What time did you come here?" continued Morse.

"About half past seven."

"And you got drunk and went out to be sick." Reluctantly Sanders agreed. "Do you usually drink on your own?"

"Not usually."

"Who were you waiting for?" Sanders did not reply. "She didn't show up?"

"No," he said flatly.

"But she did come, didn't she?"

"No, I told you. I was on my own all the time."

"But she did come, didn't she?" repeated Morse quietly. Sanders looked beaten. "She came and you saw her. You saw her in the courtyard, and she was dead."

The young man nodded.

"We'd better have a little chat, you and me," said Morse ungrammatically.

3

Thursday, 30 September

As he stood alone in the bedroom of Sylvia Kaye, Morse felt measurably relieved. The grim duties of the night were over, and he switched on the natural defence mechanism of his weary mind. He wished to forget the awakening of Mrs. Dorothy Kaye, and the summoning of her husband from his night-shift in the welding division of the Cowley car plant; the fatuous, coarse recriminations and the overwhelming hurt of their bitter, empty misery. Sylvia's mother was now under sedation, postponing the day and the reckoning; whilst Sergeant Lewis sat at headquarters learning what he could from Sylvia's father. He took many pages of careful notes but doubted if it all amounted to much. He was to join Morse in half an hour.

The bedroom was small, one of three in a neat semi-detached house in Jackdaw Court, a quiet crescent with rotting wooden fences, a few minutes' walk off the Woodstock Road. Morse sat down on the narrow bed and looked around him. He wondered if the neatness of the bed was mum's doing, for the remainder of the room betrayed the slack and untidy living of the murdered girl. A vast coloured portrait of a pop artist was pinned rather precariously above the gas fire in the chimney breast, and Morse reminded himself that he might understand young people rather better if he had a teenage family of his own; as it was, the identity of the handsome youth was cloaked in anonymity and whatever pretentions he may have had would for Morse be forever unknown. Several items of underwear draped the table and chair which, with a whitewood wardrobe, substantively comprised the only other furniture. Morse gingerly picked up a flimsy black bra lying on the chair. His mind flashed back to that first glimpse of Sylvia Kaye, rested there a few seconds and slowly returned through the tortuous byways of the last unpleasant hours. A pile of women's magazines was awkwardly stacked on the window-sill, and Morse cursorily flicked his way through make-up hints, personal problems and horoscopes. Not even a paragraph of pornography. He opened the wardrobe door and with perceptibly deeper interest examined the array of skirts, blouses, slacks and dresses. Clean and untidy. Mounds of shoes, ultra-modern, wedged, ugly: she wasn't short of money. On the table Morse saw a travel brochure for package trips to Greece, Yugoslavia and Cyprus, white hotels, azure seas and small print about insurance liability and smallpox regulations; a letter from Sylvia's employer explaining the complexities of VAT, and a diary, the latter revealing nothing but a single entry for 2 January: "Cold. Went to see *Ryan's Daughter*."

Lewis tapped on the bedroom door and entered. "Find anything, sir?" Morse looked at his cheerful sergeant distastefully, and said nothing. "Can I?" asked Lewis, his hand hovering above the diary.

"Go ahead," said Morse.

Lewis examined the diary, turning carefully through the days of September. Finding nothing, he worked meticulously through every page. "Only one day filled in, sir."

"I don't even get that far," said Morse.

"Do you think 'cold' means it was a cold day or she had a cold?"

"How do I know?" snapped Morse, "and what the hell does it matter?"

"We could find out where *Ryan's Daughter* was on in the first week of January," suggested Lewis.

"Yes, we could. And how much the diary cost and who gave it to her and where she buys her biros from. Sergeant! We're running a murder inquiry not a stationery shop!"

"Sorry."

"You may be right though," added Morse.

"I'm afraid Mr. Kaye hadn't got much to tell me, either, sir. Did you want to see him?"

"No. Leave the poor fellow alone."

"We're not making very rapid progress then."

"Oh, I don't know," said Morse. "Miss Kaye was wearing a white blouse, wasn't she?"

"Yes."

"What colour bra would your wife wear under a white blouse?"

"A lightish-coloured one, I suppose."

"She wouldn't wear a black one?"

"It would show through."

"Mm. By the way, Lewis, do you know when lighting-up time was yesterday evening?"

" 'Fraid I don't, off hand," replied Lewis, "but I can soon find out for you."

"No need for that," said Morse. "According to the diary you just inspected, yesterday, 29 September, was St. Michael and All Angels' day and lighting-up time was 6:40 p.m."

Lewis followed his superior officer down the narrow stairs, and wondered what was coming next. Before they reached the front door, Morse half turned his head: "What do you think of Women's Lib, Lewis?"

At 11:00 a.m. Sergeant Lewis interviewed the manager of the Town and Gown Assurance Company, situated on the second and third storeys above a flourishing tobacconist's shop in The High. Sylvia had worked there—her first job —for just over a year. She was a copy-typist, having failed to satisfy the secretarial college at which she had studied for two years after leaving school that the ungainly and frequently undecipherable scrawls in her short-hand notebook bore sufficient relationship to the missives originally dictated. But her typing was reasonably accurate and clean, and the company, the manager assured Lewis, had no complaints about its late employee. She had been punctual and unobtrusive.

"Attractive?"

"Well—er, yes. I suppose she was," replied the manager. Lewis made a note and wished Morse were there; but the inspector said he felt thirsty and had gone into *The Minster* across the way.

"She worked, you say, with two other girls," said Lewis. "I think I'd better have a word with them if I can."

"Certainly, officer." The manager, Mr. Palmer, seemed a fraction relieved.

Lewis questioned the two young ladies at considerable length. Neither was "a particklar friend" of Sylvia. She had, as far as they knew, no regular beau. Yes, she had boasted occasionally of her sexual exploits—but so did most of the girls. She was friendly enough, but not really "one of the girls."

Lewis looked through her desk. The usual *bric à brac*. A bit of a broken mirror, a comb with a few blonde hairs in it, yesterday's *Sun*, pencils galore, rubbers, typewriter ribbons, carbons. On the wall behind Sylvia's desk was pinned a photograph of Omar Sharif, flanked by a typewritten holiday rota. Lewis saw that Sylvia had been on a fortnight's holiday in the latter half of July, and he asked the two girls where she'd been to.

"Stayed at home, I think," replied the elder of the two girls, a quiet, serious-looking girl in her early twenties.

Lewis sighed. "You don't seem to know much about her, do you?" The girls said nothing. Lewis tried his best to elicit a little more co-operation, but met with little success. He left the office just before mid-day, and strolled over to *The Minster*.

"Poor Sylvia," said the younger girl after he had gone.

"Yes, poor Sylvia," replied Jennifer Coleby.

Lewis eventually, and somewhat to his surprise, discovered Morse in the "gentlemen only" bar at the back of *The Minster*.

"Ah, Lewis." He rose and placed his empty glass on the bar. "What's it to be?" Lewis asked for a pint of bitter. "Two pints of your best bitter," said Morse cheerfully to the man behind the bar, "and have one yourself."

It became clear to Lewis that the topic of conversation before his arrival had been horse racing. Morse picked up a copy of *Sporting Life* and walked over to the corner with his assistant.

"You a betting man, Lewis?"

"I sometimes put a few bob on the Derby and the National, sir, but I'm not a regular gambler."

"You keep it that way," said Morse, with a note of seriousness in his voice. "But look here, what do you think of that?" He unfolded the racing paper and pointed to one of the runners in the 3:15 at Chepstow: The Black Prince. "Worth a quid, would you say, sergeant?"

"Certainly an odd coincidence."

"10 to 1," said Morse, drinking deeply on his beer.

"Are you going to back it, sir?"

"I already have," said Morse, glancing up at the old barman.

"Isn't that illegal, sir?"

"I never studied that side of the law." Doesn't he want to solve this murder, thought Lewis, and as if Morse read his unspoken words he was promptly asked for a report on the deceased's position with Town and Gown. Lewis did his best, and Morse did not interrupt. He seemed rather more interested in his pint of beer. When he finished, Morse told him to get back to headquarters, type his reports, then get home and have some sleep. Lewis didn't argue. He felt dog-tired, and sleep was fast becoming a barely-remembered luxury.

"Nothing else, sir?"

"Not until tomorrow when you'll report to me at 7:30 a.m. sharp—unless you want to put a few bob on The Black Prince." Lewis felt in his pocket and pulled out 50p.

"Each way, do you think?"

"You'll kick yourself if it wins," said Morse.

"All right. 50p to win."

Morse took the 50p, and as Lewis left he saw the barman pocket the coin, and pull a further pint for the enigmatic chief inspector.

4
Friday, 1 October

Prompt at 7:30 next morning, Lewis tapped on the inspector's door. Receiving no answer, he cautiously tried the knob and peered round the door. No sign of life. He walked back to the front vestibule and asked the desk-sergeant if Inspector Morse was in yet.

"Not seen 'im."

"He said he'd be here at half-seven."

"Well, you know the inspector."

I wish I did, thought Lewis. He walked along to pick up the reports he had wearily typed out the previous afternoon, and read them through carefully. He'd done his best, but there was little to go on. He walked on to the canteen and ordered a cup of coffee. Constable Dickson, an officer whom

Lewis knew fairly well, was enthusiastically assaulting a plate of bacon and tomatoes.

"How's the murder job going, sarge?"

"Early days yet."

"Old Morse in charge, eh?"

"Yep."

"Funny bugger, isn't he?" Lewis didn't disagree. "I know one thing," said Dickson. "He was here till way gone midnight. Got virtually everyone in the building jumping about for him. I reckon every 'phone on the premises was red hot. God, he can work, that chap, when he wants to."

Lewis felt a little shame-faced. He himself had slept sweetly and soundly from six the previous evening until six that morning. He reckoned that Morse deserved his sleep, and sat down to drink a cup of coffee.

Ten minutes later a freshly-shaven Morse walked brightly into the canteen. "Ah, there you are Lewis. Sorry to be late." He ordered a coffee and sat opposite. "Bad news for you, I'm afraid." Lewis looked up sharply. "You lost your money. The constipated camel came in second."

Lewis smiled. "Never mind, sir. I just hope you didn't lose too much yourself."

Morse shook his head. "Oh no, I didn't lose anything; in fact I made a few quid. I backed it each way."

"But . . ." began Lewis.

"C'mon," said Morse. "Drink up. We've got work to do."

For the next few hours the two of them were busy sorting the reports flowing in from the wide-flung inquiries Morse had initiated the previous day. At twelve noon, Lewis felt he knew more about Sylvia Kaye than he did about his wife. He read each report with great care—Morse's orders—and felt that many of the facts were beginning to fix themselves firmly in his mind. Morse, he noticed, devoured the reports with an amazing rapidity, reminiscent of someone skipping through a tedious novel; yet occasionally he would re-read the odd report with a fascinated concentration.

"Well?" said Morse finally.

"I think I've got most things pretty straight, sir."

"Good."

"You seemed to find one or two of the reports very interesting, sir."

"Did I?" Morse sounded surprised.

"You spent about ten minutes on that one from the secretarial college, and it's only half a page."

"You're very observant, Lewis, but I'm sorry to disappoint
you. It was the most ill-written report I've seen in years,
with twelve—no less—grammatical monstrosities in ten lines!
What's the force coming to?"

Lewis didn't know what the force was coming to and
hadn't the courage to inquire into the inspector's statistical
findings on his own erratic style. He asked instead, "Do you
think we're getting anywhere, sir?"

"Doubt it," replied Morse.

Lewis wasn't so sure. Sylvia's movements on the previous
Wednesday seemed established. She had left the office in
The High at 5:00 p.m., and almost certainly walked the
hundred yards or so to the No 2 bus stop outside University
College. She had arrived home at 5:35 p.m. and had a good
meal. She told her mother she might be late home, left the
house at roughly 6:30 p.m. wearing—as far as could be
established—the clothes in which she was found. Somehow
she had got to Woodstock. It all seemed to Lewis a promising
enough starting-point for a few preliminary inquiries.

"Would you like me to get on to the bus company, sir,
and see the drivers on the Woodstock run?"

"Done it," said Morse.

"No good?" Disappointment showed in the sergeant's voice.

"I don't think she went by bus."

"Taxi, sir?"

"Improbable wouldn't you think?"

"I don't know, sir. It might not be all that expensive."

"Perhaps not, but it seems most improbable to me. If she'd
wanted a taxi, she'd have rung up from home—there's a
'phone there."

"She may have done just that, sir."

"She didn't. No 'phone call was made by any member of
the Kaye household yesterday."

Lewis was experiencing a dangerous failure of confidence. "I don't seem to be much help," he said. But Morse ignored the comment.

"Lewis, how would you go from Oxford to Woodstock?"

"By car, sir."

"She hadn't got a car."

"Get a lift with one of her friends?"

"You wrote the report. She doesn't seem to have had many girl friends."

"A boy friend, you think, sir?"

"Do you?"

Lewis thought a minute. "Bit odd if she was going with a boy friend. Why didn't he pick her up at her house?"

"Why not, indeed?"

"She wasn't picked up at home?"

"No. Her mother saw her walking away."

"You've interviewed her mother then, sir."

"Yes. I spoke to her last night."

"Is she very upset?"

"She's got broad shoulders, Lewis, and I rather like her. Of course she's terribly upset and shocked. But not quite so heartbroken as I thought she'd be. In fact I got the idea her beautiful daughter was something of a trial to her."

Morse walked over to a large mirror, took out a comb and began to groom his thinning hair. He carefully drew a few strands across the broad area of nakedness at the back of his skull, returned the comb to his pocket and asked a perplexed Sergeant Lewis what he thought of the effect.

"You see, Lewis, if Sylvia didn't go by bus, taxi or boy friend, how on earth did she ever get to Woodstock? And remember that get to Woodstock somehow she assuredly did."

"She must have hitched it, sir."

Morse was still surveying himself in the mirror. "Yes, Lewis, I think she did. And that is why," he took out the comb again and made some further passes at his straggling hair, "that is why I think I must put in a little TV appearance tonight." He picked up the 'phone and put through a call to the Chief Superintendent. "Go and get some lunch, Lewis. I'll see you later."

"Can I order anything for you, sir?"

"No. I've got to watch my figure," said Morse.

The death of Sylvia Kaye had figured dramatically in Thursday afternoon's edition of *The Oxford Mail*, and prominently in the national press on Friday morning. On Friday evening the news bulletins on both BBC and ITV carried an interview with Chief Inspector Morse, who appealed for help from anyone who had been on the Woodstock Road between 6:40 p.m. and 7:15 p.m. on the evening of Wednesday, 29 September. Morse informed the nation that the police were looking for a very dangerous man who might attack again at any time; for the killer of Sylvia Kaye, when brought to justice, would face not only the charge of wilful murder, but also the charge of sexual assault and rape.

Lewis had stood in the background as Morse faced the camera crews and joined him after his performance was over.

"That damned wind!" said Morse, his hair blown into a tufted wilderness.

"Do you really think he might kill someone else, sir?"

"Doubt it very much," said Morse.

5
Friday, 1 October

Each evening of the week, with rare exceptions, Mr. Bernard Crowther left his small detached house in Southdown Road, North Oxford, at approximately 9:40 p.m. Each evening his route was identical. Methodically closing behind him the white gate which enclosed a small, patchy strip of lawn, he would turn right, walk to the end of the road, turn right again, and make his way, with perceptible purposefulness in his stride, towards the lounge bar of *The Fletcher's Arms*. Though an articulate man, indeed an English don at Lonsdale College, he found it difficult to explain either to his disapproving wife or indeed to himself exactly what it was that attracted him to this unexceptionable pub, with its ill-assorted, yet regular and amiable clientele.

On the night of Friday, 1 October, however, Crowther would have been observed to remain quite still for several seconds after closing the garden gate behind him, his eyes downcast and disturbed as if he were pondering deep and troublous thoughts; and then to turn, against his habit and his inclination, to his left. He walked slowly to the end of the road, where, on the left beside a row of dilapidated garages, stood a public telephone-box. Impatient at the best of times, and this was not the best of times, he waited restlessly and awkwardly, pacing to and fro, consulting his watch and throwing wicked glances at the portly woman inside the kiosk who appeared ill-equipped to face the triangular threat of the gadgeted apparatus before her, an unco-operative telephone exchange and her own one-handed negotiations with the assorted coinage in her purse. But she was fighting on and Crowther, in a generous moment, wondered if one of her children had been taken suddenly and seriously ill with dad on the night-shift and no-one else to help. But he doubted whether her call was as important as the one he was about to make. News bulletins had always gripped his attention, however trivial the items reported; and the item he had watched on the BBC news at 9:00 p.m. had been far from trivial. He could remember verbatim the words the police inspector had used: "We shall be very glad if any motorist . . ." Yes, he could tell them something, for he had played his part in the terrifying and tragic train of events. But what was he going to say? He couldn't tell them the truth. Nor even half the truth. His fragile resolution began to crumble. He'd give that wretched woman another minute—one minute and no longer.

At 9:50 p.m. that same evening an excited Sergeant Lewis put through a call to Chief Inspector Morse. "A break, sir. I think we've got a break."

"Oh?"

"Yes. A witness, sir. A Mrs. Mabel Jarman. She saw the murdered girl . . ."

"You mean," interrupted Morse, "she saw the girl who was later murdered, I suppose."

"That's it. We can get a full statement as soon as we like."

"You mean you haven't got one yet?"

"She only rang five minutes ago, sir. I'm going over straightaway. She's local. I wondered if you wanted to come."

"No," said Morse.

"All right, sir. I'll have the whole thing typed up and ready for you in the morning."

"Good."

"Bit of luck, though, isn't it? We'll soon get on to this other girl."

"What other girl?" said Morse quietly.

"Well, you see, sir . . ."

"What's Mrs. Jarman's address?" Morse reluctantly took off his bedroom slippers, and reached for his shoes.

"Bit late on parade tonight, Bernard. What's it to be?"

Bernard was well liked at *The Fletcher's Arms*, always ready to fork out for his round—and more. All the regulars knew him for a man of some academic distinction; but he was a good listener, laughed as heartily as the next at the latest jokes, and himself occasionally waxed eloquent on the stupidity of the government and the incompetence of Oxford United. But tonight he spoke of neither. By 10:25 p.m. he had drunk three pints of best bitter with his usual practised fluency and got up to go.

" 'nother one before you go, Bernard?"

"Thanks, no. I've had just about enough of that horse piss for one night."

"You in the dog house again?"

"I'm always in the bloody dog house."

He walked back slowly. He knew that if the bedroom light was on, his wife, Margaret, would be reading in bed, waiting only for her errant husband to return. If there was no light, she would probably be watching TV. He came to a decision as foolish as the ones he had made as a boy when he would race a car to the nearest lamp-post. If she was in bed, he would go straight in, if she was still up, he would ring the police. He turned into the road, and saw immediately that the bedroom light was on.

Mrs. Jarman gave her testimony in a brisk, if excited, fashion. Her memory proved surprisingly clear, and Sergeant Lewis's notes grew fat with factual data. Morse left things to him. He wondered if Lewis had been right in thinking this was the big break, and considered, on reflection, that he was. He himself felt impatient and bored with the trained and thorough pedanticism with which his sergeant probed and queried the chronology of the bus-stop encounter. But he knew it had to be done and he knew that Lewis was doing it well. For three quarters of an hour he left them to it.

"Well, I want to thank you very much, Mrs. Jarman." Lewis closed his note-book and looked, in a mildly satisfied manner, towards his chief.

"Perhaps," said Morse, "I could ask you to come to see us in the morning? Sergeant Lewis will have your statement typed out, and we'd like you to have a look through it to see that he's got it all right—just a formality, you know."

Lewis stood up to go, but Morse's veiled glance told him to sit down again.

"I wonder, Mrs. Jarman," he said, "if you could do us one last favour. I'd just love a cup of tea. I know it's late but . . ."

"Why, of course, inspector. I wish you'd said so before." She hurried off and the policemen heard a spurt of water and a clatter of cups.

"Well, sergeant, you've done a good job."

"Thank you, sir."

"Now listen. That bus. Get on to it as soon as you can."

"But you said you'd checked the buses, sir."

"Well check 'em again."

"All right."

"And," said Morse, "there's that articulated lorry. With a bit of luck we can trace that."

"You think we can?"

"You've got a definite time—what else do you want, man?"

"Anything else, sir?" said Lewis in a subdued voice.

"Yes. Stay and make a few more notes. I won't be long."

The kitchen door opened and Mrs. Jarman re-appeared. "I was just wondering whether you gentlemen would like a little drop of whisky, instead of tea. I've had a bottle since Christmas—I don't usually drink myself."

"Now, now," said Morse, "you are a very resourceful woman, Mrs. Jarman." Lewis smiled wanly. He knew what was coming. *Déjà vu*.

"I think a little drop of Scotch would do me the power of good. Perhaps you'll have a drop yourself?"

"Oh no, sir, I'll have a cuppa, if you don't mind." She opened a drawer in the cupboard and brought out two glass tumblers.

"Just the one glass then, Mrs. Jarman," said Morse. "It's a pity, I know, but Sergeant Lewis here is on duty and you will appreciate that a policeman is not allowed to consume any alcoholic drink whilst on duty. You wouldn't want him to break the law, would you?"

Lewis muttered to himself.

Morse smiled into his liberal dose of whisky whilst his assistant soberly stirred a diminutive cup of wickedly dark brown tea.

"Mrs. Jarman I just want to ask you one or two more questions about what you've said to Sergeant Lewis. I hope you don't feel too tired?"

"Oh no."

"Do you remember how this 'other girl' seemed? Was she a bit cross? A bit nervous?"

"I don't think she was—well, I don't know. Perhaps she was a bit nervous."

"A bit frightened?"

"Oh no. Not that. A bit sort of, er, excited. Yes, that's it, a bit excited."

"Excited and impatient?"

"I think so."

"Now, I want you to think back. Just close your eyes if you like, and picture yourself at the bus-stop again. Can you recall anything, anything at all, that she said. She asked you if the next bus went to Woodstock. You've told us that. Anything else?"

"I can't remember. I just can't seem to remember."

"Now, Mrs. Jarman, don't rush yourself. Just relax and picture it all again. Take your time."

Mrs. Jarman closed her eyes and Morse watched her with keen anticipation. She said nothing. Morse at last broke the embarrassing silence. "What about the girl who was murdered? Did she say anything else? She wanted to hitch-hike, you said."

"Yes, she kept saying something like 'Come on.' "

" 'It'll be all right'?" added Morse.

"Yes. It'll be all right. We'll have a giggle about it in the morning."

Morse's blood froze. He remained utterly motionless. But Mrs. Jarman's memory had dredged its last.

Morse relaxed. "We've kept you up late, but you've been wonderful. And this must be a real priority brand of Scotch?"

"Oh, would you like a little drop more, sir?"

"Well, I think I wouldn't perhaps say no, Mrs. Jarman. Yes, a drop of the finest Scotch I've tasted in years."

As Mrs. Jarman turned her back to refill his glass, Morse sternly motioned Lewis to stay where he was, and for the next half hour he tried with every subtlety he knew to jog the good lady's recollection of her chance encounter with the murdered girl and her companion. But to no avail.

"Just one more thing, Mrs. Jarman. When you come to see us in the morning, we shall be holding an identity parade. It won't take more than a minute or two."

"You mean you want me to . . . Oh dear!"

At 11:45 p.m. Morse and Lewis took their leave of Mrs. Jarman. They were standing by their cars when the door of the house suddenly opened again and Mrs. Jarman came hurriedly towards Morse.

"There's just one more thing, sir. I've just remembered. When you said close your eyes and just picture things. I've thought of something. That other girl, sir. When she run, she run with a sort of splay-footed run—do you know what I mean, sir?"

"Yes I do," said Morse.

The two men returned to HQ. After inquiring whether

any further calls had come through and learning there were none, Morse called Lewis to his office.

"Well, my friend?" Morse looked pleased with himself.

"You told her we're going to have an identity parade?" asked a puzzled Lewis.

"We are. Now tell me this. What would you say was the most vital fact we learned from Mrs. Jarman?"

"We learned quite a few pieces of valuable information."

"Yes, we did. But only one fact that really made your hair stand on end, eh?" Lewis tried to look intelligent. "We learned, did we not," said Morse, "that the girls would have a bit of a giggle about it all in the morning?"

"Oh, I see," said Lewis, not seeing.

"You see what it means? They would be meeting in the morning—Thursday morning, and we know that Sylvia Kaye was in employment and we know where, do we not?"

"So the other girl works there, too."

"The evidence would seem to point very much that way, Lewis."

"But I was there, sir, and none of them said a word."

"Don't you find that very interesting?"

"I don't seem to have done a very good job, do I?" Lewis looked disconsolately down at the chief inspector's carpet.

"But don't you see," continued Morse, "we now know that one of the girls—how many were there?"

"Fourteen."

"That one of those girls is at the very least withholding vital evidence and at the best telling us a heap of lies."

"I didn't talk to them all, sir."

"Good God, man! They knew what you were there for, didn't they? One of their colleagues is murdered. A sergeant of the murder squad comes to their office. What the hell did they think you'd gone for? Service the bloody typewriters? No, you did well, Lewis. You didn't force our little girl to weave her tangled web for us. She thinks she's OK and that's how I want it." Morse got up. "I want you to get some sleep, Lewis. You've got work to do in the morning. But just before you go, find me the private address of Mr. Palmer. I think a little visit is called for."

"You're not thinking of knocking him up now, are you, sir?"

"Not only am I going to knock him up as you put it, Lewis, I am going to ask him, very nicely of course, to open up his offices for me and I am going to look through the private drawers of fourteen young ladies. It should be an exciting business."

"Won't you need a search-warrant, sir?"

"I never did understand the legal situation over search-warrants," complained Morse.

"I think you ought to have one, sir."

"And perhaps you'll let me know where the hell I find anyone to sign a warrant at this time of the night—or morning, whatever it is."

"But if Mr. Palmer insists on his legal rights . . ." began Lewis.

"I shall tell him we're trying to find out who raped and murdered one of his girls," snapped Morse, "not looking for dirty postcards from Pwllheli!"

"Wouldn't you like me to come with you, sir?"

"No. Do as I say and go to bed."

"Well, good luck, sir."

"I shan't need it," said Morse. "I know you'd never believe it, but I can be an officious bastard when I want to be. Mr. Palmer will be out of bed as if he'd got a flea in his pyjama bottoms."

But the manager of the Town and Gown Assurance Co., though condescending to get out of bed, flatly refused to get out of his pyjamas—top or bottom. He asked Morse for his authority to search his offices, and once having established that Morse had none, he proved adamant to all the cajolings and threats that Morse could muster. The inspector reflected that he had badly underestimated the little manager. After prolonged negotiation, however, a policy was finally agreed. All the staff of the Town and Gown would be assembled in the manager's office at 8:45 a.m. the following morning, where they would all be asked if they had any objection to the police opening any incoming private correspondence. If there were no objection (Palmer assured

Morse), the inspector could open all correspondence, and, if need be, make confidential copies of any letter which might be of value. Furthermore all the female employees would be asked to attend an identity parade at the Thames Valley HQ some time later the same morning. Palmer would need some time to arrange a skeleton servicing of the telephone exchange and other vital matters. It was a good job it was Saturday; the office closed at mid-day.

Perhaps, thought Morse in retrospect, things hadn't worked out too badly. He wearily drove to HQ and wondered why, with all his experience, he had rushed so wildly into such an ill-considered and probably futile scheme as he had contemplated. Yet, for all that, he thought that he had in some strange way been right. He felt in his bones that there was an urgency about this stage of the investigation. He felt he was poised for a big breakthrough, though he did not at this stage realise how many breaks-through would be required before the case was solved. Nor did he realise that in an oddly perverse way Palmer's refusal to allow him unauthorized entry to his premises had presented him with one gigantic piece of luck. For a letter, addressed to one of the young ladies in Palmer's employ, was already on its way, and no power on earth, except the inefficiency of some unsuspecting sorting clerk, could—or indeed did—prevent its prompt delivery.

Morse returned to HQ and spent the next hour at his desk. He finished at 4:15 a.m. and sat back in his black leather chair. Little point in going home now. He pondered the case, at first with a slow, methodical analysis of the facts known hitherto and then with what, if he had been wider awake, he would wish to have called a series of swift, intuitive leaps, all of which landed him in areas of twilight and darkness. But he knew that whatever had taken place on Wednesday evening had its causation in the activities of certain persons, and that these persons had been motivated by the ordinary passions of love and hate and greed and jealousy. That wasn't the puzzle at all. It was the interlocking of the jig-saw pieces, those pieces that would now be coming into his hands. He dozed off. He fitfully dreamed of an attractive red-headed barmaid and a blonde beauty with

blood all over her hair. He always seemed to dream of women.
He sometimes wondered what he would dream about if he
got himself married. Women probably, he thought.

6
Saturday, 2 October, a.m.

"What *next*?" said Judith, Mr. Palmer's confidential secretary. "Opening our letters, he said!"

"You could have said no," replied Sandra, an amiable,
feckless girl, who had, on merit, made no advance either in
status or in salary since joining the office three years ago.

"I almost did," chimed in Ruth, a flutter-lashed girl with
the brains of a butterfly. "If Bob sent me one of his real
passionate ones, coo!" She giggled nervously.

Most of the girls were young and unmarried and lived
with their parents, and because of late morning postal de-
liveries and a fear that parents might pry into matters not
concerning them, several of them had invited their corre-
spondents to address mail to the office. Indeed, so many
incoming letters were marked "Private and Confidential,"
"Personal" and the like, that an unsuspecting observer might
have surmised that the Town and Gown was the headquarters of a classified intelligence department. But Palmer
countenanced such mild abuse of his establishment with
philosophic quietude, whilst at the same time keeping a
hawk-like eye on the office telephone accounts. It seemed
to him a fair arrangement.

Each girl in her own way had been a little overawed by
Morse, and his quietly-spoken requests were conceded with
no audible murmur of dissent. Of course they all wanted to
help. In any case he was only going to get copies of the mail
and everything would be treated with the utmost confidentiality. Nevertheless Ruth had given an audible sigh of relief
on discovering that this was a morning when Bob had tem-

porarily exhausted his supply of lecherous suggestions. However broadminded they were, well . . .

"I think we all ought to help them find out about poor old Sylvia," said Sandra. For all her low-geared intellect she was a girl of ready sensitivity and had been deeply saddened, and a little frightened, by Sylvia's death. She wished in her own innocent way that she could contribute something to the inquiry, and she sensed disappointment, though little surprise, that no-one had written to her.

There were seven personal letters and two postcards for Morse to study, and as he cursorily cast his eye over each before placing it in the copying machine, he felt it was all rather foolish. Still, there was the identity parade, of which he had high hopes, although here again in the sobering light of morning the expectancy index had already fallen several points.

"Have you been on an identity parade before?" said Sandra.

"Of course not," replied Judith. "People don't get involved in murders every week, do they?"

"Just wondered."

"We do what we're told." Judith believed passionately in the virtues of authority, and she sometimes wished that Mr. Palmer, though he was very nice of course, would be just a little firmer and not quite so friendly with one or two of his employees.

"I saw one once at the pictures," said Sandra.

"I saw one on the telly," said Ruth. "Will it be like that?"

Afterwards they decided it was like that. Disappointing really. A nondescript woman walked along and looked at each of them as they spoke the words, "Do you know when the next bus is?" You couldn't really be frightened of her. Wouldn't it have been awful, though, if she'd put her hand on your shoulder? But she didn't. She'd walked past all the girls and then walked back and then walked off. That inspector—he'd been hoping, hadn't he? And that was a bit funny at the end, wasn't it? Running to the door at the far end of the yard. What was that all about?

"They got the crook in the picture," said Sandra.

"And on the telly," said Ruth.

"You shouldn't believe all you see," said Judith.

Morse was sitting in his office at mid-day, when Lewis came in. "Well, sir? Any good?"

Morse shook his head.

"No good at all?"

"She thought two or three of them might be her."

"Well, that narrows it down a bit, sir."

"Not really. I've heard defending counsels make powdered mincemeat out of witnesses who swore on their grandfathers' graves that they were absolutely *positive* about an identification. No, Lewis. It doesn't help us much, I'm afraid."

"What about your other idea, sir? You know, the girl had a funny splayed sort of run."

"Oh, we got them to run all right."

Lewis sensed he had landed on a sore point. "No good, sir." It was a statement, not a question.

"That's right, Lewis. No good. And it might have occurred, it might just have occurred, Lewis, to members of the crime squad, to me, Lewis, and to you, that all girls run in the *same ham-footed bloody way.*" He blasted the last few words at his sergeant, who waited for the hurricane to subside.

"You could do with a pint of beer, sir."

Morse looked a little happier. "You may be right."

"I've got a bit of news, sir."

"Let's have it."

"Well, the bus—that's out. I got the driver and conductor of the 6:30 p.m. 4E from Carfax. There were only a dozen or so on the bus anyway, most of them regulars. Our two girls pretty certainly didn't get to Woodstock by bus."

"We don't know for certain that both of them got to Woodstock anyway," said Morse.

"But Sylvia got there, didn't she, sir, and the other girl asked for the bus there?"

"I'm beginning to wonder if Mrs. Jarman is such a helpful witness, after all."

"I think she is, because that's only the bad news."

"You've got some *good* news?" Morse tried to sound a bit more cheerful.

"Well, it's that lorry the old girl told us about. Quite easy really to trace it. You see at Cowley there's this system with car-bodies. When they . . ."

"Yes, I know. You did a sharp job, Lewis. But cut the trimmings."

"He remembers them. A Mr. George Baker—lives in Oxford. And listen to this, sir. He saw the two girls getting into a car. A *red* car—he was sure of that. Chap driving —not a woman. He remembered because he often picks up hitchers, especially if they're girls; and he saw these two just beyond the roundabout—about fifty yards ahead. He would have given them a lift, he said, but this other car pulls up, and he has to pull out to get past. He saw the blonde all right."

"We're a despicable lot, aren't we?" said Morse. "Would you have picked them up?"

"I don't usually, sir. Only if they're in uniform. I was glad of a few lifts myself when I was in the forces."

Morse reflected carefully on the new evidence. Things were certainly moving.

"What did you say about a pint?"

They sat silently in *The White Horse* at Kidlington and Morse decided that the beer was drinkable. Finally he broke the silence. "A red car, eh?"

"Yes, sir."

"Interesting piece of research for you. How many men in Oxford own red cars?"

"Quite a few, sir."

"You mean a few thousand."

"I suppose so."

"But we could find out?"

"I suppose so."

"Such a problem would not be beyond the wit of our efficient force?"

"I suppose not, sir."

"But what if he doesn't live in Oxford?"

"Well, yes. There is that."

"Lewis, I think the beer is dulling your brain."

* * *

But if alcohol was dimming Lewis's intellectual acumen, it
had the opposite effect on Morse. His mind began to function
with an easy clarity. He ordered Lewis to take the weekend
off, to get some sleep, to forget Sylvia Kaye, and to take his
wife shopping; and Lewis was happy to do so.

Morse, not an addictive smoker, bought twenty king-sized
cigarettes and smoked and drank continuously until 2:00
p.m. What had really happened last Wednesday evening?
He was tormented by the thought that a sequence of events,
not in themselves extraordinary, had taken place; that each
event was the logical successor of the one before it; that he
knew what one or two of these events had been; that if only
his mind could project itself into a series of naturally causal
relationships, he would have it all. It needed no startling,
visionary leap from ignorance to enlightenment. Just a series
of logical progressions. But each progression landed him at
a dead end, like the drawings in children's annuals where
one thread leads to the treasure and all the others lead to
the edge of the page. Start again.

"I'm afraid I shall have to ask you to drink up," said the
landlord.

7
Saturday, 2 October, p.m.

Morse spent the afternoon of Saturday, 2 October, sitting
mildly drunk in his office. He had smoked his packet of
cigarettes by 4:30 p.m. and rang for more. His mind grew
clearer and clearer. He thought he saw the vaguest pattern
in the events of the evening of Wednesday, 29 September.
No names—no idea of names, yet—but a pattern.

He looked through the letters he had copied from the
Town and Gown: they seemed a sorry little package. Some
he dismissed immediately: not even a deranged psychiatrist
could have built the flimsiest hypotheses on five of the nine

pieces of evidence. One of the postcards read: "Dear Ruth, Weather good, went swimming twice yesterday. Saw a dead jellyfish on the beach. Love, T." How very sad to be a jellyfish, thought Morse. Only three of the communications held Morse's attention; then two; then one. It was a typewritten note addressed to Miss Jennifer Coleby and it read:

Dear Madam,
    After asessing the mny applications we have received, we must regretfully inform you that our application has been unsuccessful. At the begining of November however, further posts will become available, and I should, in all honesty, be sorry to loose the opportunity of reconsidering your position then.
    We have now alloted the September quota of posts in the Psycology Department; yet it is probable that a reliably qualified assistant may be required to deal with the routnie duties for the Principal's office.
Yours faithfully,

It was subscribed by someone who did not appear particularly anxious that his name be shouted from the housetops. An initial "G" was clear enough, but the surname to which it was floridly appended would have remained an enigma to the great Champollion himself.

So Miss Jennifer Coleby is after a new job, said Morse to himself. So what? Hundreds of people applied for new jobs every day. He sometimes thought of doing so himself. He wondered why he'd thought the letter worth a second thought. Typically badly written—unforgivable misprints. And misspellings. No-one in the schools cared much these days about the bread-and-butter mechanisms of English usage. He'd been brought up in the hard school: errors of spelling, punctuation and construction of sentences had been savagely penalised by outraged pedagogues, and this had made its mark on him. He had become pedantic and fussy and thought back on the ill-written travesty of a report he had read from one of his own staff only two days before, when he had mentally totted up the mistakes like an examiner assessing a candidate's work. "Assessing." Yes, that was wrong in this

letter—among other things. The country was becoming increasingly illiterate—for all the fancy notions of the progressive educationalists. But if his own secretary had produced
such rubbish, she would be out on her neck—today! But
she was exceptional. Julie's initials at the bottom of any letter
were the sure imprimatur of a clean and flawless sheet of
typing. Just a minute though . . . Morse looked again at the
letter before him. No reference at all. Had G. Thingamajig
typed it himself? If he had—what was he? A senior admin-
istrator of some university department? If he had . . . Morse
grew more and more puzzled. Why was there no letter heading? Was he worrying his head over nothing?

Well, there was one way of deciding the issue. He looked
at his watch. Already 5:30 p.m. Miss Coleby would probably
be at home now, he thought. Where did she live? He looked
at Lewis's careful details of the address in North Oxford.
An interesting thought? Morse began to realise how many
avenues he had not even started to explore. He put on
his greatcoat and went out to his car. As he drove the
two miles down into Oxford, he resolved that he would rid
himself as far as he could of all prejudice against Miss
Jennifer Coleby. But it was not an easy thing to do; for,
if Mrs. Jarman's memory could be trusted, the ambitious
Miss Coleby was one of the three girls who may have made
the journey to Woodstock that night with the late Miss
Sylvia Kaye.

Jennifer Coleby rented, with two other working girls, a semi-
detached property in Charlton Road where each paid a weekly
rent of £8.25, inclusive of electricity and gas. It meant a fat
rake-off of almost £25 a week for the provident landlord who
had snapped up two such properties for what now seemed
a meagre £6,500 some six years since. But it was also a
blessing for three enterprising girls who, for such a manageable outlay, were reasonably happy to share the narrow
bathroom and the even narrower lavatory. Each girl had a
bedroom (one downstairs), the kitchen was adequate for
their evening meals, and all of them used the lounge in
which to sit around, to chat and watch TV when they were
in. These arrangements, apart from the bathroom, worked

surprisingly well. Seldom were the girls in together during the day, and so far they had avoided any major confrontation. The landlord had forbidden men-friends in the bedrooms and the girls had accepted his Diktat without contention. There had, of course, been a few infractions of the ban, but the household had never degenerated into overt promiscuity. One rule the girls imposed upon themselves—no record-players; and for this, at least, their elderly neighbours were profoundly grateful. The house was kept tidy and clean, as Morse immediately saw as the door was opened by a sad girl eating a tomato sandwich.

"I've called to see Miss Coleby, if I may. Is she in?"

Dark, languorous eyes looked at him carefully, and Morse found himself tempted to wink at her.

"Just a minute." She walked leisurely away, but suddenly turned her head to ask, "Who shall I say?"

"Er, Morse. Chief Inspector Morse."

"Oh."

A cool, clean-looking Jennifer, dressed in blouse and jeans, came out to greet Morse, without apparent enthusiasm.

"Can I help you, inspector?"

"I wonder if we could have a few words together? Is it convenient?"

"It will have to be, I suppose. You'd better come in."

Morse was shown into a lounge, where Miss Dark-eyes sat pretending to be deeply engrossed in a report on the Arsenal v Tottenham match.

"Sue, this is Inspector Morse. Do you mind if we speak here?"

Sue stood up, and a little too theatrically, thought Morse, switched off the set. He observed her slow, graceful movements and smiled to himself, approvingly. "I'll be upstairs, Jen." She glanced at Morse before she left, saw the incipient smile at the corners of his mouth and afterwards swore to Jennifer that he had winked at her.

Jennifer motioned Morse to sit on the settee, and sat opposite him in an armchair.

"How can I help, inspector?"

Morse noticed a copy of Charlotte Brontë's *Villette* balancing like a circumflex accent over the arm of her chair.

"I'm having—purely routine, of course—to check the movements of all the er . . . persons . . ."

"Suspects?"

"No, no. Those who worked with Sylvia. You understand that this sort of thing has to be done."

"Of course. I'm surprised you haven't done it before." Morse was a little taken aback. Indeed, why *hadn't* he done it before? Jennifer continued. "Last Wednesday evening, I got home a bit later than usual—I went round Blackwells to spend a book-token. It was my birthday last week. I got home about six, I should think. You know what the traffic's like in the rush hour." Morse nodded. "Well, I had a bite to eat—the other girls were here—and went out about, let's see, about half-past six I should think. I got back about eight—perhaps a bit later."

"Can you tell me where you went?"

"I went to the Summertown library."

"What time does the library close?"

"Seven-thirty."

"You spent about an hour there."

"That seems to be a reasonable conclusion, inspector."

"It seems a long time. I usually spend about two minutes."

"Perhaps you're not very fussy what you read."

That's a point, thought Morse. Jennifer spoke with an easy, clear diction. A good education, he thought. But there was more than that. There was a disciplined independence about the girl, and he wondered how she got on with men. He thought it would be difficult to make much headway with this young lady—unless, of course, *she* wanted to. She could, he suspected, be very nice indeed.

"Are you reading that?"

She laid a delicately-manicured hand lightly upon *Villette*. "Yes. Have you read it?"

" 'Fraid not," confessed Morse.

"You should do."

"I'll try to remember," muttered Morse. Who was supposed to be conducting this interview? "Er, you stayed an hour?"

"I've told you that."

"Did anyone see you there?"

"They'd have a job not to, wouldn't they?"

"Yes, I suppose they would." Morse felt he was losing his way. "Did you get anything else out?" He suddenly felt a bit better.

"You'll be interested to know that I got that as well." She pointed to a large volume, also lying open, on the carpet in front of the TV set. "Mary's started to read it." Morse picked it up and looked at the title. *Who was Jack the Ripper?*

"Mm."

"I'm sure you've read that."

Morse's morale began to sag again. "I don't think I've read that particular account, no."

Jennifer suddenly smiled. "I'm sorry, inspector. I'm very much of a bookworm myself, and I have far more spare time than you, I'm sure."

"Coming back to Wednesday a minute, Miss Coleby. You say you were back about eight."

"Yes, about then. It could have been quarter past, even half past, I suppose."

"Was anyone in when you got back?"

"Yes. Sue was in. But Mary had gone off to the pictures. *Day of the Jackal* I think it was; she didn't get back until eleven."

"I see."

"Shall I ask Sue to come down?"

"No. No need to bother." Morse realised he was probably wasting his time, but he stuck it out. "How long does it take to walk to the library?"

"About ten minutes."

"But it took you almost an hour, perhaps, if you didn't get back until eight-thirty?"

Again the pleasant smile, the regular white teeth, a hint of gentle mockery around the lips. "Inspector, I think we'd better ask Sue if she remembers the time, don't you?"

"Perhaps we should," said Morse.

When Jennifer left the room Morse was looking around with sombre, weary eyes, when suddenly a thought flashed through his mind. He was deadly quick as he picked up *Villette*, turned to the inside of the cover and deftly replaced it over the arm of the chair. Sue came in, and quickly con-

firmed that as far as she could remember Jennifer had been
back in the house at some time after eight. She couldn't be
more precise. Morse got up to take his leave. He hadn't
mentioned the very thing he had come to discuss, and he
wasn't going to. That could come later.

He sat for a few minutes in the driving seat of his car and
his blood ran hot and cold. He had not quite been able to
believe his eyes. But he'd seen it in black and white, or
rather dark blue on white.

Morse knew the Oxford library routine only too well, for
he rarely returned his own irregular borrowings without
having to pay a late fine. The library worked in weeks, not
days, for books borrowed, and the day that every "week"
began was Wednesday. If a book was borrowed on a Wednesday, the date for return was exactly 14 days later—that
Wednesday fortnight. If a book was borrowed on Thursday,
the date for return was a fortnight after the following
Wednesday, 20 days later. The date-stamp was changed
each Thursday morning. This working from Wednesday to
Wednesday simplified matters considerably for the library
assistants and was warmly welcomed by those borrowers
who found seven or eight hundred pages an excessive as-
signment inside just fourteen days. Morse would have to
check, of course, but he felt certain that only those who
borrowed books on Wednesday had to return books within
the strict 14-day limit. Anyone taking out a book *on any
other day* would have a few extra days' grace. If Jennifer
Coleby had taken *Villette* from the library on Wednesday
last, the date-stamp for return would have read Wednesday,
13 October. But it didn't. *It read Wednesday, 20 October*.
Morse knew beyond any reasonable doubt that Jennifer had
lied to him about her movements on the night of the murder.
And why? To that vital question there seemed one very
simple answer.

Morse sat still in his car outside the house. From the
corner of his eye he saw the lounge curtain twitch slightly,
but he could see no-one. Whoever it was, he decided to let
things stew a while longer. He could do with a breath of
fresh air, anyway. He locked the car doors and sauntered
gently down the road, turned left into the Banbury Road

and walked more briskly now towards the library. He timed himself carefully: nine and a half minutes. Interesting. He walked up to the library door marked PUSH. But it didn't push. The library had closed its doors two hours ago.

8
Saturday, 2 October

Bernard Crowther's wife, Margaret, disliked the weekends, and effected her household management in such a way that neither her husband nor her twelve-year-old daughter nor her ten-year-old son enjoyed them very much either. Margaret had a part-time job in the School of Oriental Studies, and suspected that throughout the week she put in more hours of solid work than her gentle, bookish husband and her idle, selfish offspring put together. The weekend, *they* all assumed was a time of well-earned relaxation; but they didn't think of her. "What's for breakfast, mum?" "Isn't dinner ready yet?" Besides which, she did her week's wash on Saturday afternoons and tried her best to clean the house on Sundays. She sometimes thought that she was going mad.

At 5:30 on the afternoon of Saturday, 2 October, she stood at the sink with bitter thoughts. She had cooked poached eggs for tea ("What, again?") and was now washing up the sticky yellow plates. The children were glued to the television and wouldn't be bored again for an hour or so yet. Bernard (she ought to be thankful for small mercies) was cutting the privet hedge at the back of the house. She knew how he hated gardening, but that was one thing she was *not* going to do. She wished he would get a move on. The meticulous care he devoted to each square foot of the wretched hedge exasperated her. He'd be in soon to say his arms were aching. She looked at him. He was balding now and getting stout, but he was still, she supposed, an attractive man to some women. Until recently she had never regretted that she had married him fifteen years ago. Did she regret the children? She wasn't sure. From the time they were in arms she had been worried by her inability to gossip in easy, cosy terms with other mums about the precious little darlings. She had read a book on Mothercraft and came to the worrying conclusion that much of motherhood was distasteful to her—even nauseating. Her maternal instincts, she decided, were sadly underdeveloped. As the children grew into toddlers, she had enjoyed them more, and on occasion she had only little difficulty in convincing herself that she loved them both dearly. But now they seemed to be getting older and worse. Thoughtless, selfish and cheeky. Perhaps it was all her fault—or Bernard's. She looked out again as she stacked the last of the plates upright on the draining rack.

It was already getting dusk after another glorious day. She wondered, like the bees, if these warm days would never cease . . . Bernard had managed to advance the neatly clipped and rounded hedge by half a foot in the last five minutes. She wondered what he was thinking about, but she knew that she couldn't ask him.

The truth was, and Margaret had descried it dimly for several years now, that they were drifting apart. Was that her fault, too? Did Bernard realise it? She thought he did. She wished she could leave him, leave everything and go off somewhere and start a new life. But of course she couldn't. She would have to stick it out. Unless something tragic happened—or was it *until* something tragic happened? And then she knew she would stand by him—in spite of everything.

Margaret wiped the formica tops around the sink, lit a cigarette and went to sit in the dining-room. She just could not face the petty arguments and the noise in the lounge. She picked up the book Bernard had been reading that afternoon, *The Collected Works of Ernest Dowson*. The name was vaguely familiar to her from her school-certificate days and she turned slowly through the poems until she found the lines her class had been made to learn. She was surprised how well she could recall them:

I cried for madder music and for stronger wine,
But when the feast is finish'd and the lamps
expire,
Then falls thy shadow, Cynara! the night is thine;
And I am desolate and sick of an old passion,
Yea, hungry for the lips of my desire:
I have been faithful to thee, Cynara! in my fashion.

She read them again and for the first time seemed to catch the rhythm of their magical sound. But what did they *mean*? Forbidden fruits, a sort of languorous, illicit, painful delight. Of course, Bernard could tell her all about it. He spent his life exploring and expounding the beautiful world of poetry. But he wouldn't tell her because she couldn't ask.

It must have been an awful strain for Bernard meeting another woman once a week. How long had she known? Well, for certain, no more than a month or so. But in a strangely intuitive way, much longer than that. Six months? A year? Perhaps more. Not with that particular girl, but there may have been others. Her head was aching. But she'd taken so many codeine recently. Oh, let it ache! What a mess! her mind was going round and round. Privet hedge, poached eggs, Ernest Dowson, Bernard, the tension and deceit of the past four days. My God! What was she going to do? It couldn't go on like this.

Bernard came in. "My poor arms don't half ache!"

"Finished the hedge?"

"I'll finish it off in the morning. It's those abhorrèd shears. I shouldn't think they've been sharpened since we moved here."

"You could always take them in."

"And get 'em back in about six months."

"You exaggerate."

"I'll get it finished in the morning."

"It'll probably be raining."

"Well, we could do with a drop of rain. Have you seen the lawn? It's like the plains of Abyssinia."

"You've never been to Abyssinia."

The conversation dropped. Bernard went to his desk and

took out some papers. "I thought you'd be watching the telly."

"I can't stick being with the children."

Bernard looked at her sharply. She was near to tears. "No," he said. "I know what you mean." He looked soberly and almost tenderly at Margaret. Margaret, his wife! Sometimes he treated her so thoughtlessly, so very thoughtlessly. He walked across and laid a hand on her shoulder.

"They're pretty insufferable, aren't they? But don't worry about it. All kids are the same. I'll tell you what . . ."

"Oh, don't bother! You've made all those promises before. I don't care. I don't care, I tell you. As far as I'm concerned they can go to hell—and you with them!"

She began to sob convulsively and ran from the room. He heard her go into their bedroom above, and listened as the sobs continued. He put his head in his hands. He would have to do something, and he would have to do it very soon. He was in real danger now of losing everything. He might even have lost it already . . . Could he tell Margaret everything? She would never, never forgive him. What about the police? He'd almost told them, or, at least, he'd almost told them part of it. He looked down at Dowson's works and saw where the page was open. He knew that Margaret had been reading it and his eyes fell upon the same poem:

Surely the kisses of her bought red mouth were sweet;
But I was desolate and sick of an old passion,
  When I awoke and found the dawn was gray:
I have been faithful to thee, Cynara, in my fashion.

Yes, it had been sweet enough, it would be dishonest to pretend otherwise; but how sour it tasted now. It would have been a huge relief to have ended it all long ago, above all to have broken free from the web of lies and deceit he had spun around himself. Yet how beguiling had been the prospect of those extra-marital delights. Conscience. Damned conscience. Nurtured in a sensitive school. Fatal.

Though not a believer himself, Bernard conceded the empirical truth of the Pauline assertion that the wages of sin is death. He wanted desperately to be rid of the guilt and the remorse, and remembered vaguely from his school days in the bible-class how lustily they had all given voice to many a chorus on sin:

> *Though your sins be as scarlet, scarlet, scarlet,*
> *They shall be whiter, yea whiter than snow.*

But he couldn't pray these days—his spirit was parched and desolate. His primitive, eager religiosity was dulled now and overlaid with a deep and hard veneer of learning, culture and cynicism. He was well rehearsed in all the theological paradoxes, and the fizz of academic controversy was no longer a delight. Whiter than snow, indeed! More like the driven slush.

He walked over to the window which looked out on to the quiet road. Lights shone in most of the windows. A few people walked past; a neighbour was taking his dog to foul some other pavement. An L-driver was struggling to turn her car around, and was painfully succeeding, though the line of symmetry through MAC's Self-drive Zodiac rarely progressed more than seven or eight degrees at any one manoeuvre. More like a thirty-three-point turn, he thought. The instructor must be a patient chap. He had tried to teach Margaret to drive once . . . Still, he had made up for that. She had her own Mini now. He watched for several minutes. A man walked by, but though he thought he seemed familiar, Bernard didn't recognise him. He wondered who he was and where he was going, and kept him in sight until he turned right into Charlton Road.

As Morse had walked past, he too was wondering what to do. Best have it out with Jennifer now? He didn't know, but he thought on the whole it was. Conscious that he had not covered himself with glory at the earlier interview, he decided mentally to rehearse his new approach.

"You want to ask me some more questions?"

"Yes." Tight-lipped and masterly.

"Won't you come in?"

"Yes."

"Well?"

"Thus far you've told me nothing but a pack of lies. I suggest we start again."

"I don't know what you're talking about . . ." Slowly and pointedly he would get up from the chair and walk towards the door. He would utter not one further word. But as he opened the door, Jennifer would say, "All right, inspector." And he would listen. He thought he had a good idea of what she would tell him.

That he would have been wrong, he was not to learn for some time yet; for he discovered that Jennifer had gone out. The languid Sue, her long legs bronzed and bare, had no idea where she had gone. "Won't you come in and wait, inspector?" The full lips parted and quivered slightly. Morse both looked and felt alarmingly vulnerable. He consulted his wrist-watch for moral support. "You're very kind but . . . perhaps I'd better not."

9
Sunday, 3 October

Morse slept soundly for almost twelve hours, and awoke at 8:30 a.m. He had returned home immediately after his second call to Charlton Road with a splitting headache and a harassed mind. Now, as he blinked awake, he could scarcely believe how fresh he felt.

The last book Morse himself had taken from the library and which now lay, three weeks overdue, on his writing desk, was Edward de Bono's *A Five-Day Course in Lateral Thinking.* He had followed the course conscientiously, refused to look at any of the answers in advance, and reluctantly concluded that even the most sympathetic assessment of his lateral potential was gamma minus minus. But he had enjoyed it. Moreover he had learned that a logical, progressive, "vertical" assault upon a sticky problem might not always be the best. He had not really understood some of the jargon too well, but he had grasped the substantial points. "How can one drive a car up a dark alley if the headlights are not working?" It didn't matter what the answer was. The thing to do was to suggest *anything* a driver might conceivably do: blow the horn, take the roof rack off, lift the bonnet up. It didn't matter. The mere contemplation of futile solutions was itself a potent force in reaching the right conclusion; for sooner or later one would turn on a blinker and, hey presto!, the light would dawn. In an amateurish way Morse had tried out this technique and had surprised himself. If a name was on the tip of his tongue, he stopped thinking directly about it, and merely repeated anything he knew—the state capitals of the USA—anything; and it seemed to work.

As he lay awake he decided temporarily to shelve the murder of Sylvia Kaye. He was making progress—he knew that. But his mind lacked incision; it was going a bit stale. With a rest today (and he'd deserved one) he'd be back on mental tip-toe in the morning.

He got up, dressed and shaved, cooked himself a succulent-looking mixture of bacon, tomatoes and mushrooms, and felt good. He ran a leisurely eye through the Sunday papers, checked his pools, wondered if he was the only man in England who had picked in his "any eight from sixteen" permutation not a single score-draw, and lit a cigarette. He would sit and idle the time away until noon, have a couple of pints and get lunch out somewhere. It seemed a civilised prospect. But he was never happy without something to do, and before long was mentally debating whether to put some Wagner on the record-player or do a crossword. Crosswords were a passion with Morse, although since the death of the great Ximenes he had found few composers to please his taste. On the whole he enjoyed *The Listener* puzzles as much as any, and for this purpose took the periodical each week. On the other hand he delighted in Wagnerian opera and had the complete cycle of *The Ring*. He decided to do both, and to the opening bars of the richly-scored Prelude to *Das Rheingold*, he sat back and turned to the penultimate page of *The Listener*. This was the life. The Rhinemaidens

swam gracefully to and fro and it was a few minutes before
Morse felt willing to let the music drift away to the periphery
of his attention. He read the preamble to the crossword:

"Each of the across clues contains, in the definition, a
deliberate misprint. Each of the down clues is normal, although the words to be entered in the diagram will contain
a misprint of a single letter. Working from 1 across to 28
down the misprinted letters form a well-known quotation
which solvers . . ."

Morse read no more. He leapt to his feet. A solo horn
expired with a dying groan as he switched off the record-
player and snatched his car keys from the mantelpiece.

His in-tray was high with reports, but he ignored them. He
unlocked his cabinet, took out the file on the Sylvia Kaye
murder, and extracted the letter addressed to Jennifer Coleby. He knew there had been something wrong with the
whole thing. His mouth was dry and his hand trembled
slightly, like a schoolboy opening his O-level results:

Dear Madam,
    After asessing the mny applications we have received,
we must regretfully inform you that our application has
been unsuccessful. At the begining of November, however, further posts will become available, and I should,
in all honesty, be sorry to loose the opportunity of re-
considering your position then.
    We have now alloted the September quota of posts
in the Psycology Department; yet it is probable that a
reliably qualified assistant may be required to deal with
the routnie duties for the Principal's office.
Yours faithfully,

How wrong-headed he had been! Instead of thinking, as
he had done, with such supercilious arrogance, of the illit-
eracy and incompetence of some poor blockhead of a typist,
he should have been thinking exactly the opposite. He'd been
a fool. The clues were there. The whole thing was phoney
—why hadn't he spotted that before? When you boiled it
down it was a nonsense letter. He had first made the mistake

of concentrating upon individual mistakes and not even bothering to see the letter as a synoptic whole. But not only that. He had compounded his mistake. For if he had read the letter as a letter, he might have considered the mistakes as mistakes—*deliberate mistakes.* He took a sheet of paper and started: "asessing"—"s" omitted; "mny"—"a" omitted; "begining"—"n" omitted; "loose"—"o" inserted; "Psycology" —"h" omitted. SANOH—whatever that signified. Look again. "our"—shouldn't it be "your"? "y" omitted; "routnie"—"n" and "i" transposed. What did that give him? SAYNOHNI. Hardly promising. Try once more, "alloted"—surely two "t"s? "t" omitted. And there it was staring him in the face. The "G" of course from the signature, the only recognisable letter therein: SAY NOTHING. Someone had been desperately anxious for Jennifer not to say a word—and Jennifer, it seemed, had got the message.

It had taken Morse two minutes, and he was glad that Jennifer had been out the previous evening. He felt sure that faced with her lies about the visit to the library, she would have said how sorry she was and that she must have got it wrong. It must have been Thursday, she supposed; it was so difficult to think back to events of even the day before, wasn't it? She honestly couldn't remember; but she would try very hard to. Perhaps she had gone for a walk—on her own, of course.

But she would find things more awkward now. Strangely Morse felt little sense of elation. He had experienced an odd liking for Jennifer when they had met, and in retrospect he understood how difficult it must have been for her. But he must look the fact squarely in the face. She was lying. She was shielding someone—that someone who in all probability had raped and murdered Sylvia. It was not a pretty thought. Every piece of evidence now pointed unequivocally to the fact that it was Jennifer Coleby who had stood at Fare Stage 5 with Sylvia on the night of the 29th; that it was she who had been given a lift by a person or persons unknown (pretty certainly the former) as far as Woodstock; that there she had witnessed something about which she had been warned to keep her silence. In short that Jennifer Coleby *knew the identity of the man who had murdered Sylvia Kaye.* Morse

suddenly wondered if she was in danger, and it was this
fear which prompted his immediate decision to have Jennifer held on suspicion of being an accessory to the crime
of murder. He would need Lewis in.

He reached for his outside phone and rang his sergeant's
home number.

"Lewis?"

"Speaking."

"Morse here. I'm sorry to ruin your weekend, but I want
you here."

"Straightaway, sir?"

"If you can."

"I'm on my way."

Morse looked through his in-tray. Reports, reports, reports. He crossed through his own initials immediately, barely
glancing at such uncongenial titles as *The Drug Problem in
Britain*, *The Police and the Public*, and *The Statistics for
Crimes of Violence in Oxfordshire* (second quarter). At the
minute he was interested only in one statistic which would
doubtless, in time, appear in the statistics of violent crime
in Oxfordshire (third quarter). He'd no time for reports. He
suspected that about 95% of the written word was never
read by anyone anyway. But there were two items which
held his attention. A report from the forensic lab on the
murder weapon, and a supplementary report from the pathology department on Sylvia Kaye. Neither did more than
confirm what he already knew or at any rate suspected. The
tyre-lever proved to be a singularly unromantic specimen.
Morse read all about its shape, size, weight . . . But why
bother? There was no mystery about the lever at all. The
landlord of *The Black Prince* had spent the afternoons of
Tuesday, 28th and Wednesday, 29th tinkering with an ancient Sunbeam, and had unwittingly left his tool kit outside
the garage on the right at the back of the courtyard where
he kept the car. There were no recognisable prints—just
the ugly evidence, at one of the lever's curving ends, that
it had crashed with considerable force into the bone of a
human skull. There followed a gory analysis, which Morse
was glad to skip.

It was only a few minutes before Lewis knocked and entered.

"Ah, Lewis. The gods, methinks, have smiled weakly on our inquiries." He outlined the developments in the case. "I want Miss Jennifer Coleby brought in for questioning. Be careful. Take Policewoman Fuller with you if you like. Just held for questioning, you understand? There's no question at all of any formal arrest. If she prefers to ring up her legal advisers, tell her it's Sunday and they're all playing golf. But I don't think you'll have much trouble." On the latter point, at least, Morse guessed correctly.

Jennifer was sitting in interrogation room 3 by 3:45 p.m. On Morse's instructions, Lewis spent an hour with her, making no mention whatever of the information he had been given earlier in the afternoon. Lewis mentioned quietly that, in spite of all their inquiries, they had not been able to trace the young lady, seen by two independent witnesses, who had been with Sylvia Kaye an hour or so before she was murdered.

"You must be patient, sergeant."

Lewis smiled weakly, like the gods. "Oh, we're patient enough, miss, and I think with a little co-operation we shall get there."

"Aren't you getting any co-operation?"

"Would you like a cup of tea, miss?"

"I'd prefer coffee."

Policewoman Fuller hurried off; Jennifer moistened her lips and swallowed; Lewis brooded quietly. In the tug-of-war silence which ensued it was Lewis who finally won.

"You think I'm not co-operating, sergeant?"

"Are you?"

"Look, I've told the inspector what I know. Didn't he believe me?"

"Just what did you tell the inspector, miss?"

"You want me to go over all that again?" Jennifer's face showed all the impatience of a schoolgirl asked to rewrite a tedious exercise.

"We shall have to have a signed statement in any case."

Jennifer sighed. "All right. You want me to account for

my movements—I think that's the phrase, isn't it?—on Wednesday night."

"That's right, miss."

"On Wednesday night . . ." Laboriously Lewis began to write. "Shall I write it out for you?" asked Jennifer.

"I think I ought to get it down myself, miss, if you don't mind. I haven't got a degree in English, but I'll do my best." A quick flash of caution gleamed in Jennifer's eyes. It was gone immediately, but it had been there and Lewis had seen it.

Half an hour later, Jennifer's statement was ready. She read it, asked if she could make one or two amendments— "only spelling, sergeant"—and agreed that she could sign it.

"I'll just get it typed out, miss."

"How long will that take?"

"Oh, only ten minutes."

"Would you like me to do it? It'll only take me about two."

"I think we ought to do it ourselves, miss, if you don't mind. We have our regulations, you know."

"Just thought I might be able to help." Jennifer felt more relaxed.

"Shall I get you another cup of coffee, miss?"

"That would be nice." Lewis got up and left.

Policewoman Fuller seemed singularly uncommunicative, and for more than ten minutes Jennifer sat in silence. When the door finally opened it was Morse who entered carrying a neatly-typed sheet of foolscap.

"Good afternoon, Miss Coleby."

"Good afternoon."

"We've met before." The tide of relaxation which had reached high watermark with Lewis's departure quickly ebbed and exposed the grating shingle of her nerves. "I walked down to the library after I left you yesterday," continued Morse.

"You must enjoy walking."

"They tell me walking is the secret of perpetual middle age."

With an effort, Jennifer smiled. "It's a pleasant walk, isn't it?"

"It depends which way you go," said Morse.

Jennifer looked sharply at him and Morse, as Lewis earlier, noted the unexpected reaction. "Well, I would like to stay and talk to you, but I hope you will let me sign that statement and get back home. There are several things I have to do before tomorrow."

"I hope Sergeant Lewis mentioned that we have no authority to keep you against your will?"

"Oh yes. The sergeant told me."

"But I shall be very grateful if you can agree to stay a little longer."

The back of Jennifer's throat was dry. "What for?" Her voice was suddenly a little harsher.

"Because," said Morse quietly, "I hope you will not be foolish enough to sign a statement which you know to be false"—Morse raised his voice—"and which I know to be false." He gave her no chance to reply. "This afternoon I gave instructions for you to be held for questioning since I suspected, and still suspect, that you are withholding information which may be of very great value in discovering the identity of Miss Kaye's murderer. That is a most serious offence, as you know. It now seems that you are foolish enough to compound such stupidity with the equally criminal and serious offence of supplying the police with information which is not only inaccurate but demonstrably false." Morse's voice had risen in crescendo and he ended with a mighty thump with his fist upon the table between them.

Jennifer, however, did not appear quite so abashed as he had expected.

"You don't believe what I told you?"

"No."

"Am I allowed to ask why not?" Morse was more than a little surprised. It was clear to him that the girl had recovered whatever nerve she may have lost. He clearly and patiently told her that she could not possibly have taken out her library books on Wednesday evening, and that this could be proved without any reasonable doubt. "I see." Morse waited for her to speak again. If he had been mildly surprised at her previous question, he was flabbergasted by her next. "What were *you* doing at the time of the murder last Wednesday evening, inspector?"

What was he doing? He wasn't quite sure, but any such admission would hardly advance his present cause. He lied. "I was listening to some Wagner."

"Which Wagner."

"*Das Rheingold.*"

"Is there anyone who could back up your story? Did anyone see you?"

Morse surrendered. "No." In spite of himself, he had to admire the girl. "No," he repeated, "I live on my own. I seldom have the pleasure of visitors—of either sex."

"How very sad."

Morse nodded. "Yes. But you see, Miss Coleby, I am not as yet suspected of dressing up in women's clothes and standing at the top of the Woodstock Road hitching a lift with Sylvia Kaye."

"And *I* am?"

"And you are."

"But presumably I'm not suspected of raping and murdering Sylvia?"

"I hope you will allow me a modicum of intelligence."

"You don't understand."

"What's that supposed to mean?"

"Hasn't it occurred to you that Sylvia probably enjoyed being raped?" There was bitterness in her tone, and her cheeks were flushed.

"That seems to assume that she was raped *before* she died, doesn't it?" said Morse quietly.

"I'm sorry—that was a horrid thing to say."

Morse followed up his advantage. "My job is to discover what happened from the moment Sylvia and her friend—*and I believe that was you*—got into a red car on the other side of the Woodstock roundabout. For some reason this other girl has not come forward, and I don't think the reason's very hard to find. *She knew the driver of the car,* and she's protecting him. She's probably frightened stiff. But so was Sylvia Kaye frightened stiff, Miss Coleby. More than that. She was so savagely struck on the back of the head that her skull was broken in several places and lumps of bone were found in her brain. Do you like the sound of that?

It's an ugly, horrible sight is murder and the trouble with murder is that it usually tends to wipe out the only good witness of the crime—the victim. That means we've got to rely on other witnesses, normal ordinary people most of them, who accidentally get caught up at some point in the wretched business. They get scared; OK. They'd rather not get mixed up in it; OK. They think it's none of their business, OK—but we've got to rely on some of them having enough guts and decency to come forward and tell us what they know. And that's why you're here, Miss Coleby. I've got to know the truth."

He took the statement that Jennifer had made and tore it into pieces. But he could not read her mind. As he had been speaking she had been gazing through the window of the little office into the outside yard, where the day before she had stood with her office colleagues.

"Well?"

"I'm sorry, inspector. I must have caused you a lot of trouble. It was on Thursday that I went to the library."

"And on Wednesday?"

"I did go out. And I did go on the road to Woodstock—but I didn't get as far as Woodstock. I stopped at *The Golden Rose* at Begbroke—that's what, about two miles this side of Woodstock. I went into the lounge and bought a drink—a lager and lime. I drank it out in the garden and then went home."

Morse looked at her impatiently. "In the dark, I suppose."

"Yes. About half past seven."

"Well—go on."

"What do you mean—'go on'? That was all."

"Do you want me to . . ." began Morse, his voice fuming. "Fetch Lewis!" he barked. Policewoman Fuller read the gale warning and hurried out.

Jennifer appeared untroubled, and Morse's anger subsided.

It was Jennifer who broke the silence. "You mustn't be too angry with me, inspector." Her voice had become little more than a whisper. Her hand went to her forehead and for a while she closed her eyes. Morse looked at her closely

for the first time. He had not noticed before how attractive
she could be. She wore a light-blue summer coat over a
black jumper, with gloves in matching black. Her cheek
bones were high and there was animation in her face, her
mouth slightly open revealing the clean lines of her white
teeth. Morse wondered if he could ever fall for her, and
decided, as usual, that he could.

"I've been so flustered, and so frightened."

He had to lean forward slightly to catch her words. He
noticed that Lewis had come in and motioned him silently
to a chair.

"Everything will be all right, you see." Morse looked at
Lewis and nodded as the sergeant prepared to take down
the second draft of the evidence of Miss Jennifer Coleby.

"Why were you frightened?" asked Morse gently.

"Well, it's all been so strange—I don't seem to be able to
wake up properly since . . . I don't seem to know what's real
and what's not. So many funny things seem to be happening." She was still sitting with her head in her hand, looking
blankly at the top of the table. Morse glanced at Lewis.
Things were almost ready.

"What do you mean—'funny things'?"

"Just everything really. I'm beginning to wonder if I know
what I *am* doing. What am I doing *here*? I thought I'd told
you the truth about Wednesday—and now I realise I didn't.
And there was another funny thing." Morse watched her
keenly. "I had a letter on Saturday morning telling me I'd
not been chosen for a job—*and I don't even remember ap-
plying for it*. Do you think I'm going mad?"

So that was going to be her story! Morse experienced the
agony of a bridge player whose ace has just been covered
by the deuce of trumps. The two policemen looked at each
other, and both were conscious that Jennifer's eyes were on
them.

"Well, now." Morse hid his disappointment and disbelief
as well as he was able. "Let's just get back to Wednesday
night, shall we? Can you repeat what you just told me? I
want Sergeant Lewis to get it down." His voice sounded
exasperated.

Jennifer repeated her brief statement and Lewis, like the inspector before him, looked temporarily bewildered.

"You mean," said Morse, "that Miss Kaye went on to Woodstock, but that you only went as far as Begbroke?"

"Yes, that's exactly what I mean."

"You asked this man to drop you at Begbroke?"

"What man are you talking about?"

"The man who gave you a lift."

"But I didn't get a lift to Begbroke."

"You *what*?" shrieked Morse.

"I said I didn't get a lift. I would never hitch-hike anyway. I think you ought to know something, inspector. *I've got a car.*"

While Lewis was getting the second statement typed, Morse retreated to his office. Had he been wrong all along? If what Jennifer now claimed was true, it would certainly account for several things. On the same road, on the same night and one of her own office friends murdered? Of course she would feel frightened. But was that enough to account for her repeated evasions? He reached for the 'phone and rang *The Golden Rose* at Begbroke. The jovial-sounding landlord was anxious to help. His wife had been on duty in the lounge on Wednesday. Could she possibly come down to Kidlington Police HQ? Yes. The landlord would drive her himself. Good. Quarter of an hour, then.

"Do you remember a young lady coming in to the lounge last Wednesday? On her own? About half-past seven time?"

The richly-ringed and amply-bosomed lady wasn't sure.

"But you don't often get women coming in alone, do you?"

"Not often, no. But it's not all *that* unusual these days, inspector. You'd be surprised."

Morse felt that little would surprise him any more. "Would you recognise someone like that? Someone who just dropped in one night?"

"I think so, yes."

Morse rang Lewis, who was still waiting with Jennifer in the interview room.

"Take her home, Lewis."

The landlady of *The Golden Rose* stood beside Morse at the inquiry desk as Jennifer walked past with Lewis.

"That her?" he asked. It was his penultimate question.

"Yes. I think it is."

"I'm most grateful to you," lied Morse.

"I'm glad I could help, inspector."

Morse showed her to the door. "I don't suppose you happen to remember what she ordered, do you?"

"Well, as a matter of fact, I think I do, inspector. It was lager and lime, I think. Yes, lager and lime."

It was half an hour before Lewis returned. "Did you believe her, sir?"

"No," said Morse. He felt more frustrated than depressed. He realised that he had already landed himself in a good deal of muddle and mess by his own inadequacies. He had refused the offer of the auxiliary personnel available to him, and this meant that few of the many possible leads had yet been checked and documented. Sanders, for example—surely to any trained officer the most obvious target for immediate and thorough investigation—he had thus far almost totally ignored. Indeed, even a superficial scrutiny of his conduct of the case thus far would reveal a haphazardness in his approach almost bordering upon negligence. Only the previous month he had himself given a lecture to fellow detectives on the paramount importance in any criminal investigation of the strictest and most disciplined thoroughness in every respect of the inquiry *from the very beginning*.

And yet, for all this, he sensed in some intuitive way (a procedure not mentioned in his lecture) that he was vaguely on the right track still; that he had been right in allowing Jennifer to go; that although his latest shot had been kicked off the line, sooner or later the goal would come.

For the next hour the two officers exchanged notes on the afternoon's interrogation, with Morse impatiently probing Lewis's reactions to the girl's evasions, glances, and gestures.

"Do you think she's lying, Lewis?"

"I'm not so sure now."

"Come off it, man. When you're as old as I am you'll recognise a liar a mile off!"

Lewis remained doubtful: he was by several years the older man anyway. Silence fell between them.

"Where do we go from here, then?" said Lewis at last.

"I think we attack down the other flank."

"We do?"

"Yes. She's shielding a man. Why? Why? That's what we've been asking ourselves so far. And you know where we've got with that line of inquiry? Nowhere. She's lying, I know that; but we haven't broken her—not yet. She's such a good liar she'd get any damned fool to believe her."

Lewis saw the implication. "You could be wrong, sir."

Morse blustered on, wondering if he was. "No, no, no. We've just been tackling the case from the wrong angle. They tell me, Lewis, that you can climb up the Eiger in your carpet slippers if you go the easy way. Now we've got to try the hard way."

"How do we do that, sir?"

"We've been trying to find out who the other girl was, because we thought she could lead us to the man we want."

"But according to you we *have* found her."

"Yes. But she's too clever for us—and too loyal. She's been warned to keep her mouth shut—not that she needed much telling, if I'm any judge. But we're up against a brick wall for the time being, and there's only one alternative. The girl won't lead us to the man? All right. We find the man."

"How do we start on that?"

"I think we shall need a bit of Aristotelian logic, don't you?"

"If you say so, sir."

"I'll tell you all about it in the morning," said Morse.

Lewis paused as he reached the door. "That identification of Miss Coleby, sir. Did you think it was satisfactory—just to take the landlady's word for it?"

"Why not?"

"Well, it was all a bit casual, wasn't it? I mean, it wasn't exactly going by the book."

"What book?" said Morse.

Lewis decided that his mind had got itself into a quite sufficient muddle for one day, and he left.

Morse's mind, too, was hardly functioning with crystalline lucidity; yet already emerging from the mazed confusion was the germ of a new idea. He had suspected from the start that Jennifer Coleby was lying; would have staked his professional reputation upon it. But he could have been wrong, at least in one respect. He had tried to break Jennifer's story, but had he been trying to break it *at the wrong point*?

What if all she had told him was perfectly true? . . . The same revolving pro's and con's passed up and down before his eyes like undulating hobby-horses at a fairground, until his own mind, too, was in a dizzying whirl and he knew that it was time to give it all a rest.

10
Wednesday, 6 October

The cocktail lounge of *The Black Prince* was seldom busy for the hour after opening time at 11:00 a.m., and the morning of Wednesday, 6 October, was to prove no exception. The shock-wave of the murder was now receding and *The Black Prince* was quickly returning to normality.

It was amazing how quickly things sank into the background, thought Mrs. Gaye McFee as she polished another martini glass and stacked it neatly among its fellows. But not really; only that morning an incoming air-liner had crashed at Heathrow with the loss of seventy-nine lives. And every day on the roads . . .

"What'll it be, boys?" The speaker was a distinguished-looking man, about sixty years old, thick set, with silvery-grey hair and a ruddy complexion. Gaye had served him many times before and knew him to be Professor Tompsett (Felix to his friends, who were rumoured not to be legion) —emeritus Professor of Elizabethan Literature at Oxford

University, and the recently-retired vice-principal of Lonsdale College. His two companions, one a gaunt, bearded man in his late twenties, the other a gentle-looking bespectacled man of about forty-five, each ordered gin and tonic.

"Three gin and tonics." Tompsett had an incisive, imperative voice, and Gaye wondered if he got his college scout to stir his morning coffee.

"Hope you're going to enjoy life with us, young Melhuish!" Tompsett laid a broad hand on his bearded companion's shoulder, and was soon engrossed in matters which Gaye was no longer able to follow. A group of American servicemen had come in and were losing no time in quizzing her about the brands of lager, the menu, the recent murder, and her home address. But she enjoyed Americans, and was soon laughing good-naturedly with them. As usual, the lager-pump was producing more froth than liquid substance and Gaye noticed, waiting patiently at the other end of the bar, the bespectacled member of the Oxford triumvirate.

"Shan't be a second, sir."

"Don't worry. I'm in no great rush." He smiled quietly at her, and she saw the glimmer of a twinkle in his dark eyes, and she hurriedly squared the account with the neighbourly Americans.

"Now, sir."

"We'd all like the same again, please. Three gins and tonics." Gaye looked at him with interest. The landlord had once told her that if anyone ordered "gins and tonics" instead of the almost universal "gin and tonics"—he really *was* a don. She wished he would speak again, for she liked the sound of his voice with its sarft Glarcestershire accent. But he didn't. Nevertheless, she stayed at his end of the bar and lightly repolished the martini glasses.

"Whatawe done to you, honeybunch?" and similar endearing invitations emanated regularly from her other clients, but Gaye quietly and tactfully declined their ploys; she watched instead the man from Gloucestershire. Tompsett was in full flow.

"He didn't even go to my inaugural when he was up. What do you think of that, Peter, old boy."

"Don't blame him really," said Peter. "We all sit and salivate over our own prose, Melhuish, and we kid ourselves it's bloody marvellous."

The Professor of Elizabethan Literature laughed good-humouredly and half-drained his glass. "Been here before, Melhuish?"

"No, I haven't. Rather nice, isn't it?"

"Bit notorious now, you know. Murder here last week."

"Yes, I read about it."

"Young blonde. Raped and murdered, right in the yard out there. Pretty young thing—if the newspapers are anything to go by."

Melhuish, newly-appointed junior fellow at Lonsdale, very bright and very anxious, was beginning to feel a little more at home with his senior colleagues.

"Raped, too, was she?"

Tompsett drained his glass. "So they say. But I've always been a bit dubious myself about this rape business."

"Confucius, he say girl with skirt up, she run faster than man with trousers down, eh?"

The two older men smiled politely at the tired old joke, but Melhuish wished he hadn't repeated it: off-key, over-familiar. Gaye heard the clear voice of Tompsett rescuing the conversation. He was no fool, she thought.

"Yes, I agree with you, Melhuish. We mustn't get too serious about rape. God, no. Happens every day. I remember a couple of years back there was a young gal here—you'd remember her, Peter—quick, clear mind, good worker, marvellous kid. She was taking Finals and had eight three-hour papers. She'd done her seventh paper on the Thursday morning—no it was the Friday, or was it . . . but that's beside the point. She took her last but one paper in the morning with just one more fence to jump in the afternoon. Well, she went off to her digs out at Headington for lunch and—begger me!—she got raped on her way back. Just think of the shock for the poor lass. You remember, Peter? Anyway, she insisted on taking the last paper and do you know, Melhuish—she did better on the last paper than she'd done on all the others!"

Melhuish laughed heartily and took the empty glasses.

"You make it up as you go along," muttered Peter.

"Well, it was a good story, wasn't it?" said Tompsett.

Gaye lost the thread of their talk for a few minutes, and when she picked it up again, it was clear that the conversation had taken a slightly more serious turn. They always said that gin was a depressant.

"... not necessarily raped *before* being murdered, you know."

"Oh, shut up, Felix."

"Bit revolting, I know. But we all read the Christie business, didn't we? Wicked old bugger, he was!"

"Do they think that's what happened here?" asked Melhuish.

"Do you know, I might have been able to tell you that," said Tompsett. "Old Morse—good chap!—he's in charge of the case, and we've had him at the college guest-evenings. He was invited tonight, but he had to cry off. Had a minor accident." Tompsett laughed. "Fell off a ladder! Christ, who'd ever believe it? Here's a chap in charge of a murder inquiry and he falls off a bloody ladder!" Tompsett was highly amused.

The Americans had renounced all hope and the bar had emptied now. The three men walked across to the table by the window.

"Well, we'd better see what they can offer us for lunch," said Peter. "I'll get the menu."

Gaye held out a large expensive-looking folder and presented it, already opened, like a neophyte offering the collect for the day to an awesome priest.

Peter looked through quickly, a gentle cynicism showing on his face. He looked up at Gaye and found her watching him. "Do you recommend 'Don's Delight' or 'Proctor's Pleasure'?" He asked it in an undertone.

"I shouldn't have the steak if I were you," her voice as quiet as his.

"Are you free this afternoon?"

She weighed up the situation for several seconds before nodding her head, almost imperceptibly.

"What time shall I pick you up?"

"Three o'clock?"

"Where?"

"I'll be just outside."

* * *

At four o'clock the two lay side by side in the ample double-bed in Peter's rooms in Lonsdale College. His left arm was around her neck, his right hand gently caressing her breasts.

"Do you believe a young girl can get raped?" he asked.

Gaye considered the problem. Contented in mind and in body, she lay for a while contemplating the ornate ceiling. "It must be jolly difficult for the man."

"Mm."

"Have you ever raped a woman?"

"I could rape you, any day of the week."

"But I wouldn't let you. I wouldn't put up any resistance."

He kissed her full lips again, she turned eagerly towards him.

"Peter," she whispered in his ear, "rape me again!"

The 'phone blared suddenly, shrill and urgent in the quiet room. Blast!

"Oh, hullo Bernard. What? No. Sitting idling, you know. What? Oh, tonight. Yes. Well, about seven, I think. Why not call in for me? We can have a quick drink together. Yes. Felix? Oh, he's well tanked-up already. Yes. Yes. Well, look forward to it. Yes. Bye."

"Who's Bernard?"

"Oh, he's an English don here. Good chap. Pretty bad sense of timing, though."

"Does he have a set of rooms like this?"

"No, no. He's a family man is Bernard. Lives up in North Oxford. Quiet chap."

"*He* doesn't rape young girls then?"

"What, Bernard? Good lord no. Well, I don't think so . . . ."

"You're a quiet man, Peter."

"Me?" She fondled him lovingly, and abruptly terminated all further discussion of Mr. Bernard Crowther, quiet family man of North Oxford.

2
Search for a Man

11
Wednesday, 6 October

Beginning its life under a low (Head Room 12 ft) railway bridge, and proceeding its cramped and narrow way for several hundred yards past shabby rows of terraced houses that line the thoroughfare in tight and mean confinement, the Botley Road gradually broadens into a spacious stretch of dual carriageway that carries all west-bound traffic towards Faringdon, Swindon and the sundry hamlets in-between. Here the houses no longer shoulder their neighbours in such grudging proximity, and hither several of the Oxford businessmen have brought their premises.

Chalkley and Sons is a sprawling, two-storeyed building, specialising in household fittings, tiling, wallpaper, paint and furniture. It is a well-established store, patronised by many of the carpenters (discount), the interior-decorators (discount), and almost all the do-it-yourselfers from Oxford. At the farthest end of the ground-floor show-rooms there is a notice informing the few customers who have not yet discovered the fact that the Formica Shop is outside, over the yard, second on the left.

In this shop a young man is laying a large sheet of formica upon a wooden table, a table which has a deep, square groove cut longitudinally through its centre. He pulls towards him, along its smoothly-running gliders, a small automatic saw, and carefully lines up its wickedly polished teeth against his pencilled mark. Deftly he flicks out a steel ruler and checks his measurement. He appears content with a rapid mental calculation, snaps a switch and, amid a grating whirr, slices through the tough fabric with a clean and deadly swiftness. He enjoys that swiftness! Several times he repeats the process: lengthways, sideways, narrowly, broadly, and stacks the measured strips neatly against the wall. He looks at his watch; it is almost 12:45 p.m. An hour and a quarter. He locks the sliding doors behind him, repairs to the staff washroom, soaps his hands, combs his hair and, with little regret, temporarily turns his back upon the premises of Mr. Chalkley and his sons. He pats a little package which bulges slightly in the right-hand pocket of his overcoat. Still there.

Although his immediate destination is no more than ten minutes' walk away, he decides to take a bus. He crosses the road and traverses in the process as many lines, continuous, broken, broad, narrow, yellow, white, as one may find in the key to an ordnance-survey map; for the Oxford City Council has escalated its long war of attrition against the private motorist and has instituted a system of bus-lanes along the Botley Road. A bus arrives almost immediately, and the dour Pakistani one-man crew silently discharges his manifold duties. The young man always hopes that the bus is fairly full so that he may sit beside one of the mini-skirted, knee-booted young girls returning to the city; but today it is almost empty. He sits down and looks mechanically around him.

He alights at the stop before the railway bridge (where the bus must make a right-hand detour to avoid a scalping from the iron girders), threads his way to a dingy street behind the shabby rows of houses, and enters a small shop. The legend above the door of Mr. Baines's grimy, peeling shop-front reads "Newsagent and Tobacconist." But such is the nature of Mr. Baines's establishment that he employs no cohorts of cheeky boys and girls to deliver his morning and evening newspapers, nor does his stock of tobacco run to more than half a dozen of the more popular brands of cigarettes. He sells neither birthday cards nor ice-cream nor confectionery. Mr. Baines—yes, he is a shrewd man—calculates that he can make as much profit from one swift, uncomplicated transaction as from the proceeds of one day's paper rounds, or from the sale of a thousand cigarettes. For Mr. Baines is a dealer in hard pornography.

Several customers are standing along the right-hand side of the narrow shop. They flick their way through a bewildering variety of gaudy, glossy girlie magazines, with names that ring with silken ecstasies: *Skin* and *Skirt* and *Lush* and *Lust* and *Flesh* and *Frills*. Although the figures of the scantily-clad models which adorn the covers of these works are fully and lewdly provocative, the browsers appear to riffle the pages with a careless, casual boredom. But this is the appearance only. A notice, in Mr. Baines's own hand, warns every potential purveyor of these exotic fruits that "the books are to be bought"; and Mrs. Baines sits on her hard stool behind the counter and keeps her hard eyes upon each of her committed clients. The young man throws no more than a passing glance at the gallery of thrusting nakedness upon his right and walks directly to the counter. He asks, audibly, for a packet of twenty Embassy and slides his package across to Mrs. Baines; which lady, in her turn, reaches beneath the counter and passes forward a similar brown-paper parcel to the young man. How Mr. Baines himself would approve! It is a single, swift, uncomplicated transaction.

The young man stops at the *Bookbinder's Arms* across the road and orders bread and cheese and a pint of Guinness. He feels his usual nagging impatience, but gloats inwardly in expectation. Five o'clock will soon be here and the journey to Woodstock is infinitely quicker now, with the opening of the new stretch of the ring-road complex. His mother will have his cooked meal ready, and then he will be alone. In his own perverted way he has grown almost to enjoy the anticipation of it all, for over the last few months it has become a weekly ritual. Expensive, of course, but the arrangement is not unsatisfactory, with half-price back on everything returned. He drains his Guinness.

Sometimes he still feels guilty (a little)—though not so much as he did. He realises well enough that his dedication to pornography is coarsening whatever sensibilities he may once have possessed; that his craving is settling like some cancerous, malignant growth upon his mind, a mind crying out with ever-increasing desperation for its instant, morbid gratification. But he can do nothing about it.

Prompt at 2:00 p.m. on Wednesday, 6 October, Mr. John Sanders is back in the formica shop, and once more the gyrating saw, whining in agony, can be heard behind the sliding doors.

On Wednesday evenings during term-time the Crowther household was usually deserted from 7:00 p.m. to 9:00 p.m.

Mrs. Margaret Crowther joined a small group of earnest middle-aged culture-vultures in a WEA evening class on Classical Civilisation; weekly the children, James and Caroline, swelled the oversubscribed membership of the Wednesday disco at the nearby Community Centre; Mr. Bernard Crowther disliked both pop and Pericles.

On the night of Wednesday, 6 October, Margaret left the house at her usual time of 6:30 p.m. Her classes were held about three miles away in the Further Education premises on Headington Hill, and she was anxious to secure a safe and central parking-lot for the proudly-sparkling Mini 1000 which Bernard had bought for her the previous August. Diffidently she backed out of the garage (Bernard had agreed to leave his own 1100 to face the winter's elements in the drive) and turned into the quiet road. Although still nervous about her skills, especially in the dark, she relished the little drive. There was the freedom and independence of it all— it was her car, she could go wherever *she* wanted. On the by-pass she took her usual deep breath and concentrated inordinately hard. Car after car swished by her on the outside lane, and she fought back her instinctive reaction to raise her right foot from its gentle pressure on the accelerator and to cover the brake pedal. She was conscious of the headlights of all the oncoming cars, their drivers, she was sure, brashly confident and secure. She fiddled with her safety belt and daringly glanced at the dashboard to ensure that her lights were dipped. Not that she ever had them on full anyway, for fear that in the sudden panic of dipping them she would press the switch the wrong way and turn them off altogether. At the Headington roundabout she negotiated the lanes competently, and uneventfully covered the remainder of her journey.

When she had first considered committing suicide, the car had seemed a very real possibility. But she now knew that she could never do it that way. Driving brought out all her primitive instincts for safety and self-preservation. And anyway, she couldn't smash up her lovely new Mini. There were other ways . . .

She parked carefully, getting in and out of the car several times before she was perfectly happy that it was as safely ensconced and as equi-distanced from its neighbours as she could manage, and entered the large, four-storeyed, glass-fronted building that ministered to the needs of the city's maturer students. She saw Mrs. Palmer, one of her class-mates, starting up the stairs to Room C26.

"Hullo, Mrs. Crowther! We all missed you last week. Were you poorly?"

"What's wrong with those two?" asked James.

A quarter of an hour after Margaret's departure, Bernard Crowther had caught the bus down to Lonsdale College, where he dined one or two nights a week. The children were alone.

"Not unusual, is it?" said Caroline.

"They hardly talk to one another."

"I 'spect all married people get like that."

"Didn't used to be like that."

"*You* don't help much."

"Nor do you."

"Wha' do you mean?"

"Ah—shut up!"

"You misery."

"F— off!"

These days their conversation seldom lasted longer. With a few minor permutations and, in the presence of mum and dad, a few concessions to conventional middle-class moral-ity, their parents had heard it many times. It worried Mar-garet deeply and infuriated Bernard, and each wondered secretly if all children were as vicious, ill-tempered and unco-operative as their own. Not that James and Caroline were uppermost in either parent's mind this Wednesday evening.

As one of the senior fellows of his college, Bernard had naturally been invited to the memorial jamboree for the ex-vice-principal who had retired the previous summer. The dinner was to begin at 7:30 p.m., and Bernard arrived in Peter's rooms with half an hour to spare. He poured himself a gin and vermouth and sat back in a faded armchair. He thought he liked Felix Tompsett—the old sod! Certainly he ate too much, and drank too much and, if many-tongued

rumour could be believed (why not?), he had done a lot of
other things too much. But he was a good "college man";
it was on his advice that the college had bought up a lot of
property in the early sixties and his understanding of interest
rates and investment loans was legendary. Odd really, thought
Bernard. He finished his gin and shrugged into his gown.
Preprandial sherry would be flowing in the Senior Common
Room, and the two friends made their way thither.

"Well, Bernard! How are you, old boy?" Felix's smile beamed
a genuine welcome to his old colleague.

"Can't grumble," replied Bernard lamely.

"And how's that lovely wife of yours?"

Bernard grabbed a sherry. "Oh fine, fine."

"Lovely woman." Felix mused on. He had obviously begun
to celebrate his own commemoration with pre-meditated
gusto, but Bernard couldn't match his bonhomie. He thought
of Margaret as the conversation burbled around him . . . He
tuned in again just in time to laugh convincingly at Felix's
discovery of a recent inscription on the wall of the gents in
the *Minster* bar.

"Bloody good, what?" guffawed Felix.

The party moved next door and sat down to the evening's
feast. Bernard always felt that they had far too much to eat,
and tonight they had far, far too much to eat. As he struggled
his way through the grapefruit cocktail, the turtle soup, the
smoked salmon, the tournedos Rossini, the gateau, the cheese
and the fruit, he thought of the millions in the world who
had not eaten adequately for weeks or even months, and
saw in his mind the harrowing pictures of the famine victims
of Asia and Africa . . .

"You're quiet tonight," said the chaplain, passing Bernard
the claret.

"Sorry," said Bernard. "It must be all this food and drink."

"You must learn to take the gifts the good Lord showers
upon us, my boy. You know, as I get older I must confess
to the greater appreciation of two things in life—natural
beauty and the delights of the belly."

He leaned back and poured half a glass of vintage claret
towards his vast stomach. Bernard knew that some men

were naturally fat—all to do with the metabolic rate, or something. But there were no fat men in Belsen . . .

But whatever other confessions the good chaplain may have been about to divulge were cut short by the toast to Her Majesty and the clearing of the Principal's throat as he rose to his feet to begin his ecomium of Felix Tompsett. They had all heard it all before. A few necessary alterations in the hackneyed, hallowed phrases—but basically the same old stuff. Felix would be leaving holes in so many aspects of college life; it would be difficult to fill the holes . . . Bernard thought of Margaret. Why not leave the bloody holes unfilled . . . One of the foremost scholars of his generation . . . Bernard looked at his watch. 9:15 p.m. He couldn't go yet. Anecdotes and laughter . . . Bernard felt pretty sure they would all be reminded of that incident when a disgruntled undergraduate had pissed all over Felix's carpet two years ago . . . Back to the academic stuff. Top-of-the-head. Phoney . . . His work on the Elizabethan lyric poets . . . why, the old bastard had spent most of his time doing firsthand research on the historic inns of Oxfordshire. Or with the women . . . For the first time Bernard wondered if Felix had made any overtures to Margaret. He'd better not . . .

Felix spoke well. Slightly drunk, amiable, civilised—quite moving really. Come on! 9:45 p.m. The presentation was made and the company broke up by 10:00 p.m. Bernard rushed out of college and ran through the Broad to St. Giles, where he found a taxi immediately. But even before the taxi stopped, he saw some movement outside the darkened house. His heart raced in panic-stricken despair. James and Caroline stood beside the front door.

"You might have . . ." began Caroline.

Bernard hardly heard. "Where's your mother?" His voice was hard and urgent.

"Don't know. We thought she must have been with you."

"How long have you been waiting?" He spoke with a clipped authority the children had seldom heard.

" 'Bout half an hour. Mum's always been here before . . ."

Bernard opened the front door. "Ring up the tech. at Headington. Ask if they've finished."

"You do it, Caroline."

Bernard brought his right hand with vicious force across James's face. "Do it!" he hissed.

He went to the gate. No-one. He prayed for the sound of a car, any car. Car! A cold sweat formed on his forehead as he darted to the garage. The door was locked. He found the key. His hand shook convulsively. He opened the door.

"What on earth are you doing?"

Bernard started, and in his heart blessed all the gods that were and are and are to be. "Where the hell have you been?" In a fraction of a second his terrible, agonised fear had flashed to anger—relieved, fierce, beautiful anger.

"As a matter of fact the starter-motor's gone on the Mini. I couldn't get anyone to fix it and in the end I had to catch a bus."

"You could have let me know."

"Oh yes, of course. You want me to ring round all the garages, then you, and then presumably the kids." Margaret herself was becoming very angry. "What's all the fuss about? Just because *I'm* late for a change!"

"The children have been waiting no end of a time."

"So what!" Margaret stormed into the house, and Bernard heard the high-pitched voices within. He closed the front gate and then the garage. He locked and bolted the front door. He felt happy, happier than he had felt for many days and many hours.

12
Wednesday, Thursday; 6, 7 October

Morse did not know what had persuaded him, after seven months of promises and prevarications, to fill in the ragged gaping hole above the kitchen door where the electrician had led in the wires for a new power-point. Everything had been wrong from the start anyway. The Polyfilla powder, purchased some two years previously, had hardened into a solid block of semi-concrete within its packet; the spatula he used for cracking eggs and filling cracks had mysteriously vanished from the face of the earth; and the primitive household steps never had stood four-square on their rickety legs. Perhaps he had taken inspiration from Mr. Edward de Bono and his recipe for lateral thought. But whatever the motive for his sudden urge to see the wretched hole filled in, Morse had taken a vertical plunge, like some free-fall parachutist, from the top of the steps, when the cord restraining the uprights to a functional 30° angle suddenly snapped and the whole apparatus collapsed into a straight line beneath him. Like Hephaestus, thrown o'er the crystal battlements, he landed with an agonising jolt upon his right foot, lay with a feeling of nausea for two or three minutes, wiping the cold sweat which formed upon his brow, and finally limped his way to the front room and lay breathing heavily on the settee. After a while the foot was a little easier and he felt somewhat reassured; but half an hour later the swelling began and a fitful, sharp pain nagged away at his instep. He wondered if he could drive, but knew it would be foolish to try. It was 8:30 p.m. on Tuesday, 5 October. Only one thing for it. He hobbled and hopped across to the telephone and rang Lewis, and within the half hour he was sitting disconsolately in the accident room of the Radcliffe Infirmary, waiting for the result of the X-ray. A young boy sitting on the bench next to Morse was wringing his left hand in some agony (car door) and two men badly injured in a road accident were wheeled by for priority treatment. He felt a little less depressed.

He was finally seen by an almost unintelligible Chinese doctor who held up his X-ray pictures to the light with the disinterestedness of a bored guest having a casual glance at one of the holiday slides of his host. "Nobrocken. Creep-ancrushes." From the competent nurse into whose hands he was now delivered, Morse gathered that no bones were broken and that the treatment prescribed was crêpe bandage and hospital crutches.

He expressed his thanks to nurse and doctor as he swung

along diffidently towards the waiting Lewis. "You," shouted the doctor after him. "You, Mr. Morse. Nowork twodays. You rest. OK?"

"I think I shall be all right, thanks," said Morse.

"You, Mr. Morse. Youwangebetter, eh? Nowork. Two days. Rest. OK?"

"OK." Oh God!

Morse hardly slept through Tuesday night; he had a vicious toothache in each of the toes on his foot. He swallowed Disprin after Disprin and finally towards dawn dozed off from sheer exhaustion. Lewis called several times during the prolonged agonies of Wednesday and watched the inspector fall into a blessedly-deep sleep at about 9:00 p.m.

When Lewis greeted him the next morning, Morse felt better; and because he felt better, his mind reverted to the murder of Sylvia Kaye, and because his mind was not now wholly preoccupied with the tribulations of his right foot, he felt a great depression grow upon him. He felt like a quiz contestant who had almost got some of the answers right, had others on the tip of his tongue, but had finished up with nothing. One always longed to start again . . .

He lay with these troubled thoughts on his mind. Lewis was fussing around. Good old Lewis. They'd all be having a good laugh at the station, he thought. Humiliating, falling off a ladder. Well he hadn't fallen *off* a ladder. He'd fallen *through* one.

"Lewis! You told everybody what happened, I suppose?"

"Yes, sir."

"Well?"

"They think you're making it up. They think you've got gout really. You know—too much port."

Morse groaned. He could picture himself limping round with every other person stopping him to inquire into the circumstances of the disaster. He'd write it all out, have it photocopied, and distribute the literature around the station.

"Still painful, sir?"

"Of course it bloody well is. You've got millions of nerve endings all over your bloody toes. You know that, don't you?"

"I had an uncle, sir, who had a beer barrel run over his toes."

"Shut up," winced Morse. The thought of anything, let alone a beer barrel, being within three feet of his injured foot was quite unbearable. Beer barrel, though. Morse was getting better.

"Are the pubs open yet?"

"Fancy a drink, sir?" Lewis looked pleased with himself.

"Wouldn't mind a jar."

"As a matter of fact I brought a few cans in last night, sir."

"Well?"

Lewis found some glasses, and positioning a chair a goodly distance from "the foot," poured out the beer.

"Nothing new?" asked Morse.

"Not yet."

"Mm."

The two men drank in silence. Some of the answers almost right . . . others on the tip of his tongue . . . What, wondered Morse, if he had been right, or almost right? If only he could start again . . . Suddenly he sat up, forgot his incapacity, yelped "Oh, me foot!" and leaned back again into his nest of pillows. He *could* start again, couldn't he? "Lewis. I want you to do me one or two favours. Get me some writing paper—it's in the writing-desk downstairs; and what about some fish and chips for lunch?"

Lewis nodded. As he went off for the writing paper Morse interrupted him.

"Three favours. Open a few of those cans."

A thought had been floating around in Morse's mind for several days, elusive as a bar of soap in a slippery bath. In the beginning was the thought, and the thought became word and Morse unwrapped the text carefully and read the message. *Im Anfang war die Hypothese*. In the beginning was the hypothesis. But before formulating any hypothesis, even of the most modest order, Morse decided that he would feel sharper in body, mind and spirit with a good wash and a shave. Slowly and painfully he got out of bed, tacked crabwise around the walls and ended up by hopping over the last few feet of the bathroom floor. It took him almost an hour to complete his toilet, but he felt a new man. He retraced his irregular progress and gently heaved his right foot into a comfortable niche alongside a spare pillow stuffed down at the bottom of the bed. He felt exhausted but wonderfully refreshed. He closed his eyes and fell fast asleep.

Lewis wondered if he should wake him, but the pungent smell of fried batter and vinegar saved him the trouble.

"What's the time, Lewis? I've been asleep."

"Quarter past one, sir. Do you want the fish and chips on a plate? Me and the wife always eat 'em off the paper— seems to taste better somehow."

"They say it's the newsprint sticking to the chips," replied Morse, taking the oily package from his sergeant and tucking in with relish. "You know, Lewis, perhaps we've been going about this case in the wrong way."

"We have, sir?"

"We've been trying to solve the case in order to find the murderer, right?"

"I suppose that's the general idea, isn't it?"

"Ah, but we might get better results the other way round."

"You mean . . ." But though Morse waited it was clear that Lewis had no idea whatsoever what he meant.

"I mean we ought to find the murderer in order to solve the case."

"I see," said Lewis, unseeing.

"I'm glad you do," said Morse. "It's as clear as daylight— and open some of these bloody curtains, will you?"

Lewis complied.

"If," continued Morse, "if I told you who the murderer was and where he lived, you could go along and you could arrest him, couldn't you?" Lewis nodded vaguely and wondered if his superior officer had caught his skull on the kitchen sink before landing on his precious right foot. "You could, couldn't you? You could bring him here to see me, you could keep him at a safe distance from my grievous injury—and he could tell us all about it, eh? He could do all our work for us, couldn't he?"

Morse jabbered on, his mouth stuffed with fish and chips, and with genuine concern Lewis began to doubt the inspector's sanity. Shock was a funny thing; he'd seen it many times in road accidents. Sometimes two or three days afterwards some of the parties would go completely ga-ga. They'd recover of course . . . Or had Morse been drinking? Not the beer. The opened cans were still unpoured. A heavy responsibility suddenly seemed to descend on Lewis's shoulders. He was sweating slightly. The room was hot, the autumn sun bright upon the glass of the bedroom window.

"Can I get you anything, sir?"

"Yep. Flannel and soap and towel. By Jove, your wife's right, Lewis. I'll never eat 'em off a plate again."

A quarter of an hour later a bewildered sergeant let himself out of the front door of Morse's flat. He felt a little worried and would have felt even more so if he had been back in the bedroom at that moment to hear Morse talking to himself, and nodding occasionally whenever he particularly approved of what he heard coming from his own lips.

"Now my first hypothesis, ladies and gentlemen, and as I see things the most vital hypothesis of all—I shall make many, oh yes, I shall make many—is this: that the murderer is living in North Oxford. You will say this is a bold hypothesis, and so it is. Why should the murderer not live in Didcot or Sidcup or even Southampton? Why should he live in North Oxford? Why not, coming nearer home, why not just in Oxford? I can only repeat to you that I am formulating a hypothesis, that is, a supposition, a proposition, however wild, assumed for the sake of argument; a theory to be proved (or disproved—yes, we must concede that) by reference to facts, and it is with facts and not with airy-fairy fancies that I shall endeavour to bolster my hypothesis. *Im Anfang war die Hypothese*, as Goethe might have put it. And please let it not be forgotten that I am Morse of the Detective, as Dickens would have said. Oh yes, a detective. A detective has a sensibility towards crime—he feels it; he must feel it before he can detect it. There are indications which point to North Oxford. We need not review them all here, but the *ambience* is right in North Oxford. And if I am wrong, why, no harm is done to our investigation. We are propounding a hypothesis, that is, a supposition, a proposition, however wild . . . I've said all that before, though. Where was I, now? Oh yes. I wish you to accept, provisionally, dubiously, hopelessly if needs be, my premier hypothesis. The murderer is a resident of North Oxford. Now I mentioned facts, and I shall not disappoint you. Aristotle classified the animals, I believe, by subdividing them, and subdivision will be our method of procedure. Aristotle, that great man, divided and subdivided—species, sub-species, genera (Morse was getting lost) genera, species, sub-species and so on until he reached—what did he reach?—*the individual specimen of the species.*" (That sounded better.) "I, too, will divide. In North Oxford there are, let us say, 'x' number of people. Now we further hypothesise that our murderer is a male. Why can we be confident of this fact? Because, ladies and gentlemen, the murdered girl was *raped.* This is a *fact*, and we shall bring forward at the trial the evidence of eminent medical personnel to . . ." Morse was tiring a little, and fortified himself with another can of beer. "As I was saying, our murderer is male. We can therefore divide our number x by, let us say, er, four—leaving the women and children out of our reckoning. Now can we subdivide again, you will ask? Indeed, we can. Let us guess at the age of our murderer. I put him—I am diffident, and you will accuse me of formulating sub-hypotheses—between 35 and 50. Yes, there are reasons . . ." But Morse decided to skip them. They weren't all that convincing, perhaps, but he had reasons, and he wished to sustain the impetus of his hypothesis. "We may then further subdivide our number x by two. That seems most reasonable, does it not? Let us continue. What else can we reasonably hypothesise? I believe—for reasons which I realise may not be fully acceptable to you all—that our suspect is a married man." Morse was feeling his way with an increasing lack of confidence. But the road ahead was already clearing; the fog was lifting and dissipating in the sun, and he resumed with his earlier briskness. "Now this means yet a further diminution in the power of x. Our x is becoming a manageable unit, is it not? But not yet is the focus of our *camera hypothetica* fixed with any clear delineation upon our unsuspecting quarry. But wait! Our man is a regular drinker, is he not? It is surely one of our more reasonable claims, and gives to our procedure not only the merits of hypothetical plausibility, but also of extreme probability. Our case is centred upon *The Black Prince*, and one does not visit *The Black Prince* in order to consult the tax inspector." Morse was wilting again. His foot was throbbing again with rhythmic pain, and his mind wandered off for a few minutes. Must be those Disprin. He closed his eyes and continued his forensic monologue within his brain.

He must, too, surely he must, figure in at least the top 5% of the IQ range? Jennifer wouldn't fall for an ignorant buffoon, would she? That letter. Clever chap, well-schooled. *If* he wrote it. If, if, if. Carry on. Where's our x now? Go on. He must be attractive to women. Yet who can say what attracts those lovely creatures? But yes. Say yes. Subdivide. Cars! God, he'd forgotten cars. Not everyone has a car. About what proportion? Never mind, subdivide. Just a minute— *red* car. He felt slightly delirious. Just a fraction longer . . . That really would be a significant sub-division. The x was floating slowly away, and now was gone. The pain was less vicious. Comfortable . . . almost . . . comfortable . . .

He was woken at 4:00 p.m. by Lewis's inability to manage the front door without a disturbing clatter. And when Lewis anxiously put his head round the bedroom door, he saw Morse scribbling as furiously as Coleridge must have scribbled when he woke up to find, full grown within his mind, the whole of *Kubla Khan.*

"Sit down, Lewis. Glad to see you." He continued to write with furious rapidity for two or three minutes. Finally he looked up. "Lewis, I'm going to ask you some questions. Think carefully—don't rush!—and give me some intelligent answers. You'll have to guess, I know, but do your best."

Oh hell, thought Lewis.

"How many people live in North Oxford?"

"What do you call 'North Oxford,' sir?"

"I'm asking the questions, you're answering 'em. Just think generally what *you* think North Oxford is; let's say Summertown and above. Now come on!"

"I could find out, sir."

"Have a bloody guess, man, can't you?"

Lewis felt uncomfortable. At least he could see that only three of the beer cans were empty. He decided to plunge in. "Ten thousand." He said it with the assurance and unequivocal finality of a man asked to find the sum of two and two.

Morse took another sheet of paper and wrote down the number 10,000. "What proportion of them are men?"

Lewis leaned back and eyed the ceiling with the confidence of a statistical consultant. "About a quarter."

Morse wrote down his second entry neatly and carefully beneath the first: 2,500. "How many of those men are between 35 and 50?"

Quite a lot of retired people in North Oxford, thought Lewis, and quite a lot of young men on the estates. "About half, no more."

The third figure was entered: 1,250. "How many of them are married, would you say?"

Lewis considered. Most of them, surely? "Four out of five, sir."

Morse formed the figures of his latest calculation with great precision: 1,000.

"How many of them regularly go out for a drink—you know what I mean—pubs, clubs, that sort of thing?"

Lewis thought of his own street. Not so many as some people thought. The neighbours on either side of him didn't—mean lot! He thought of the street as a whole. Tricky this one. "About half."

Morse revised his figure and went on to his next question. "You remember the letter we had, Lewis. The letter Jennifer Coleby said she knew nothing about?" Lewis nodded. "If we were right in thinking what we did, or what I did, would you say we were dealing with a man of high intelligence?"

"That's a big if, isn't it, sir?"

"Look, Lewis. That letter was written by our man—just get that into your head. It was the big mistake he made. It's the best clue we've got. What the hell do they pay us for. We've got to follow the clues, haven't we?" Morse didn't sound very convinced, but Lewis assured him that they had to follow the clues. "Well?"

"Well what, sir?"

"Was he an intelligent man?"

"Very much so, I should think."

"Would you think of writing a letter like that?"

"Me? No, sir."

"And you're pretty bright, aren't you sergeant?"

Lewis squared his shoulders, took a deep breath and decided not to minimise his intellectual capacity. "I'd say I was in the top 15%, sir."

"Good for you! And our unknown friend? You remember he not only knows how to spell all the tricky words, he knows how to mis-spell them, too!"

"Top 5%, sir."

Morse wrote down the calculation.

"What proportion of middle-aged men are attractive to women?" Silly question! Morse noticed the derision in Lewis's face. "You know what I mean. Some men are positively repulsive to women!" Lewis seemed unconvinced. "I know all about these middle-aged Romeos. We're all middle-aged Romeos. But some men are more attractive to women than others, aren't they?"

"I don't get many falling for me, sir."

"That's not what I'm asking you. Say something, for God's sake!"

Lewis plunged again. "Half? No, more than that. Three out of five."

"You're sure you mean that?"

Of course he wasn't sure. "Yes."

Another figure. "How many men of this age group have cars?"

"Two out of three." What the hell did it matter?

Morse wrote down his penultimate figure. "One more question. How many people own red cars?"

Lewis went to the window and watched the traffic going by. He counted. Two black, one beige, one dark blue, two white, one green, one yellow, one black. "One in ten, sir."

Morse had shown a growing excitement in his manner for the last few minutes. "Phew! Who'd have believed it? Lewis, you're a genius!"

Lewis thanked him for the compliment and asked wherein his genius lay. "I think, Lewis, that we're looking for a male person, resident in North Oxford, married—probably a family, too; he goes out for a drink fairly regularly, sometimes to Woodstock; he's a well-educated man, may even be a university man; he's about 35 to 45, as I see him, with a certain amount of charm—certainly, I think a man some of the young ladies could fall for; finally he drives a car—to be precise a red car."

"He'd be as good as anyone, I suppose."

"Well, even if we're a bit out here and there, I'd bet my bottom dollar he's pretty likely to fit into most of those categories. And, do you know, Lewis, *I don't think there are many who fall into that category*. Look here." He passed over to Lewis the sheet of paper containing the figures.

North Oxford?	10,000
Men?	2,500
35–50?	1,250
Married?	1,000
Drinker?	500
Top 5%?	25
Charm?	15
Car?	10
Red Car?	1

Lewis felt a guilty sense of responsibility for the remarkable outcome of these computations. He stood by the window in the fading light of afternoon, and saw two red cars go by one after the other. How many people *did* live in North Oxford? Was he really in the top 15%? 25% more likely. "I'm sure, sir, that we could check a lot of these figures." Lewis felt constrained to voice his suspicions. "I don't think you can just fiddle about with figures like that, anyway. You'd need to . . ." He had a dim recollection of the need for some statistical laws operating on data; the categories had to be ordered and reduced in logical sequence; he couldn't quite remember. But it was all little more than an elaborate game to amuse a fevered brain. Morse would be up in a day or so. Better look after him and humour him as best he could. But was there any logic in it? Was it all *that* stupid? He looked again at the paper of figures and another red car went by. There were nine "ifs." He stared gloomily out of the window and mechanically counted the next ten cars. Only one red one! North Oxford was, of course, the biggest gamble. But the fellow had to live somewhere, didn't he? Perhaps the old boy was not so cuckoo as he'd thought. He looked at the sheet yet again . . . The other big thing was that letter. *If* the murderer had written it.

"What do you think then, Lewis?"

"Might be worth a go."

"How many men do you want?"

"We'd need to do a bit of thinking first, wouldn't we?"

"What do you mean?"

"The local authorities could help a good deal. First we'd need some up-to-date lists of residents."

"Yes. You're right. We need to think it through before we do anything."

"That's what I thought, sir."

"Well?"

"We could get straight on to it in the morning, sir, if you felt up to it."

"Or we could get straight on to it now if *you* felt up to it?"

"I suppose we could."

Lewis rang his long-suffering spouse, and conferred with Morse for the next two hours. After he had left, Morse reached for a bedside 'phone and was lucky to find the Chief Superintendent still in his office. And half an hour later Morse was still talking, and ruefully cursing himself for having forgotten to reverse the charges.

13
Saturday, 9 October

On the morning of Saturday, 9 October Bernard Crowther sat at his desk in his front room reading Milton, but not with his usual thrilled enjoyment. He was lecturing on *Paradise Lost* this term and in spite of his thorough and scholarly mastery of the work he felt he should do a little more homework. Margaret had caught the bus to Summertown to do her shopping and his car was ready outside to pick her up at mid-day. The children were out. Goodness knew where.

He was surprised to hear the front door bell ring, for they had few callers. Butcher perhaps. He opened the door.

"Why, Peter! What a surprise! Come in, come in." Peter Newlove and Bernard had been firm friends for years. They had arrived at Lonsdale College the same term and since then had enjoyed a warm and genuine relationship. "What brings you here? Not very often we have the pleasure of seeing you in North Oxford. I thought you played golf on Saturday mornings, anyway."

"I couldn't face it this morning. Bit chilly round the fairways, you know." The weather had turned much colder the last two days, and the autumn had suddenly grown old. The day seemed bleak and sour. Peter sat down. "Working on Saturday morning, Bernard?"

"Just getting ready for next week."

Peter looked across at the desk. "Ah. *Paradise Lost*, Book I. I remember that. We did it for higher certificate."

"You've read it since, of course."

"*From morn to noon he fell, from noon to dewy eve, a summer's day.* What about that?"

"Very fine." Bernard looked out of the window and saw the white hoar-frost still unmelted on his narrow lawn.

"Is everything all right, Bernard?" The man from Gloucestershire spoke with an abrupt kindliness.

"Course everything's all right. Why did you say that?" It was clear to Peter that everything was far from right.

"Oh, I don't know. You just seemed a bit on edge on Wednesday night. Scuttled away like a startled hare after the dinner."

"I'd forgotten that Margaret would be late, and I knew the kids would be waiting outside."

"I see."

"Was it that obvious?"

"No, not really. I was watching you, that's all. You didn't seem your old self when we had a drink together, and I thought you might be a bit under the weather." Bernard said nothing. "Everything OK with you and, er, Margaret?"

"Oh, yes. Fine. I've got to collect her, by the way, at twelve. What's the time now?"

"Half-past eleven." Peter rose to his feet.

"No, don't go! We've got time for a quick drink. What'll you have?"

"Are you going to have one?"

"Of course I am. Whisky?"

"Fine."

Bernard withdrew to the kitchen to get the glasses, and Peter stood in front of the window, looking out into the narrow street. A car, white and pale blue, with a light (not flashing) on the roof and marked in bold black lettering across its side, was parked across the way, two or three doors to the left. It had not been there when Peter arrived. As he watched, a police constable, with a black and white chequered band around his flat, peaked hat, was coming out of a front gate. A middle-aged woman walked with him and the two were talking freely, pointing between them to every point of the compass. More talk and further pointing arms. Was she pointing here? The constable had a list in his hand and he was clearly checking some names. The woman stood with her apron around her, clutching her arms about her middle to keep warm and chattering interminably on.

Bernard came in, the glasses clattering a little on the tray. "Say when!"

"I see you've got a few criminals in the road, Bernard."

"What did you say?" Bernard looked up sharply.

"Is the law always prowling around here like this?" Peter got no further. The door bell rang twice; shrill, peremptory. Bernard opened the door and stood face to face with the young constable.

"Can I help you, officer?"

"Yes, I think so, sir, if you will. Won't take more'n a minute. Is this your car, sir?" He pointed to the red 1100 outside.

"Yes, it is."

"Just checking, sir. We've had a lot of cars stolen recently. Just checking." He made a note in his book. "Can you remember the registration number, sir?"

Mechanically Bernard recited the number.

"That's yours all right then, sir. Have you got your log-book handy, sir?"

"Is it necessary?"

"Well, it is rather important, if you don't mind, sir. We're checking as thoroughly as we can."

Peter heard the conversation through the open door and felt strangely worried. Bernard came in and poked about haphazardly in his desk. "Where the hell's Margaret . . . They're checking on stolen cars, Peter. Shan't be a minute." He looked ashen, and could find nothing. "I'm sorry, officer," he called. "Come in a minute, will you?"

"Thank you, sir. Don't worry if you can't put your hand on the log-book, sir. You can give me the information yourself quite easily."

"What do you want to know?"

"Full name, sir?"

"Bernard Michael Crowther."

"Age, sir?"

"Forty-one."

"Married, sir?"

"Yes."

"Children?"

"Two."

"Occupation?"

"University lecturer."

"That's about all, sir." He closed his book. "Oh, just one more thing. Have you left your car unlocked recently? You know what I mean. Is it locked now, for example?"

"No, I don't think so."

"No, it isn't, sir. I tried all the doors before I called. It's an open invitation to car thieves, you know."

"Yes, I'm sure you're right. I'll try to remember."

"Do you use your car much, sir?"

"Not a great deal. Running around a bit in Oxford. Not much really."

"You don't take it out when you go for a drink, for example?"

Peter thought he saw the daylight. Bernard had been drinking and driving, had he?

"No, not very often," answered Bernard. "I usually go round to *The Fletcher's*. It's not far; I always walk there."

"Would you take the car if you went drinking outside Oxford, sir?"

"I'm afraid I would," said Bernard slowly, in a helpless sort of way.

"Well, don't drink too much, sir, if you're driving. But I'm sure you know all about that." The constable glanced quickly round the room and looked drily at the two large tumblers of whisky; but he said nothing more until he reached the door. "You don't know anyone else in the road who's got a red car, do you, sir? I've got to make a few more inquiries."

Bernard thought, but his mind was swimming. He couldn't think of anybody. He closed his eyes and put his left hand on his forehead. Every day in term time he walked to the far end of the road. Red car? Red car? His was the only one, he was pretty sure of that.

"Well don't worry, sir. I'll just make one or two more, er . . . Anyway, thank you for your help, sir." He was gone. But not, Peter noticed, to make any more inquiries in that particular road. He walked straight to the police car (left unlocked) and immediately accelerated away.

Some ten minutes later as he drove along to Woodstock, Peter Newlove was glad he'd never married. The same woman—thirty, forty, fifty years! Not for him. He couldn't imagine poor old Bernard jumping into bed that afternoon for a riotous half-hour romp with Margaret. Whereas . . . He thought of Gaye undressing, and his right foot pressed hard upon the accelerator.

An immensely excited Constable McPherson rushed across the forecourt of the Thames Valley HQ where earlier the same morning he had seen poor old Morse staggering painfully along, his arms encircling the shoulders of two of his burly mates. Wow! McPherson felt like a man with eight draws up on the treble-chance pool. As he had driven the few miles from North Oxford to Kidlington, he sensed a feeling of unprecedented elation. For the last four years his uniformed career had been uniformly undistinguished; he had apprehended no significant villain; he had witnessed no memorable breach of either the civil or the criminal code. But blessed indeed he was today! As he had neared the Banbury Road roundabout he had switched on the wailing siren and the winking blue light, and had delighted in the deference accorded to him by his fellow motorists. He felt mightily important. Why not? He *was* mightily important —for today, at least.

Inside the station, McPherson debated for a second or two. Should he report to Lewis? Or should he report his intelligence direct to the inspector? The latter course seemed on reflection the more appropriate, and he made his way along the corridors to Morse's door, knocked and just caught the muffled "come in" from the other side.

"And what can I do for you, constable?"

McPherson made his report with an accuracy and incisiveness that was impressive, and Morse congratulated him upon the prompt and efficient discharge of his duty. McPherson, though mightily gratified with the compliment, was a little surprised that Morse himself seemed not immediately anxious to summon the cohorts of the law. But he'd done his own job—done it well.

"Excuse me if I don't stand up—gout, you know—but . . ." He shook McPherson's hand warmly. "It won't go unnoticed, believe me."

After McPherson's departure, Morse sat silently and thoughtfully for a few minutes. But so he had been sitting when the constable had entered. It would have been so disappointing for McPherson to have known, and anyway McPherson had been the immediate cause. No, he could never have had the heart to confess that Mr. Bernard Crowther had telephoned in at 11:45 a.m. wishing, he said, to make a statement.

Crowther had insisted that he should present himself, that on no account were the police to collect him, that he expected the authorities at least to allow to a witness, coming forward voluntarily with what might be valuable information, the normal courtesy of not being picked up like a common felon. Morse had agreed, and Bernard promised to be with him at 2:30 p.m.

* * *

Morse found himself apologising for his immobility and his
first impression of Crowther was surprisingly agreeable. The
man was nervous—that was plain for all to see; but there
was an odd charm and dignity about the fellow; that sort of
middle-aged schoolmaster-type that some of the girls might
have a crush on.

"Look, inspector—you are a chief inspector, I think—I
have never in my life been inside a police station until
this moment. I am not conversant with normal police practice and procedure. So I have taken the precaution of writing out, very rushed, I'm afraid, the statement I wish
to make."

14
Saturday, 9 October

On the evening of Wednesday, September 29th, I left my
house in Southdown Road at 6:45 p.m. I drove my car to
the roundabout at the north end of the Banbury Road, where
I turned left and travelled the four hundred yards or so along
Sutherland Avenue to the roundabout at the northern end
of the Woodstock Road. Here I turned off the A40 and took
the road north to Woodstock. Night was already drawing in
and I switched the side-lights on, in common, I noticed,
with the majority of the other motorists. Yet although it was
that awkward half light in which it is most difficult to drive,
it was not dark enough for full head-lights; it was certainly
not dark enough for me to miss two young girls standing a
little way beyond the roundabout on the grass verge alongside the self-service filling-station. The girl nearer to the
road I saw clearly. She was an attractive girl with long fair
hair, white blouse, short skirt and a coat over her arm. The
other girl had walked on a few yards and had her back
towards me; she seemed to be quite happy to leave the
business of getting a lift to her companion. But she had

darkish hair, I think, and if I remember correctly was a few inches taller than her friend.

I must now try to be completely honest with you. I have often been guilty of romantic day-dreams, even vaguely erotic day-dreams, about picking up some wildly attractive woman and finding her a rare and disturbing combination of brains and beauty. In my silly imaginings the preliminary and diffident skirmishing would lead gradually but inevitably to the most wanton delights. But this, remember, has always been a day-dream and I mention it simply to excuse myself for having stopped at all. I shouldn't feel guilty and apologetic about such things; yet in all honesty I do feel so, and have always felt so.

But that is by the way. I leaned over and opened the nearside front door and said that I was going to Woodstock, if that would help. The blonde girl said something like "Oh, super." She turned round to her companion and said (I think), "What did I tell you?" and got into the front seat beside me. The other girl opened the rear door and got in also. What conversation there was was desultory and disappointing. The girl beside me reiterated at intervals that this was "a real bi' of luck" (she had a typical Oxford manner of speech) because she had missed the bus; I think the girl sitting in the back spoke only once and that was to ask the time. I mentioned as we passed the gates of Blenheim Palace that "this was about it," and I understood that it would do them fine. I dropped them as soon as we reached the main street, but I didn't notice where they went. It was natural for me to believe, as I did, that they were going to meet their boy friends.

There is little more to say. What I have written above is a true record of the events which, as I now realise, later in the evening led up to the murder of one of the girls I had driven.

I have just re-read what I have written and am conscious that it perhaps says little which can help your investigation. I am also aware that my statement will give rise to two questions: first, why was I myself going to Woodstock on the night of 29 September, and second, why did I not come forward earlier with my evidence? The two questions are really one, and I shall feel a great weight off my shoulders to be able to answer it; nevertheless, it is my earnest hope that what I have to say can be treated by the police with the strictest confidentiality, since other people, themselves completely innocent, would be hurt beyond telling if it were to become generally known.

For the last six months or so I have been having an affair with another woman. We have been able to meet regularly once a week, almost always on Wednesday evenings, when my wife and children are away from home and when no awkward questions are likely to arise. On Wednesday, 29th, I was on my way to meet this woman by the side gates of Blenheim Palace at 7:15 p.m. I parked my car outside the *Bear Hotel* and walked there. She was waiting. We walked into Blenheim gardens, beside the lake, and through the trees—it is a most beautiful spot. It was, of course, dangerous for us, since so many people from Oxford go out for a meal in Woodstock. But we were always careful, and the element of risk was itself perhaps part of the excitement.

I need say no more. I read the account of the murder and later watched Detective Chief Inspector Morse make his appeal on television. I wish you to know that I almost telephoned there and then; in fact I waited outside a telephone-box in Southdown Road for several minutes that same evening with a firm resolve to come forward immediately. But this is making excuses, and I have none to offer. I fully understand, as you will, that I have not, even at this late stage, come forward of my own volition. When a police constable called at my home this morning, I realised that you were on to me, and thought it best to offer this statement straightaway. I perpetuated to my wife the rigmarole which the constable had given me about stolen cars, and I told her that I would be coming here. I would do anything in the world to avoid hurting her (yet, it is probable, I know, that I have hurt her already), and I should be most grateful if any part of my statement not relevant to the strict terms of the inquiries you are conducting can be kept secret.

That I am genuinely sorry for the inconvenience and needless extra work which I have caused, will, I trust, be obvious from what I have said here. If it is not, let me hasten to state now my profound apologies for my selfish and cowardly course of action.

I am,

Your humble servant,

Bernard Michael Crowther.

Morse read the statement slowly. When he had finished he looked across the table at Crowther, then looked down again at the statement and re-read it with even greater concentration. When he had finished, he leaned back in his black leather chair, carefully picked up his injured right foot, put it across his left knee and rubbed it lovingly.

"I've hurt my foot, Mr. Crowther."

"Have you? I'm sorry to hear that. My medical friends say that feet and hands are about the worst things to knock about—something to do with the multiplicity of nerve-endings."

He had a pleasant voice and manner. Morse looked him fully in the eyes. For several seconds neither man flinched, and Morse thought he saw a basic honesty in the man. But he could not conceal from himself a draining sense of disappointment and anticlimax; like Constable McPherson he had thought of a big pools win, only to find that instead of "telegrams required" the forecast was very low. "Yes." He picked up the conversation. "I shan't be walking round Blenheim Park tonight, sir."

"Nor shall I," said Bernard.

"Very romantic, I should think, having a bit on the side like that."

"You make it sound very crude."

"Wasn't it?"

"Perhaps so."

"Are you still seeing her?"

"No. My philandering days are over now, I hope."

"Have you seen her since that night?"

"No. It's all off. It seemed better."

"Does she know that you picked the two girls up?"

"Yes."

"Is she upset—that it's all over, I mean?"

"I suppose so, a bit."

"What about you?"

"To be truthful, it's a great relief. I'm not a very accomplished Casanova and I hated all the lying."

"You realise, of course, that it would help a great deal if this young lady—is she young, by the way?"

For the first time Bernard hesitated. "Fairly young."

"If this young lady," continued Morse, "would come forward and corroborate your evidence?"

"Yes. I know it would."

"But you don't want that."

"I'd rather you disbelieved my story than dragged her into it."

"You're not going to tell me who she is? I can promise you that I will handle the business myself."

Bernard shook his head. "I'm sorry. I can't do that."

"I could try to find her, you know," said Morse.

"I couldn't stop that."

"No, you couldn't." Morse moved his foot carefully back to the cushion strategically placed under his desk. "You could be withholding vital evidence, Mr. Crowther." Bernard said nothing. "Is she married?" persisted Morse.

"I'm not going to talk about her," he said quietly, and Morse sensed a steely resolve in the man.

"Do you think I could find her?" His foot shot with pain, and he picked it up again. Oh, what the hell, he thought; if this bit of stuff likes him to tickle her tits under the trees, what's that got to do with me? Bernard had not answered and Morse changed his tack. "You realise, I'm sure, that this other girl, the one who sat in the back seat, she's the one who might be able to give us a line?" Crowther nodded. "Why do you think we haven't heard from her?"

"I don't know.'

"Can't you think of any reason?"

Bernard could, that was clear, but he did not put his thoughts into words.

"You can, can't you, Mr. Crowther? Because it could be exactly the same reason which accounted for your reluctance to come forward." Bernard nodded again. "She could tell us, perhaps, who Sylvia Kaye's boy friend was, where she was going to meet him, what they were going to do—she might be able to tell us such a lot, don't you think?"

"I didn't get the idea they knew each other very well."

"Why do you say that?" asked Morse sharply.

"Well, they didn't chatter much together. You know how young girls do: pop music, dances, discos, boy friends—they just didn't talk much—that's all."

"You didn't catch her name?"

"No."

"Have you tried to think if Sylvia used her name?"

"I've tried to tell you all I can remember. I can't do any more."

"Betty, Carole, Diana, Evelyn . . . no?" Bernard remained impassive. "Gaye, Heather, Iris, Jennifer . . ." Morse could not make out the mildest flicker of response in Bernard's eyes. "Had she got nice legs?"

"Not so nice as the other's, I don't think."

"You noticed those?"

"What do you think? She was sitting next to me."

"Any erotic day-dreams?"

"Yes," said Crowther, with a fierce burst of honesty.

"It's a good job it's not a criminal offence," sighed Morse, "otherwise we'd all be inside." He noticed a light smile play for a brief second on Crowther's worried face. *I can see him being attractive to some women,* thought Morse. "What time did you get home that night?"

"About a quarter to nine."

"Was that the usual time, you know, because of, er, your, er, wife and so on?"

"Yes."

"An hour a week, was that it?"

"Not much longer."

"Was it worth it?"

"It seemed so—at the time."

"You didn't call at *The Black Prince* that evening?"

"I've never been in *The Black Prince*." It sounded very definite. Morse looked down at the statement again and noticed the beautifully-formed handwriting; it seemed a pity to type it out. He questioned Crowther for a further half an hour, and gave it up soon after 4:00 p.m.

"We shall have to keep your car here a while, I'm afraid."

"You will?" Crowther sounded disappointed.

"Yes, we might just find something, you know—hair, that sort of thing. They can do wonderful things these days, our forensic boys." He got up from his chair and asked Crowther for his crutches. "I'll promise you one thing," said Morse. "We'll keep your wife out of it. I'm sure you can make up something to tell her. After all, you're used to that sort of thing, aren't you, sir?"

Morse limped out behind Crowther and ordered the desk sergeant to get some transport. "Leave your car keys with me please, sir," said Morse. "You should have the car back early next week." The two men shook hands and Crowther was to wait only a few minutes before he was ushered into a police car. Morse watched him go with mixed feelings. He felt he'd handled things satisfactorily. He needed to think now, not to talk.

He summoned assistance and was helped across to Crowther's car. The doors were open. He struggled his way into the nearside front seat and sat back, manoeuvring his foot as carefully as he could, and stretching his legs as far as possible in front of him. He closed his eyes and pictured the legs of Sylvia Kaye, long, tanned, finely-formed, rising up to her brief skirt. He thought she might have leaned back, too. "Hot pants!" he said, almost to himself.

"Pardon, sir?" said the sergeant who had helped him into the car.

By an odd coincidence (or was it?) Studio 2 in Walton Street was presenting a double sexploitation bill whose titles were calculated to titillate even the most jaded appetite. The first, 2:00–3:05 p.m., was *Danish Blue* (not, judging from the mounds of female flesh that burst their bounds in the stills outside, a film about the manufacturing of cheese) and from 3:20–5:00 p.m. the main attraction of the week, entitled *Hot Pants*.

At 5:00 p.m. the earlier addicts were leaving, and a small group of men stood inside the foyer waiting for admission. One of these would normally have joined the early brigade, for this was for him a weekly occurrence. But he had been needed by Messrs. Chalkley and Sons for two hours' overtime in the formica shop. He would not, this week, be able to stay round and see the programme twice; but the films seldom met his inflated expectations or the infinite promise of the coming-shortly trailers. On these occasions he seldom looked about him, and it was just as well in the late afternoon of Saturday, 9 October, that once again he averted his eyes from his fellow voyeurs. For standing no more than four feet away from him, ostensibly checking the times of the next programme, but keeping himself carefully and unobtrusively out of the limelight, was the sergeant seconded to Detective Chief Inspector Morse for the inquiry into the murder of Sylvia Kaye. Lewis thought that this was one of Morse's more rewarding assignments, and he suspected that, but for his accident, his chief might well have undertaken it himself.

15
Monday, 11 October

The weekend drifted by, and the leaves continued to fall. Morse was feeling more cheerful; he could not put a good deal of weight on to his foot, and on Monday morning, deciding that he could exchange his crutches for a pair of sticks, he arranged for McPherson to drive him down to the Radcliffe Infirmary Outpatients' (Accident) Department.

He questioned McPherson closely as they drove. What impression had he formed of Crowther? What had been Crowther's immediate reactions? What was he like at home did he think? What had he been doing when McPherson called? Morse found the young constable surprisingly intelligent and observant, and told him so. Furthermore he

found a good deal in the information he had been given that
interested him and aroused his curiosity.

"What had he been reading—did you manage to see?"

"No, sir. But books on literature, I think. You know, poetry." Morse let it pass.

"He had a writing-desk, you say?"

"Yes, sir. You know, papers all over it."

Morse mentally resolved not to count up the "you knows"
he'd had so far and the "you knows" he was surely going to
get. "Was there a typewriter there?" He said it casually
enough.

"Yes. You know, one of those portable things."

Morse said no more. Waved through the narrow yards of
the Infirmary, that seemed in conspiracy to prevent too many
injured citizens from gaining immediate access to the Out-
patients' Department, the police car parked itself, with no
objections from porters, orderlies or traffic wardens, on a
broad stretch of concrete marked "Ambulances Only." A
policeman's parking lot was sometimes not an unhappy one.
Morse had foreseen the swopping of crutches for sticks as
a straightforward transaction; but it was not to be. There
appeared to be an unbreached egalitarianism in the world
of all injured brothers, and Morse was constrained to take
his proper place and wait his proper time whilst the proper
formalities were completed. He sat on the same bench, skipped
through the same old edition of *Punch*, and felt the same
impatience; he heard the same Chinese doctor, his sang-
froid seemingly disturbed by the inability of a little boy to
sit still: "Youwannagetbetter, li'l boy, youbetter sidstill."

Morse stared gloomily at the floor and found himself
watching the nurses' legs go by. Not much to make the
blood boil really. Except one pair—beautiful! Morse would
like to have seen the rest of the delicious damsel, but she
had walked swiftly past. Fat, so-so, thin, so-so—and then
those legs again and this time they stopped miraculously in
front of him.

"I hope you're being looked after all right, Inspector Morse?"

The inspector was visibly stunned. He looked up slowly,
straight and deep into the sad, come-hither face of darling
Dark-eyes, co-resident of the cool Miss Jennifer Coleby. "You

remember me?" said Morse; a little illogically, thought the girl standing directly above him.

"Don't you remember *me*?" she asked.

"How could I forget you?" said the inspector, slipping at last into a smooth forward gear. How lovely she was! "You work here?"

"If I may say so, inspector, you must have asked a great many more intelligent questions in your time." She wore her uniform becomingly—and Morse always thought a nurse's uniform did more for a girl than all the fine feathers of the fashion houses.

"No, not very bright, was it?" he confessed. She smiled —delightfully.

"Have a seat," said Morse, "I'd like to have a chat with you. We didn't say much before, did we?"

"I'm sorry, inspector. I can't do that. I'm on duty."

"Oh." He was disappointed.

"Well . . ."

"Just stay a minute," said Morse. "You know, I really would like to see you, some time. Can I see you when you come off duty?"

"I'm on duty until six."

"Well, I could meet . . ."

"At six I shall go home and have a quick meal, and then at seven . . ."

"You've got a date."

"Well, let's say I'm busy."

"Lucky bugger," mumbled Morse. "Tomorrow?"

"Not tomorrow."

"Wednesday?" Morse wondered mournfully if the progression through the remaining days of the week was anything more than a hollow formality; but she surprised him.

"I could see you on Wednesday evening, if you like."

"Could you?" Morse sounded like an eager schoolboy. They arranged to meet in *The Bird and Baby* in St. Giles at 7:30 p.m. Morse tried to sound more casual: "I can take you home, of course, but perhaps it would be better not to pick you up. You can get a bus all right?"

"I'm not a child, inspector."

"Good. See you then." She turned away. "Oh, just a minute," called Morse. She walked back to him. "I don't know your name yet, Miss . . ."

"Miss Widdowson. But you can call me Sue."

"Is that just for special friends?"

"No," said Miss Widdowson. "Everyone calls me Sue."

For the first week of the case Morse had felt confident in his own abilities, like a schoolboy with a tricky problem in mathematics to work out who had the answer book secretly beside him. From the very beginning of the case he thought he had glimpsed a Grand Design—he would have to juggle about a bit with the pieces of evidence that came to hand, but he knew the pattern of the puzzle. For this reason he had not, he realised, considered the evidence *qua* evidence, but only in relation to his own prejudiced reconstruction of events. And having failed to work out an answer to his problem which bore the faintest similarity to the agreed solution in the answer book, he was now beginning seriously to wonder if, after all, the answer book was wrong. Sometimes on the eve of a big horse-race he had read through the list of runners and riders, closed his eyes and tried to visualise the headlines on the sports page of the following morning's newspaper. He'd had little success with that, either. Yet he still thought he was on the right track. He was, as he saw himself, a persevering man, although he was wide awake to the possibility that to Lewis (sitting across the table now) his perseverance might well be considered stubbornness, and to his superiors sheer pig-headedness.

In fact Lewis was not at that moment considering the stubbornness of his chief at all; he was contemplating with great distaste the orders he had just received.

"But do you think it's proper to do it this way, sir?"

"I doubt it," said Morse.

"But it's not legal, surely?"

"Probably not."

"But you want me to do it." Morse ignored the non-question. "When?"

"You'd have to make sure he was out first."

"How do you suggest . . . ?"

Morse interrupted him. "Christ man, you're not in apron strings. Use your nous!"

Lewis felt angry as he walked across to the canteen and ordered a cup of coffee.

"What's the matter, sarge?" Constable Dickson was eating again.

"That bloody man Morse—that's what's the matter," muttered Lewis, setting down his cup with such vigour that half the contents slopped messily into the saucer.

"I see you like your coffee half and half, sarge," said Dickson. "Half in the cup and half in the saucer." He was highly amused.

McPherson walked in and ordered coffee. "Solved the murder yet, sergeant?"

"No we bloody haven't," snapped Lewis. He got up and left the grey-looking apology untouched—half in the cup and half in the saucer.

"What's eating him?" asked McPherson. "God, he don't know how lucky he is. Damn good chap, Inspector Morse. I tell you, if he don't get to the bottom of that Woodstock business, nobody will."

It was a nice compliment and Morse could have done with it. After Lewis had left, he sat for a long time, his hands together in front of his face, fingertips to fingertips, eyes closed, as if praying to some benign divinity for light along the darkening path. But Morse had long ago, albeit unwillingly, discounted the existence of any supernatural agency. He was fishing patiently in the troubled waters of his mind.

He got his bite about 4:30 p.m., and limped across to the file on the Woodstock murder. Yes, they were both there. He took them out and read them again—for the umpteenth time, it seemed. He must be right. He had to be. But still he wondered if he was.

The first thing (but it was a minnow, not a shark) that arrested his attention was that in both the letter from the (pretty certainly) bogus employer, and in the statement made by Crowther, the writer had used the form "I should." Morse, not as conversant as he should have been with some of the niceties of English grammar, more often than not—almost always now he thought of it—used the form "would." He could hear himself dictating: "Dear Sir, I would be very glad to . . ." Ought he to have said "I should?" He reached for Fowler's *Modern English Usage.* There it was: "The verbs *like, prefer, care, be glad, be inclined,* etc. are very common in first-person conditional statements (*I should like to know* etc.). In these *should,* not *would,* is the correct form in the English idiom." Well, thought Morse, we learn something new every day. But somebody knew all about it already. So he should, though; he was an English don, wasn't he? What about Mr. G—undecipherable who had something to do with a mis-spelt Psychology Department? (Blast—he'd not even checked that yet.) But Mr. G was a university man, too, wasn't he? said a still small voice at the back of Morse's mind. A very little minnow! Interesting though.

He read the documents yet again. Just a minute. Hold on. Yes. This wasn't a minnow. Surely not! "Yet it is not improbable . . ." The phrase appeared in each document. A mannered phrase. "Yet" standing at the beginning of its clause; not the commonest of syntactical structures. And what about "not improbable." That was a figure of speech Morse had learned at school. "St. Paul was a citizen of no mean city." He consulted Fowler again. That was it. *Litotes.* Parallel expressions raced through his mind. "Yet it is probable . . ."; "but it is probable/likely . . ."; "But it may be . . ."; "Maybe . . ."; "I think . . ."; "But I think . . ." Odd. Very odd. A very mannered phrase.

And there was another coincidence. The phrase "in all honesty" also appeared in each letter. What would he himself have written? "Frankly," "honestly," "to be frank," "truthfully"? Come to think of it, it didn't mean very much at all. Three little weasel words. The letter really was most odd. Had his first appraisal of its significance been over-sophisticated, too clever-clever? But people *did* do that sort of thing. Wives and husbands did it in war-time, communicating to each other a wealth of factual data unsuspected by the army censors. "I'm sorry to hear little Archie's got the croup. Will write again soon," might well have concealed the military intelligence that Trooper Smith was to be posted from Aldershot to Cairo next Saturday. Fanciful? No! Morse believed that he had been right.

The evening shadows fell across his desk, and he replaced the Woodstock file and locked the cabinet. The answer was slowly coming, and it seemed to be the answer in the answer book.

16
Tuesday, 12 October

On Tuesday morning at 11:00 a.m., half an hour after Crowther had boarded a bus to the city centre, a small business van, bearing the legend "Kimmons Typewriters" drew up outside the Crowther residence in Southdown Road. A man, wearing a lightweight grey jacket with "Kimmons" embroidered across the pocket, alighted from the van and walked through the white gate, past the scraggy lawn, and knocked. Margaret Crowther, wiping her hands on her apron, opened the door.

"Yes?"

"Mr. Crowther live here, please?"

"Yes."

"Is he in?"

"No, not at the minute."

"Oh. You Mrs. Crowther?"

"Yes."

"Your husband rang to ask us to look at his typewriter. He said the carriage was getting stuck."

"Oh, I see. Come in, will you?"

The typewriter man rather ostentatiously took from his pocket a small box, containing, one must have supposed, the requisite tools of the trade, stepped with an obvious diffidence into the narrow hallway and was ushered into the room off the righthand side of the hall where Bernard Crowther spent so much of his time considering the glories of the English literary heritage. He spotted the typewriter immediately.

"Do you need me?" Mrs. Crowther seemed anxious to resume her culinary duties.

"No, no. Shan't be more than a few minutes—unless it's really wonky." His voice sounded strained.

"Well, call me when you've finished. I'm only in the kitchen."

He looked carefully around, made a few perfunctory tappings on the typewriter, slid the carriage tinkling to and fro several times, and listened carefully. He could hear the clink of plates and saucers; he felt fairly safe and very nervous. Quickly he slid open the top drawer on the right of the small desk: paper-clips, biros, rubbers, elastic bands—nothing very suspicious. Systematically he tried the two lower drawers, and then the three on the left. All pretty much the same. Wadges of notes clipped together, bulky agendas for college meetings, file-cases, writing paper, more writing paper and yet more—ruled, plain, headed, foolscap, folio, quarto. He repeated his pathetic little pantomime and heard, in welcome counter-point, an answering clatter of crockery. He took one sheet from each of the piles of writing paper, folded them carefully and put them into his inside pocket. Finally taking one sheet of quarto he stood it in the typewriter, twiddled the carriage and quickly typed two lines of writing:

After asessing the mny applications we have received, we must regretfully inform you that our application.

Mrs. Crowther showed him to the door. "Well, that should be all right now, Mrs. Crowther. Dust in the carriage-bearings, that's all." Lewis hoped it sounded all right.

"Do you want me to pay you?"

"No. Don't bother about that now." He was gone.

At twelve noon Lewis knocked on Bernard Crowther's door in the second court of Lonsdale College and found him finishing a tutorial with a young, bespectacled, long-haired undergraduate.

"No rush, sir," said Lewis. "I can wait perfectly happily until you've finished."

But Crowther had finished. He had met Lewis the previous Saturday, and was anxious to hear whatever must be heard. The youth was forthwith dismissed with the formidable injunction to produce an essay for the following tutorial on "Symbolism in *Cymbeline*," and Crowther shut the door. "Well, Sergeant Lewis?"

Lewis told him exactly what had occurred that morning; he made no bones about it and confessed that he had not enjoyed the subterfuge. Crowther showed little surprise and seemed anxious only about his wife.

"Now, sir," said Lewis. "If you say you expected a man from Kimmons to come and look at your typewriter, no harm's been done. I want to assure you of that."

"Couldn't you have asked me?"

"Well, yes, sir, we could. But I know that Inspector Morse wanted to make as little fuss as possible."

"Yes, I'm sure." Crowther said it with an edge of bitterness in his voice. Lewis got up to go. "But why? What did you expect to find?"

"We wanted to find out, sir, if we could, on what machine a certain, er, a certain communication was written."

"And you thought I was involved?"

"We have to make inquiries, sir."

"Well?"

"Well what, sir?"

"Did you find out what you wanted?"

Lewis looked uneasy. "Yes, sir."

"And?"

"Shall we say, sir, that we didn't find anything at all, er —at all incriminating. That's about the position, sir."

"You mean that you thought I'd written something on the typewriter and now you think I didn't."

"Er, you'd have to ask Inspector Morse about that, sir."

"But you just said that the letter wasn't written on . . ."

"I didn't say it was a letter, sir."

"But people do write letters on typewriters don't they, sergeant?"

"They do, sir."

"You know, sergeant, you're beginning to make me feel guilty."

"I'm sorry, sir. I didn't mean to do that. But in a job like ours you've got to suspect everybody really. I've told you all I can, sir. Whatever typewriter we're looking for wasn't the one in your house. But there's more than one typewriter in the world, isn't there, sir?"

Crowther did not contest the truth of the assertion. A large bay window gave a glorious view on to the silky grass of the second court, smooth and green as a billiard table. Before the window stood a large mahogany desk, littered with papers and letters and essays and books. And in the centre of this literary clutter there sat, four-square upon the desk, a large, ancient, battered typewriter.

On his way back to Kidlington Lewis drove through the broad tree-lined sweep of St. Giles and took the right fork to follow the Banbury Road up through North Oxford. As he passed the large engineering block on his right, he saw a tallish woman in dark slacks and a long heavy coat walking along, every few steps sticking out a thumb in what seemed a particularly demoralised and pessimistic way. She had long blonde hair, natural by the look of it, reaching half way down her back. Lewis thought of Sylvia Kaye. Poor kid. He passed the blonde just as she turned her head, and he blinked hard. What a world we live in! For the lovely blonde had a lovely beard and side-whiskers down to his chin. Interesting thought . . .

Morse had been unable to conceal his exasperation when Lewis had reported to him earlier and when, with ridiculous rapid certitude, he had established that the letter on which he had pinned his faith had neither been written on Crowther's personal typewriter nor on any of the brands of writing paper so carefully filched from Crowther's personal store. His one worry then had been to paper over the cracks of irregularity in police procedure, and it was for this reason that he had immediately despatched Lewis to talk to Crowther. To the report of this interview he listened with care, if without enthusiasm, when Lewis returned at 1:00 p.m.

"Not the happiest of mornings then, sergeant."

"No. I'd rather not do that sort of thing again, sir."

Morse sympathised. "I don't think we've done any harm though, have we, Lewis? I'm not worried so much about Crowther—he's hardly been above-board with us, has he? But Mrs. Crowther . . . could have been tricky. Thanks, anyway." He spoke with genuine feeling.

"Never mind, sir. At least we tried." Lewis felt much better.

"What about a drink?" said Morse. The two men went off in lighter spirits.

It had occurred to neither of the policemen that women of the intelligence and experience of Mrs. Margaret Crowther would do anything but automatically and unquestioningly accept the *bona fides* of any Tom, Dick and Harry of a tradesman. Furthermore, Mrs. Crowther had herself been a confidential secretary before she married Bernard; in fact the typewriter was hers and that very morning she herself had typed out two letters on the same machine, one addressed to her husband and one addressed to Inspector Morse, c/o Thames Valley Police HQ., Kidlington. The typewriter was in perfect order, she knew that; and she had seen the nervous man from Kimmons Typewriters as he had slid open the drawers of Bernard's desk. She wondered what he was looking for, but she didn't really care. In a gaunt, weary way she had even smiled as she closed the door behind him. She would fairly soon be ready to post the two letters. But she wanted to be sure.

Morse worked at his desk through most of the afternoon. The report on Crowther's car had come in, but appeared to signify little. One long blonde hair, heavily peroxided, was found on the floor behind the near-side driving seat, but that was about it. No physical traces whatsoever of the second girl. Several other reports, but again nothing that appeared to advance the progress of the investigation. He turned his attention to other matters. He had to appear the next morning in the Magistrates' Court: there were briefs and memoranda to read. His mind was grateful to have, for a change, some tangible data to assimilate and he worked through the material quite oblivious to the passage of time. When he looked at his watch at 5:00 p.m. he was surprised how swiftly the afternoon had gone by. Another day over—almost. New day tomorrow. For some reason he felt contented and he wondered to himself if that reason had anything to do with Wednesday and Sue Widdowson.

He rang Lewis, who was about to go home. Yes, of course he could come along. Perhaps he could just ring his long-suffering wife? She'd probably just got the chips in the pan. "You say, Lewis, that Crowther has got another typewriter in his rooms in college. I think we ought to check. Well?"

"Anything you say, sir."

"But you'd like to do it straight this time, wouldn't you?"

"I think that would be best, sir."

"Anything you say, Lewis."

Morse knew the Principal of Lonsdale College fairly well and he rang him up there and then. Lewis was a little surprised at Morse's request. The chief really was doing it properly this time. He listened to the monologue. "How many typewriters would there be? Yes. Yes. Including those . . . Yes. As many as that? But it could be done? Well that would be an enormous help, of course . . . You'd rather it that way? No, doesn't matter to me . . . By the end of the week? Good. Most grateful. Now listen carefully . . ."

Morse gave his instructions, iterated his thanks at inordinate length, and beamed at his sergeant when he finally cradled the 'phone. "Co-operative chap that, Lewis."

"Not much option, had he?"

"Perhaps not. But it will save us a lot of time and trouble."

"You mean save *me* a lot of time and trouble."

"Lewis, my friend, we're a team you and me, are we not?" Lewis nodded a grudging assent. "By the end of the week we shall have evidence from every typewriter in Lonsdale College. What about that?"

"Including Crowther's?"

"Of course."

"Wouldn't it have been a bit easier . . ."

"To fire straight at the bull's eye? It would. But you said you wanted to do this in accordance with the great unprejudiced principles of English law, did you not? We haven't got a thing on Crowther. He's probably as innocent as my Aunt Freda."

Since Lewis had never seen or heard of the said Aunt Freda he refrained from direct comment. "Do you think Crowther's our man, sir?"

Morse stuck his thumb in the corner of his mouth. "I don't know, Lewis. I just don't know."

"I had a bit of an idea today, sir," said Lewis after a pause. "I saw what I thought was a girl and when I got close and she turned round she wasn't a she, she was a he."

"You explain yourself very succinctly, sergeant."

"But you know what I mean."

"Yes, I do. When we were boys we tried to look like boys; if you looked like a girl you were a cissy. Nowadays you've got young fellows with eye make-up and handbags. Makes you wonder."

But Morse hadn't quite seen his point and Lewis filled in the picture. He was no ideas man, he'd always realised that, and felt great diffidence in putting his notion forward. "You see, sir, I was just thinking. We know Mrs. Jarman saw the two girls" (he needn't have gone on, but Morse held his peace) "at the bus-stop. She must have been right, surely. She actually spoke to one of them and the other one was Sylvia Kaye. All right. The next thing is that the lorry driver, Baker, saw the girls being picked up at the other side of the roundabout by a man in a red car. But it was getting dark. He said they were two girls. *But he might have been wrong.* I could have sworn I saw a girl this morning—but I was wrong. Everybody has been dazzled by Sylvia—all the eyes were on her and no wonder. But what if the lorry driver had seen Sylvia and another person, and what if this other person looked like a girl but wasn't. *The other person could have been a man.* Remember, sir, the other girl Mrs. Jarman saw was wearing slacks, and the descriptions we had from Baker fitted so well we thought they must be the same two people. But what if the other girl decided in the end not to hitch-hike to Woodstock. What if she caught up with Sylvia, told her she wasn't going to bother to go to Woodstock after all, and what if Sylvia met up with some man, probably someone she knew anyway, who'd been waiting for a lift before she got there, and the two of them hitched together. I know you've probably thought of this anyway, sir," (Morse gave no indication either way—he hadn't) "but I thought I ought to mention it. We've been trying to find the man who did this and I just thought he might have been in the car with Sylvia all along."

"We've got Crowther's evidence you know, sergeant," said Morse slowly.

"I know, sir. I'd like to see that again if I could. As I remember it he didn't have *much* to say about his second passenger, did he?"

"No, that's true," admitted Morse. "And I can't help thinking he knows more than he's told us anyway." He walked over to the filing cabinet, took from his files the statement of Bernard Crowther, read the first sheet, passed it over to Lewis, and read the second. When both men had finished, they looked at each other over the table.

"Well, sir?"

Morse read it out: " 'The girl nearer to the road I saw clearly. She was an attractive girl with long fair hair, white blouse, short skirt and a coat over her arm. The other girl had walked on a few yards and had her back towards me; she seemed to be quite happy to leave the business of getting a lift to her companion. But she had darkish hair, I think, and if I remember correctly was a few inches taller than her friend . . .' What do you think?"

"Not very definite is it, sir?"

Morse searched for the other relevant passage: " 'I think the girl sitting in the back spoke only once and that was to ask the time . . .' You may have got something, you know," said Morse.

Lewis warmed to his theory. "I've often heard, sir, that when a couple are hitching the girl shows a leg, as it were, and the man keeps out of the way. You know, suddenly shows himself when the car stops and it's too late for the driver to say no."

"That didn't happen here though, sergeant."

"No. I know that, sir. But it fits a bit doesn't it: 'seemed quite happy to leave the business of getting a lift to her companion.'" Lewis felt he should quote his evidence, too.

"Mm. But if you're right, what happened to the other girl?"

"She could have gone home, sir. Could have gone any-where."

"But she wanted to go to Woodstock very badly, didn't she, according to Mrs. Jarman."

"She could have got to the bus-stop."

"The conductor doesn't remember her."

"But when we asked him we were thinking of two girls, not one."

"Mm. Might be worth checking again."

"And another thing, sir." The tide was coming in inex-orably and was lapping already at the sand-castles of Morse's Grand Design.

"Yes?"

"I hope you don't mind me mentioning it, sir, but Crowther says that the other girl was a few inches taller than Sylvia." Morse groaned, but Lewis continued, remorseless as the tide. "Now Sylvia Kaye was 5'9", if I remember it right. If the other girl was Jennifer Coleby she must have been wear-ing stilts, sir. She's only about 5'6", isn't she—"

"But don't you see, Lewis? That's the sort of thing he *would* lie about. He's trying to put us off. He wants to protect this other girl."

"I'm only trying to go on the evidence we've got, sir."

Morse nodded. He thought seriously that he should take up schoolteaching—primary school would be about his level; spelling, he thought, the safest bet. Why hadn't he thought about that height business before? But he knew why. In the Grand Design it was Crowther who had been the guilty man.

And now the waves were curling perilously close to the last of the sand-castles; had already filled the moat and breached the rampart. It was 6:00 p.m., and Lewis's second batch of chips was getting cold.

Morse limped out of the building with Lewis, and the two stood talking by the sergeant's car for several minutes. Lewis felt rather like a pupil in Morse's putative primary school who had caught his master out in the spelling of a simple word, and he hesitated to mention a little thing that had been on his mind for several days. Should he keep it for tomorrow? But he knew that Morse had a busy day in front of him at the courts. He plunged in.

"You know the letter, sir, addressed to Jennifer Coleby?"

Morse knew it by heart. "What about it?"

"Could there have been some fingerprints on the original copy?"

Morse heard the question and stared blankly into the middle distance. At last he shook his head sadly. "Too late now."

The primary school became a distinctly firmer prospect as the minutes ticked by. The sand-castle lurched forward and prepared to topple headlong. It was time someone else took over; he would see the Commissioner.

A police car stopped a few yards from him. "Want some help, sir?"

"I'm all right, thanks." Morse shook off his gloom. "I'll be back in training next week. You'll see me in the first-team squad for the next home game."

The constable laughed. "Bit of a nuisance, though. Especially when you can't drive."

Morse had almost forgotten his car. It had been locked up for over a week now. "Constable, jump in the front with me, will you? It's high time I had a try." He climbed into the driving seat, waggled his right foot over the brake and accelerator, pushed the foot with firmness on the brake-pedal, and decided he could cope. He started the engine, drove off round the yard, tested his ability to do the right things, came to a stop, got out and beamed like an orphan handed a teddy bear.

"Not bad, eh?" The constable helped Morse into the building and along to his office.

"You'll be able to use your car again tomorrow, won't you, sir?"

"I think I shall," said Morse.

He sat down and thought of tomorrow. The Commissioner. In the afternoon would be best, perhaps. He rang

the Commissioner's number, but there was no reply. He
was seeing someone else, too, in the evening. He was looking forward to seeing Sue Widdowson—it was little use
pretending he wasn't. But what a mess he'd made of it.
The Bird and Baby indeed! Why on earth hadn't he invited
her to *The Elizabeth* or *The Sorbonne* or *The Sheridan*. And
why hadn't he arranged to pick her up, like any civilised
man would have done? Hang Jennifer Coleby! It wasn't too
late, though, was it? She would be home by now. He looked
at his watch: 6:30 p.m. *The Oxford Mail* lay on his desk
and he scanned the entertainments page. *Hot Pants* and
Danish Blue, he noticed, had been retained for a second
week "by public demand." He could have taken her to the
pictures, of course. Perhaps not to Studio 2, though. Res-
taurants. Not much there. Then he spotted it. "*Sheridan
Dinner Dance*: double ticket—£6. 7:30–11:30 p.m. Bar. Dress
informal." He rang *The Sheridan*. Yes, a few double tickets
still available, but he would have to collect them tonight.
Could he ring back in a quarter of an hour or so? Yes. They
would keep a double ticket for him.

Jennifer Coleby's telephone number was somewhere in
the file and he soon found it. He thought over what he was
to say. "Miss Widdowson"—that would be best. He hoped
that Sue would answer.

Brrr Brrr. He felt excited. Fool.

"Yes?" A young girl's voice, but whose? The line crackled.

"Is that Oxford 54385?"

"Yes, it is. Can I help you?" Morse's heart sank. It was
unmistakably the cool, clear voice of Jennifer Coleby. Morse
tried in some inchoate way to speak as if he wasn't Morse.
"I want to speak to Miss Widdowson if she's there, please."

"Yes, she is. Who shall I say is calling?"

"Oh tell her it's one of her old school friends," replied the
un-Morselike voice.

"I'll get her straightaway, Inspector Morse."

"Sue! Su-ue!" he heard her shouting. "One of your old
school friends on the line!"

"Hello. Sue Widdowson here."

"Hello." Morse didn't know what to call himself. "Morse
here. I just wondered if you'd like to make it *The Sheridan*

tomorrow night instead of going for a drink. There's a dinner-dance on and I've got tickets. What do you say?"

"That'd be lovely." Morse thought he liked her voice. "Absolutely lovely. Several of my friends are going. Should be great fun."

Oh no! thought Morse. "Not too many, I hope. I don't want to have to share you with a lot of others, you know." He said it lightly with a heavy heart.

"Well, quite a few," admitted Sue.

"Let's make it some other place, shall we? Do you know anywhere?"

"Oh, we can't do that. You've got the tickets anyway. We'll enjoy it—you'll see."

Morse wondered if he would ever learn to tell the truth. "All right. Now I can pick you up, if you like. Would that suit you?"

"Oh, yes please. Jenny was going to run me down in her car—but if you . . ."

"All right. I'll pick you up at 7:15."

"7:15 it is then. Is it long dresses?" Morse didn't know. "Never mind—I can easily find out."

From one of your many friends, doubtless, thought Morse. "Good. Looking forward to it."

"Me, too." She put down the receiver and Morse's own endearing adieu was left unspoken. Was he really looking forward to it? They were usually a bit of an anti-climax, these things. Still it would do him good. Or serve him right. He didn't much care. He'd have a decent meal anyway, and it would be good to hold a young girl in his arms again, tripping the light fantastic . . . Oh hell! He'd forgotten all about that. He was going out of his mind, the stupid, senseless fool that he was. He could no more invite the fair Miss Widdowson to share the delights of a dreamy waltz than invite a rabbi to a plate of pork. He hobbled to the inquiry desk. "Get me a car, sergeant."

"There'll be one in a few minutes, sir. We've got to . . ."

"Get me a car now, sergeant. And I mean *now*." The last word resounded harshly through the open hall and several heads turned round. The desk sergeant reached for the 'phone. "I'll be waiting outside."

"Want some help, sir?" The desk sergeant was a kindly man, and had known the inspector for several years. Morse waited by the desk. He was angry with himself and he had many reasons for feeling so. But why he should think he had a right to take things out on one of his old friends he could not imagine. He cursed his own selfishness and discourtesy.

"Yes, sergeant, I could do with some help." It had not been Morse's day.

17
Wednesday, 13 October, a.m.

A freak storm struck the Oxford area in the early hours of Wednesday morning, demolishing chimneys, blowing down television-aerials and lifting roof-tiles in its path. The 7:00 a.m. news reported a trail of devastation in Kidlington, Oxon, where a Mrs. Winifred Fisher had a narrow escape when the roof of a garage broke its moorings and crashed through an upstairs window. "I just can't describe it," she said. "Terrifying." The portable radio stood on the bedside table along with a telephone and an alarm clock which, at 6:50 a.m., had wakened Morse from a long, untroubled sleep.

He got out of bed when the news had finished and peered through the curtains. At least his own garage seemed intact. Funny, though, that the storm had not awakened him. Gradually the memory of yesterday's events filtered through his consciousness and settled like a heavy sediment at the bottom of his mind. Gone were the flights of angels that had guarded him in sleep and he sat on the edge of his bed fingering the rough stubble on his chin and wondering what this day would bring. Increasingly, as the case progressed, the graph of his moods was resembling a jagged mountain range, peaks and valleys, troughs and elations.

At a quarter to eight he was shaved, washed and dressed, and feeling fresh and confident. He swilled out the dregs from his late-night cup of Horlicks, rinsed his late-night whisky glass, filled the kettle and turned his attention to a major problem.

For the last few days he had worn, around his wounded foot, an outsize white plimsoll, loosely laced, and slit down the heel. It was time to get back to something normal. He was loath to appear in the court in such eccentric footwear and he could hardly believe that Miss Widdowson would be overjoyed with a semi-plimsolled escort at the dance. He had two pairs of shoes only and a dangerously low supply of suitable socks; and with such limited permutations of possibilities, the prospect of being presentably shod that day was somewhat remote. He slipped his faithful battered plimsoll back on, and decided to buy a large pair of shoes from M and S, his favourite store. It was going to be an expensive day. He drank a cup of tea, and looked out of the window. His dustbin lid was leaning against the front gate, with litter everywhere. He must remember to have a look at the roof-tiles . . .

In retrospect he thought he had got yesterday's events out of all perspective; he had been standing too close to the trees, and now he thought he saw again the same familiar wood, labyrinthine, certainly, as before—but still the same. He was feeling his old resilient self, or almost so. But the drastic course of action he had contemplated—what about that? He would have to consider things again; he had a more immediate problem on his mind. Where were his pen, his comb and his wallet. Amazingly, and with deep relief, he found them all in the same heap on the bedroom mantel-piece.

The faithful old Lancia was still there. It had been a good buy. Powerful, reliable, and 300 miles on a full tank. He had often thought of changing it but never had the heart. He eased himself into the narrow gap between the door of the driver's seat and the whitewashed wall of the garage. It was always a tricky manoeuvre and he was getting no thinner. But it felt good to sit at the wheel again. He gave the old girl a bit more choke than usual—after all she had been standing idle for a week—and pressed the starter. Chutter . . . chutter . . . chutter . . . chutter. No. Bit more choke?

But he mustn't flood her. Again. Chutter . . . chutter . . .
chutter . . . chutter . . . chutter . . . Odd. He'd never had much
difficulty before. Third time lucky, though. Chutter . . .
chutter . . . chutter. Battery must be getting a bit low. Oh
dear. Give her a minute or two's rest. Let her get her breath
back. This time, then! Chutter . . . chutter . . . Bugger! Once
more. Chutt . . . "Just my bloody luck," he said to himself.
"How the hell am I supposed to get about without . . ." He
stopped and shivered involuntarily. A grey dawn was break-
ing in his mind and the purple mysteries of the morning
were shot with the rays of the rising sun. "Bliss was it in
that dawn to be alive." Wordsworth, wasn't it? It had been
in *The Times* crossword last week. The waves were at last
receding from the beach. The white crests of the breakers
rolled ceaselessly and tirelessly towards the shore, but their
strength was gone. He saw the Grand Design before him
and the last little sand-castle had survived the mighty sea.

The manager of Barker's garage in Oxford was so impressed by Inspector Morse's courteous call upon his services that a new battery was on its way in ten minutes, and
installed in fifteen. The clouds were high and white and the
sun shone brightly. Open weather, as Jane Austen would
have called it. Morse retrieved the dustbin lid, and meticulously gathered up all the litter from his garden.

The university city of Oxford was busy this morning, the
third full day of the Michaelmas term. First-year undergraduates, with spankingly-new college scarves tossed over
their shoulders, eagerly explored the bookshops of The Broad,
and a trifle self-consciously strode down the High into the
crowded Cornmarket, into Woolworths and Marks and
Spencer and thence, according to taste, into the nearest pubs
and coffee shops. At 1:00 p.m. Morse was sitting on a chair
in the self-service men's shoe department in the basement
of M and S. He normally took size 8, but was now experi-
menting with patience and determination. Size 9 seemed of
little use, and after considerable trafficking in stockinged
feet between the show counter and his chosen chair, he
plumped for size-10 black leather slip-ons. They seemed
huge and were, of course, potentially useless in the long

run. But who cared? He could wear two pairs of socks on his left foot. Which reminded him. He paid for the shoes, adjusted his plimsoll, much to the bewilderment of a large, morose-looking cashier, who looked as if she might wear size 10 herself, and proceeded to the hosiery counter where he purchased half a dozen gaudy pairs of lightweight socks. If he had been able, he would have walked out into Corn-market with a light step. The car was functioning, the courts were finished, the case was flourishing.

Others, too, were making their purchases. Trade was thriving this morning, and not only in the large stores in the main streets in Oxford city-centre. At about the same time that Morse, the megapode, tucked his purchases beneath his arm, one further swift, uncomplicated transaction was being effected in the run-down back street behind the Botley Road, and it could be argued that this time, at least, John Sanders had struck the better bargain.

18
Wednesday, 13 October, p.m.

At Lonsdale College Wednesday, 13 was the first full guest-night of the Michaelmas term and Bernard Crowther left home a little earlier than usual. At 6:15 p.m. he knocked on Peter Newlove's rooms and walked in, not waiting for a reply.

"That you, Bernard?"

"It's me."

"Pour yourself a drink. Shan't be a minute."

Bernard had passed the Lodge as he came in and had picked up three letters from his pigeon-hole. Two he opened raggedly and relegated cursorily to his jacket pocket. The third was marked "confidential," and contained a card "From the Principal":

"The police, in the course of their investigations into the recent murder at Woodstock, are anxious to trace the provenance of a typed letter which has come into their possession and which they think may be material evidence in their inquiries. I have been asked by the police to see that every typewriter in the college is checked and I am asking all my colleagues to comply with this request. The Bursar has agreed to undertake this duty and it is my view, and also that of the Vice-Principal, that we must readily accede to this proper request. I have therefore informed Chief Inspector Morse, who is heading the murder inquiries, that we as a collegiate body are most anxious to co-operate in any way possible. The Bursar has an inventory of all college typewriters; but there may be private typewriters in the rooms of several fellows, and I ask that information concerning them should be given to the Bursar immediately. Thank you for your help."

"What's up, Bernard? Don't you want a drink?" Peter had come in from the bathroom and stood combing his thinning hair with a thinning comb.

"Have you had one of these?"

"I have indeed received a communication from our revered and reverend Principal, if that's what you mean."

"What's it all about?"

"Don't know, dear boy. Mysterious though, isn't it?"

"When's the great investigation due?"

"Due? It's done. At least mine is. Little girl came in this afternoon—with the Bursar, of course. Typed out some cryptic message and then she was gone. Pity really. Lovely little thing. I must try to spend a bit more time in the Bursary."

"I shan't be able to help much myself, I'm afraid. That bloody thing of mine was manufactured in the middle ages and hasn't had a ribbon in it for six months. I think it's what they call 'seized-up,' anyway."

"Well, that's one suspect less, Bernard. Now are you going to have a drink or not?"

"Don't you think we shall have enough booze tonight?"

"No, dear boy, I don't." Peter sat down and pulled on an expensive pair of heavy, brown brogues: size 10s, but not purchased from the self-service shoe department at Marks and Spencer.

* * *

"We've just got time for a quick one, I think." It was almost
7:30 p.m. "What would you like?"

"Dry sherry for me, please. I shan't be a minute. Must
powder my nose." She went off to the cloak-room. There
were only a few people in the lounge bar and Morse, served
without delay, took the drinks over to the corner of the room
and sat down.

The Sheridan was the most fashionable of the Oxford
hotels and most visiting stars of stage, screen, sport and
television found themselves booked in at this well-appointed,
large, stone building just off the bottom of St. Giles. A striped
canopy stretched out over the pavement and a flunkey stood
his station beside the gleaming name-plate on the shallow
steps leading down to the street from the revolving doors.
Morse suspected that the management kept a red carpet
rolled up somewhere on the premises. Not that it had been
rolled out this evening; in fact he had been unable to find
any parking space at all in the hotel's narrow yard and had
been forced to park his car along St. Giles. It wasn't perhaps
the best of starts, and they had said little to each other.

He watched her as she came back. She had parted with
her coat and walked with enviable elegance towards him,
her long deep-red velvet dress gently affirming the lines
of her graceful body. And suddenly, sweetly his heart beat
stronger, and their eyes met and she smiled. She sat beside
him and he was aware again, as he had been as she sat
beside him in the car, of the strange and subtle promise of
her perfume.

"Cheers, Sue."

"Cheers, inspector."

He didn't know what to do about this name trouble. He
felt like an ageing schoolmaster meeting one of his old pupils
and being rather embarrassed by the "sirs" in every other
sentence, and yet feeling it phoney to have it otherwise. He
let the "inspectors" pass. Things could change, of course.
Morse offered her a cigarette but she declined. As she sipped
her sherry Morse noticed the long and delicately-manicured
fingers: no rings, no nail-polish. He asked her about her

day's work and she told him. It was all a little strained. They finished their drinks and walked out of the lounge and up the stairs to the Evans Room, Sue lifting her dress slightly as she negotiated the stairs, and Morse trying to forget the tightness in his right shoe and frenziedly arching the left foot to prevent the shoe from falling off completely.

The room was arranged with subdued and delicate decorum: around a small, well-polished dance-floor tables were set at regular intervals, the silver cutlery gleaming on the white tablecloths and a red candle lit on each table, the blue and yellow flames tapering into a slimness, almost as exquisite, thought Morse, as Sue Widdowson herself. Several couples were already seated and it was sadly clear to Morse that some of her wretched friends were among them. A small band played some languorous melody that lingered in the mind and as they were shown to their table a young couple took the floor, blithely and obliviously, feeding deep upon each other's eyes.

"You've been here before?"

Sue nodded, and Morse followed the young couple with his eyes and decided not to give too free a rein to his imagination. A waiter came to them with the menu, and Morse welcomed the diversion.

"Do they throw in the wine?"

"We get a bottle between us."

"Is that all?"

"Isn't that enough?"

"Well, it's a special occasion, isn't it?" Sue was noncommittal. "What about a bottle of champagne?"

"You've got to drive me home, remember?"

"We could get a taxi."

"What about your car?"

"Perhaps the police will pick it up." Sue laughed and Morse saw her white teeth and the fullness of her lips. "What do you say?"

"I'm in your hands, inspector." Would you were, he thought.

Several other couples were now dancing and Sue was watching them. "You enjoy dancing?" Sue kept her eyes on the dancers and nodded. A young Adonis waved a hand in their direction.

" 'lo Sue. All right?" Sue raised a hand in greeting.

"Who's that?" asked Morse aggressively.

"Doctor Eyres. He's one of the housemen at the Radcliffe."
She seemed almost hypnotised by the scene. But she turned
back into Morse's orbit with the arrival of the champagne,
and after a while the conversation took a freer course. Morse
chattered as amiably and interestingly as he could and Sue
seemed pleasantly relaxed. They ordered their meal, and
Morse poured another glass of champagne. The band stopped;
the couples on the floor clapped half-heartedly for a few
seconds and retired to the perimeter tables. Dr. Eyres and
his heavily-mascaraed young brunette made their way towards Morse's table, and Sue seemed glad to see them.

"Doctor Eyres this is Inspector Morse." The two men shook
hands. "And this is Sandra. Sandra this is Inspector Morse."
The leaden-eyed Sandra, it transpired, was also a nurse and
worked with Sue at the Radcliffe Infirmary. The band resumed its plangent strains.

"Mind if I had this dance with Sue, inspector?"

"Of course not," smiled Morse. You lousy, lecherous med-
ico. Sandra sat down and looked at Morse with obvious interest in her eyes.

"I'm awfully sorry not to be able to ask you to dance," he
said, "but I've had an accident with my foot. Nearly better,
though."

Sandra was sympathy itself. "Oh dear. How did that
happen?"

For the fiftieth time in the last seven days Morse repeated the attendant circumstances of his escapade. But
his mind was all on Sue. As she escorted the houseman
to the floor he thought of Coleridge:

> The bride hath paced into the hall,
>   Red as a rose is she.

He watched them dance; he saw Sue's arms closely round
her partner's neck, her body close to his; and then his cheek
was brushing her hair, her head happily resting on his shoulder. Morse felt sick of a jealous dread. He turned his eyes
away from the smooching couples. "Do you know, I reckon

I could just about cope with this dance myself," he said.
"May I?" He took her hand, led her to the floor and, firmly
placing his right arm round her waist, drew her towards
him. Rapidly, however, he realised the extent of his own
stupidity. His injured foot was working like a dream, but
lacking the confidence to lift his other foot more than a
centimetre off the dance-floor he was soon kicking his partner's toes with monotonous and ill-received regularity. Mer-
cifully the dance was quickly over, and mumbling profuse
apologies about his ill-educated feet Morse slopped his way
back to the haven of his table. Sue was still talking in an
animated way to Doctor Eyres, and after Sandra had rejoined
them, the trio erupted into peals of laughter.

Ten minutes earlier Morse had anticipated that even the
most succulent steak would taste tonight as dry as the Dead
Sea apples, but he tucked into his meal with a will. At least
he could eat. Even if he couldn't dance, even if he'd forgotten
how middle-aged he'd now become, even if Sue was yearn-
ing for someone else, he could still eat. And jolly good it
was. They said little and when something was said, as they
drank their coffees, it came as a big surprise.

"Why did you ask me out, inspector?"

Morse looked at her, the hair light-brown and lifted softly
from her face, her face itself all freshness and delight, the
cheeks now faintly flushed with wine; and above all the
magic of those wide and doleful eyes. Had he asked her with
any firm purpose? He wasn't sure. He put his elbows on the
table, rested his chin on his clasped hands. "Because I find
you so very beautiful and I wanted to be with you."

Sue looked at him for several seconds, her eyes unblinking
and gentle. "Do you mean that?" she asked quietly.

"I don't know if I meant it when I asked you. But I mean
it now—I think you know I do." He spoke simply and calmly
and he held her eyes with his own as he spoke. He saw two
splendid tears forming on her lower lids and she reached
across and laid her hand upon his arm.

"Come and dance with me," she whispered.

The floor was crowded and they did little more than sway
slowly to the sweet, low rhythm of the band. Sue leaned her
head lightly against his cheek and Morse felt with a won-

derful joy the moisture of her eyes. He wished the world
would stop and that this heavenly moment could be launched
on the eternal seas. He kissed her ear and said some awkward, loving things, and Sue nuzzled deeper and deeper
into his arms and pulled him even more closely to her. They
stood together as the music ended, and Sue looked up at
him. "Can we go now, please. Somewhere on our own?"

Morse remembered little of the next few minutes. He had
waited in a dream-like state beside the revolving doors and
arm-in-arm the two had slowly walked along St. Giles towards the car.

"I want to talk to you," said Sue when they were sitting
in the car.

"I'm listening."

"You know when you said that you might not have
meant . . . might not have meant what you said. Oh, I'm
getting all muddled. What I mean is—you did want to ask
me something, didn't you?"

"Did I?" asked Morse.

"You know you did. About Jennifer. That's where we both
came in, wasn't it? You thought she'd got something to do
with the Woodstock murder . . ." Morse nodded. "And you
wanted to ask me about her boy friends and that sort of
thing."

Morse sat silently in the darkness of his car. "I'm not going
to ask you now, Sue. Don't worry." He put his arm around
her and drew her towards him and tenderly kissed the softest,
heavenliest lips that ever the Almighty made. "When can
we meet again, Sue?" As soon as he had spoken he knew
that something was wrong. He felt her body tauten; she
moved away from him, felt for her handkerchief and blew
her nose. She was on the verge of tears. "No," she said, "we
can't."

Morse felt a hurt that he had never known before, and
his voice was strained and unbelieving. "But why? Why?
Of course we can meet again, Sue."

"We can't." Her voice for the moment seemed matter-of-
fact and final. "We can't meet again, inspector, because . . .
because I'm engaged to be married." She just managed to
blurt out the last word before burying her head on Morse's

shoulder and bursting into anguished tears. Morse kept his arm tightly around her and listened with unfathomable sadness to her convulsive sobs. The front window had steamed over with their breath and Morse perfunctorily wiped away the moisture with the back of his right hand. Outside he saw the massive outer wall of St. John's College. It was only 10:00 p.m. and a group of undergraduates were laughing gaily outside the Porter's Lodge. Morse knew it well. He'd been an undergraduate there himself; but that was twenty years ago and life since then had somehow passed him by.

They drove in silence up to North Oxford and Morse pulled up the Lancia directly in front of Sue's front door. As he did so the door opened and Jennifer Coleby came out with her car-keys in her hand, and walked towards them.

"Hello, Sue. You're home early, aren't you?"

Sue wound the window down. "We didn't want to get stopped for drinking and driving."

"Are you coming in for a coffee?" asked Jennifer. The question was directed obliquely through the car window to Morse.

"No. I think I'd better get home."

"See you in a minute then," said Jennifer to Sue. "Just going to put the car away." She climbed into a smart little Fiat and drove smoothly off to her rented garage in the next street.

"Good little cars, Fiats," said Morse.

"No better than English cars, are they?" asked Sue. She was bravely trying not to make a fool of herself again.

"Very reliable, I'm told. And even if something does go wrong, there's a good agent pretty near, isn't there?" Morse hoped he sounded casual enough, but he didn't really care.

"Yes, right on the doorstep, really."

"I've always found Barkers pretty good myself."

"She does, too," said Sue.

"Well, I suppose I'd better go."

"Are you sure you won't come in for some coffee?"

"Yes. I'm quite sure."

Sue took his hand and held it lightly in her own. "You know I shall cry myself to sleep, don't you?"

"Don't say that." He didn't want to be hurt any more.

"I wish you were going to sleep with me," she whispered. "I wish you were going to sleep with me for ever, Sue."

They said no more. Sue got out of the car, waved as the Lancia slowly moved off, and turned towards the front door, her face blinded with tears.

Morse drove to Kidlington with a heavy heart. He thought of the first time he had seen Miss Dark-eyes and now he thought of the last. Would things had been otherwise! He thought of the saddest line of poetry he had ever read:

Not a line of her writing have I, not a thread of her hair

and felt no better for the thought. He didn't want to go home; he had never realised before how lonely he had become. He stopped at *The White Horse*, ordered a double whisky and sat down in an empty corner. She hadn't even asked his name . . . He thought of Doctor Eyres and his dark-eyed Sandra and supposed, without a hint of envy, that they were probably getting into bed by now. He thought of Bernard Crowther and doubted if his illicit liaisons with his girl in Blenheim Park were tinged with half the sadness that he himself now felt. He thought of Sue and her fiancé and hoped he was a good fellow. He bought another double whisky and, maudlin and fuddled, left soon after the landlord shouted time.

He put away the car with exaggerated care and heard the 'phone ringing before he could open the door. His heart raced. He rushed into the hall just as the 'phone stopped. Was it her? Was it Sue? He could always ring back. What was the number? He didn't know. It was in his files at Police HQ. He could ring there. He picked up the 'phone—and put it down. It wouldn't be Sue. If it was, she could ring back. She'd probably been ringing all the time he'd been sitting in *The White Horse*. Blast it. Ring again, Sue. Just to let me hear you speak. Ring again, Sue. But the telephone rang no more that night.

19
Thursday, 14 October

Bernard Crowther had a hangover on Thursday morning. He would be lecturing in the Schools at 11:00 a.m. and he contemplated his notes on "Influences on Milton's Poetical Style" with a growing sense of apprehension. Margaret had brought him a cup of hot black coffee at a quarter to nine; she always knew—and usually said so. She had been up since half-past six, cooked the children's breakfast, washed some shirts and blouses, made the beds, hoovered the bedrooms and she was now putting on her coat in the hall. She put her head round the door. "You all right?" How Bernard hated the reminder!

"Fine."

"Do you want anything from town—milk of magnesia tablets?" They seemed perpetually in a state of eruptive belligerence, staring at each other over a long-disputed frontier. Margaret! Margaret! He wished he could talk to her.

"No. No thanks. Look, Margaret, I've got to go down myself pretty soon. Can you wait a few minutes?"

"No. Must be off. You home for lunch?"

What was the point? "No. I'll have a bite to eat in college." He heard the front door bang and watched her as she walked quickly to the end of the road and round the corner and out of sight. He went to the kitchen, filled a glass with cold water and dropped in two tablets of soluble Disprin.

Morse and Lewis conferred from nine to ten that morning. There were several loose ends to tie up and several interesting trails to follow. At least, that's how Morse explained things to Lewis. After Lewis had left him, he had a call from a young reporter on *The Oxford Mail*, as a result of which a brief paragraph would appear in the evening edition. Routine answers. He couldn't tell anyone much, but he tried to sound as confident as he could. It was good for morale.

He got the Kaye file and spent the next hour re-reading the documents in the case. At 11:00 a.m. he put the file away, reached for the Oxford and District telephone directory, looked under the Cs for the number he wanted, and rang the manager of Chalkley and Sons, Botley Road. He was unlucky. John Sanders had not come in that morning; his mother had 'phoned—bad cold or something.

"What's your opinion of him?" asked Morse.

"He's all right. Quiet, little bit surly, perhaps. But most of them are these days. Works well enough, I think."

"Well, I'm sorry to have bothered you. I wanted a quick word with him, that's all."

"About this murder at Woodstock?"

"Yes. He found the girl, you know."

"Yes. I read about it and of course everyone tried to talk to him about it."

"Did he have much to say?"

"Not really. Didn't seem to want to talk. Understandable, I suppose."

"Yes. Well, thanks once again."

"You're very welcome. Do you want his home address?"

"No thanks. I've got it here."

Lewis was rather more fortunate. Mrs. Jarman was at home, dusting the stairs.

"But I don't understand, sergeant. I'm *sure* they were both girls."

Lewis nodded. "Just checking up on one or two things."

"But I spoke to one of them, as you know, and the other poor girl—well, you know . . . And I thought they were *about* the same height; but it's ever so difficult to remember you know . . ." Yes, Lewis knew. He left her to dust the stairs.

He found the bus conductor drinking coffee in the canteen at Gloucester Green.

"*One* girl getting on the bus? But you said *two* before."

"Yes, I know. But we've got an idea that perhaps only one got on."

"Sorry. I can't remember. I am sorry, honest—but it's a long time ago now."

"Yes. Don't worry. As I said—just an idea. If you do happen to think of anything . . ."

"Of course."

George Baker was digging his garden. " 'Allo mate. I seen you before."

"Sergeant Lewis Thames Valley Police."

"Ah. Course. Wha' can a do forya?"

Lewis explained his visit but George's answer was only marginally less discouraging than those of the others.

"We-ell, I s'pose it *could* a been a fella, bu' swipe me mate, I could a swore as both of 'em was women."

Memories were fading and the case was growing stale. Lewis went home for lunch.

At 2:00 p.m. he was ushered into the office of the car service manager of Barkers Garage on the Banbury Road, where he spent more than an hour working his way methodically through hundreds of carbon copies of work-sheets, customers" invoices, booking-ledgers and other sundry records of car repairs for the weeks beginning September 22 and 27. He found nothing. He spent a further hour going back to the beginning of September, increasingly conscious that his task was futile. Miss Jennifer Coleby, although she had an account with Barkers, had not brought in her car for any repairs or service since July. She had bought the car new from the garage over three years ago; HP nearly finished; no trouble with payments; no serious mechanical faults. 6,000 service on 14 July, with a few oddments put right. £13.55. Bill paid July 30.

Lewis was disappointed if not surprised. Morse seemed to have a bee in his bonnet about this Coleby woman. Perhaps this would put him off for good? But he doubted it. He walked over the road to the newsagents and bought the evening newspaper. A caption near the bottom righthand corner of the front page caught his eye:

WOODSTOCK KILLING
BREAKTHROUGH NEAR

"Following intensive activity, police are quietly confident that the killer of Sylvia Kaye, found raped and murdered at

The Black Prince, Woodstock, on the night of 29 September will soon be found. Chief Inspector Morse of the Thames Valley HQ, who is heading the murder inquiry, said today that several key witnesses had already come forward and he considered that it would only be a matter of time before the guilty party was brought to justice."

Lewis thought it must be a hoax.

The confident head of the murder inquiry, if ever invited to take his eight discs to a desert island, would have answered "Committees" to the inevitable question about what he would be most glad to have got away from. The meeting called for this Thursday afternoon to consider pensions, promotions and appointments stretched on and on like an arid desert. His only contribution throughout was a word of commendation for Constable McPherson. It seemed a justifiable excuse for contravening his customary and caustic taciturnity. The meeting finally broke up at five minutes past five, when he yawned his way back to his office and found Lewis reading the prospects for Oxford United's visit to Blackpool the following Saturday.

"Seen this, sir?" Lewis handed him the newspaper and pointed to the caption portending judgement-day for the Woodstock killer.

Morse read the item with weary composure. "They do twist things a bit, these reporters, don't they?"

Sue Widdowson's day, too, dragged drearily by. She'd wanted desperately to talk to Morse again last night. Who knows what she might have said? Was his 'phone out of order? But in the cold light of morning she had realised how foolish it would have been. David was coming on Saturday for the weekend, and she would be meeting him at the station at the usual time. Dear David. She had received another letter that morning. He was so nice and she liked him so very much. But . . . No! She had just *got* to stop thinking of Morse. It had been almost impossible. Sandra had been full of questions and Doctor Eyres had patted her bottom far too intimately, and she was lousily, hopelessly miserable.

* * *

Mrs. Amy Sanders was worried about her son. He had seemed listless and off-colour for a week or so now. In the past he had taken the odd day or two off work, and more than once she had had to lay it on a bit thick in describing to Messrs Chalkley the symptoms of some fictitious malady which had temporarily stricken her dear boy. But today she was genuinely concerned. John had been sick twice during the night and was lying shivering and sweating when she had called him at 7:00 a.m. He had eaten nothing all day and, against her son's wishes, she had rung the doctor's surgery at 5:00 p.m. No, she had not thought it urgent, but would be most grateful if the doctor could call some time.

The bell rang at 7:30 p.m. and Mrs. Sanders opened the front door to find a man she had never seen before. Still, the doctors these days were always changing around.

"Does Mr. John Sanders live here?"

"Yes. Come in, doctor. I'm ever so glad you could call."

"I'm not a doctor, I'm afraid. I'm a police inspector."

The landlord of *The Bell* at Chipping Norton took the booking himself at 8:30 p.m. He consulted the register and picked up the 'phone again.

"For tomorrow night and Saturday night, you said?"

"Yes."

"I think we can do that all right, sir. Double room. Do you want a private bathroom?"

"That would be nice. And a double bed if you've got one. We never seem to sleep well in these twin beds."

"Yes. We can do that."

"I'm afraid I shan't have time to confirm it in writing."

"Oh don't worry about that, sir. If you could just let me have your name and address."

"Mr. and Mrs. John Brown, Hill Top, Eaglesfield (all one word), Bristol."

"I've got that."

"Good. My wife and I look forward to seeing you. We should be there about five."

"We hope you'll enjoy your stay, sir."

The landlord put down the 'phone and wrote the names

of Mr. and Mrs. J. Brown into the booking register. His wife had once added up the number of John Browns booked into *The Bell*: in one month alone there were seven. But it wasn't his job to worry too much about that. Anyway, the man had sounded most polite and well educated. Nice voice, too: West Countryish—rather like his own. And there must be one or two quite genuine John Browns somewhere.

20
Friday, 15 October, a.m.

Morse woke up late on Friday morning. *The Times* was already on the floor in the hall and one letter was protruding precariously through the letter box. It was a bill from Barkers—£9.25. He stuck it, with several of its fellows, behind the clock on the mantelpiece.

The car purred into life at the first gentle touch. He had the sticks in the back of the car and decided to run down to the Radcliffe Infirmary before going to the office. As he joined the patiently-crawling, never-ending line of traffic in the Woodstock Road, he debated his course of action. He could see her quite by chance, of course—as he had last time; or he could ask for her. But would she want that? He longed just to *see* her again and, dammit!, she would be there. What could be more natural? He had dreamed about Sue the previous night, but in a vague, elusive sort of way which had left her standing in the forecourt of his mind. *Had* it been her on the 'phone on Wednesday night?

He turned off, across the traffic, into the yard of the Radcliffe, stopped on double yellow lines, collared the nearest porter, gave him the sticks and the promissory note of the bearer to return the same, and told him to see to it. Police!

The road was clear as he left Oxford and he cursed himself savagely every other minute. He should have gone in— stupid fool. He knew deep down he wasn't a stupid fool, but it didn't help much.

Lewis was waiting for him. "Well, what's the programme, sir?"

"I thought we'd take a gentle bus-ride a little later, Lewis." Ah well. His not to reason why. "Yes. I thought we'd go to Woodstock on the bus together. What about that?"

"Has the car konked out again?"

"No. Going like a dream. So it should. Had a bill for the bloody battery this morning. Guess how much."

"Six, seven pounds."

"Nine pounds twenty-five!"

Lewis screwed up his nose. "Cheaper if you'd gone to the tyre and battery people up in Headington. They don't charge for any labour. I've always found them very good."

"You sound as if you're always having car trouble."

"Not really. Had a few punctures lately, though."

"Can't you change a tyre yourself?"

"Well yes. Course I can. I'm not an old woman you know, but you've got to have a spare."

Morse wasn't listening. He felt the familiar tingle of the blood freezing in his arms. "You're a genius, sergeant. Pass me the telephone directory. Consult the yellow pages. Here we are—only two numbers. Which shall we try first?"

"What about the first one, sir?"

A few seconds later Morse was speaking to Cowley Tyre and Battery Services. "I want to speak to the boss of the place. It's urgent. Police here." He winked at Lewis. "Ah, hullo. Chief Inspector Morse here. Thames Valley . . . No, no. Nothing like that . . . Now, I want you to look up your records for the week beginning 27 September . . . Yes. I want to know if you supplied a battery or mended a puncture for a Miss Jennifer Coleby. C-O-L-E-B-Y. Yes. It might have been any day—probably Tuesday or Wednesday. You'll ring me back? Get on with it straightaway, please. It's most urgent. Good. You've got my number? Good. Cheers." He rang the second number and repeated the patter. Lewis was turning over the Sylvia Kaye file that lay open on Morse's desk. He studied the photographs—large, glossy, black and white photographs with amazingly clear delineation. He looked again at the shots of Sylvia Kaye as she lay that night in the yard of *The Black Prince*. She'd been really something, he thought. The white blouse had been torn sharply on the left-hand side, and only the bottom of the four buttons remained fastened. The left breast was fully revealed and Lewis was strongly reminded of the provocative poses of the models in the girlie magazines. It could almost have been an erotic experience—looking through those pictures; but Lewis remembered the back of the blonde head and the cruelly-shattered skull. He thought of his own darling daughter—thirteen now; she was getting a nice little figure . . . God, what a world to bring up children in. He hoped and prayed that she would be all right, and he felt a deep and burning need to find the man who did all that to Sylvia Kaye.

Morse had finished.

"Can you put me in the picture, sir?" asked Lewis.

Morse sat back and thought for a few minutes. "I suppose I ought to have told you before, Lewis. But I couldn't be sure—well, can't be sure now—about one or two things. Pretty well from the beginning I thought I had a good idea of the general picture. I thought it was like this. Two girls want a lift to Woodstock and we've got some fairly substantial evidence that they *were* picked up—*both* of them." Lewis nodded. "Now neither the driver nor the other girl came forward. The question I asked myself was 'why?' Why were both these people anxious to keep quiet? There were pretty obvious reasons why *one* of them should keep his mouth shut. But why both? It seemed most improbable to me that the pair of them could be partners in crime. So. What are we left with? One very strong possibility, as I saw it, was that they knew each other. But that didn't seem quite good enough, somehow. Most people don't withhold evidence, certainly don't tell complicated lies, just because they know each other. But what if they have, between them, some guilty reason for wanting to keep things very quiet indeed? And what if such a guilty reason is the fact that they know each other rather *too* well? What if they are—not to put too fine a point on things—having an affair with each other? The situation's not so good for them, is it? With a murder in the background—not so good at all." Lewis wished he'd get on with it. "But let's go back a bit. On the face of it our evidence suggested from the word go that the encounter between the two girls and the driver of the car was pure chance: Mrs. Jarman's evidence is perfectly clear on that point. Now we have discovered, after a good deal of unnecessary trouble, who the driver of the red car was: Crowther. In his evidence he admits that he is having an affair with another woman and that the venue for these extramarital excursions is Blenheim Park. Furthermore, again on his own evidence, he was going to see his lady-love on the night of Wednesday, 29 September. Now at this point I took a leap in the dark. What if the lady-love was one of the girls he picked up?"

"But . . ." began Lewis.

"Don't interrupt, Lewis. Now, was the lady-love Sylvia Kaye? I don't think so. We know that Mr. John Sanders had a date, however vague, with Sylvia on the 29th. It doesn't prove things one way or the other, but Sylvia is the less likely choice of the two. So. We're left with our other passenger—Miss, or Mrs. X. It is clear from Mrs. Jarman's evidence that Miss X seemed anxious and excited, and I think no-one gets too anxious and excited about going to Woodstock unless that person has a date, and an important date at that, and not very much time to spare. Crowther said an hour or so at the most, remember?"

"But . . ." He thought better of it.

"We also learned from what Mrs. Jarman said that Sylvia knew the other girl. There was that business of having a giggle about it in the morning. So, we try the place where Sylvia works and we find an extraordinary, quite inexplicable letter written to Miss Jennifer Coleby, who has become my odds-on favourite for the Miss X title. I agree that the evidence of the letter is not conclusive; worth following up though. She's a clever girl, our Jennifer. She has two spanners to throw in the works. First, she seems to have been at a pub this side of Woodstock instead of in Blenheim Park; second—and this really worried me and still does—why does she have to bus to Woodstock, or hitch-hike, if she's got a car? Which, as we know, she has. It seemed a fatal objection. But is it? *My* car wouldn't start on Wednesday morning because the battery was flat. You said that *you* had a few punctures recently and you said you could mend them. You said you were not an old woman. Now Jennifer Coleby is not an old woman—but *she's a woman*. What if she discovered that her car wouldn't start? What would she do? Ring up her garage. That was pretty obvious and hence your visit to Barkers, where you drew a blank. I thought I saw the light, though, this morning. I had a bill for my car-battery and you mentioned the tyre and battery people. The real question then is *when* did Jennifer discover her car was out of order? Surely not before she got back from work, at about 5:30 p.m. Now not many garages these days are going to do much at that time; the staff has all gone. But your little tyre and battery men don't work, methinks, to union hours, and they are worth trying. I must assume that Jennifer could get no-one to see to her car that night—not because they couldn't do it, but because they *couldn't do it in time*. She may not have discovered the trouble until about 6:15 or 6:30 p.m. But I think she tried to get something done—and failed. Well, what's she to do? Naturally, she can get a bus. She's never had to bus before, but she's seen the Woodstock buses often enough and that's why I believe it was Jennifer who was seen at Fare Stage 5 on the night Sylvia was murdered. She meets an impatient fellow-traveller, Sylvia, and the two of them decide to hitch-hike. They walk past the roundabout and a car stops: Crowther's car. It's hardly a coincidence, is it? He's got to get to Woodstock, too, and he's bound to be going there at roughly the same time as Jennifer. Whether he knew it was her—it was getting fairly dark—I just don't know. I suspect he did." Morse stopped.

"And what happened then, do you think, sir?"

"Crowther has told us what happened for the next few miles."

"Do you believe him?"

Morse sat thoughtfully and didn't answer immediately. The 'phone rang. "No," said Morse, "I don't believe him." Lewis watched the inspector. He could not hear what was being said on the other end of the line. Morse listened impassively.

"Thank you very much," he said finally. "What time would be convenient? All right. Thank you." He put down the 'phone, and Lewis looked at him expectantly.

"Well, sir?"

"I told you Lewis. You're a genius."

"Her car *was* out of order?"

Morse nodded. Miss Jennifer Coleby rang the Cowley Tyre and Battery Co. at 6:15 p.m. on the evening of Wednesday, 29 September. She said it was urgent—a very flat front-tyre. They couldn't get there until sevenish and she said that was too late."

"We're making headway, sir."

"We are, indeed. Now what about our bus-ride?"

The two men caught the 11:35 4A to Woodstock. It was half-empty and they sat in the front seat on the upper deck. Morse was silent and Lewis mulled over the strange developments in the case. The bus made good speed and stopped only four times before reaching Woodstock. At the third of these stops Morse gave his sergeant a dig in the ribs and Lewis looked out to see where they were. The bus had pulled into a shallow lay-by just outside Begbroke, at a large, thatched house with its garden crowded with tables and chairs set under brightly-striped umbrellas; he bent his head down to the bottom of the side window to see the name of the public house and read the two words *Golden Rose*.

"Interesting?" said Morse."

"Very," replied Lewis. He thought he might as well say something.

They alighted at Woodstock and Morse led the way. "Ready for a pint, sergeant?"

They walked into the cocktail-bar of *The Black Prince*. "Good morning, Mrs. McFee. You won't remember me, I suppose?"

"I remember you very well, inspector."

"What a memory," said Morse.

"What can I get for you, gentlemen?" She was clearly not amused.

"Two pints of best bitter, please."

"Official business?" Her dislike of Morse's manner was not quite enough to stifle her natural curiosity.

"No. No. Just a friendly visit to look at you again." He's in good spirits this morning, thought Lewis.

"I see from the paper that you're hoping . . ." she fumbled for the words.

"We're making progress, aren't we, sergeant?"

"Oh yes," said Lewis. After all, he was the other half of those intensive inquiries.

"Don't they ever give you a few hours off?" asked Morse.

"Oh, they're very good really." She was softening a little towards him; it was always nice to be reminded how hard she worked. "As a matter of fact I've got tonight and all of Saturday and Sunday off."

"Where shall we go?" asked Morse.

The hostess smiled professionally. "Where do you suggest, inspector?" Good for you, my girl, thought Lewis.

Morse asked for the menu and studied it in some detail.

"What's the food like here?" asked Morse.

"Why don't you try it?"

Morse appeared to consider the possibility but asked instead if there was a good fish-and-chip shop nearby. There wasn't. Several customers had come in and the policemen left by the side entrance and walked into the yard. To their right, a car was sitting up on its haunches, with each of the front wheels off. Underneath the car, suitably protected from the grease and oil, and wielding a formidable wrench, lay the landlord of *The Black Prince*, and by his side the folding tool-box which had so recently housed a long and heavy tyre-spanner.

Unnoticed by Morse and Lewis as they left the premises, a young man had entered the cocktail-bar and ordered a tonic water. Mr. John Sanders had apparently made a sufficient recovery from his bouts of shivery fever to join once more in the social life of Woodstock, if not to resume his duties with Messrs Chalkley and Sons.

On the bus journey back Morse was deeply engrossed in a Midland Counties bus time-table and a map of North Oxford. Occasionally he looked at his watch and made a brief entry

in a note-book. Lewis felt hungry. It had been a pity about
the fish-and-chip shop.

21
Friday, 15 October, p.m.

A bulky envelope marked "confidential" arrived on Morse's
desk at 3:30 that afternoon—"from the Principal." He had
done a very careful and thorough job—that was quite clear.
There were ninety-three typewriters, it appeared, in Lonsdale College. Most of them belonged to the college and had
found their various ways into the rooms of the fellows; over
twenty were the personal property of members of the college.
Ninety-three sheets of paper, each numbered, were neatly
arranged beneath a bull-dog clip. Two further sheets, stapled
together, provided the key to the typewritten specimens,
and, appropriately enough, the Principal's typewriter was
given the no. 1 designation. Morse riffled the sheets. It was
going to be a bigger job than he'd thought, and he rang the
laboratory boys. He learned it would take an hour or so.

Lewis had spent most of the afternoon typing his reports
and did not return to Morse's office until 4:15 p.m.

"You hoping to have the weekend off, Lewis?"

"Not if there's something you want me for, sir."

"I'm afraid we have rather a lot to do. I think it's time we
had a little confrontation, don't you?"

"Confrontation?"

"Yes. A gentle little confrontation between a certain Miss
Coleby and a certain Mr. Crowther. What do you think?"

"Might clear the air a bit."

"Ye-es. Do you think the old establishment could run to
four clean cups of coffee in the morning?"

"You want me to join you?"

"We're a team, Lewis, my boy. I've told you that before."
Morse rang Town and Gown and asked for Mr. Palmer.

"Hew shell I see is calling?" It was the prim little Judith.

"Mister Plod," said Morse.

"Howld on, please, Mr. Plod . . . you're threw."

"I didn't quite catch your name, sir? Palmer here."

"Morse. Inspector Morse."

"Oh, hullo, inspector." Stupid girl!

"I want to have a word with Miss Coleby. Confidential. I wonder if . . ."

Palmer interrupted him. "I'm awfully sorry, inspector. She's not here this afternoon. She wanted to spend a long weekend in London and, well . . . we do occasionally show a little er flexibility, you know. It sometimes helps the er the smooth running . . ."

"London, you say?"

"Yes. She said she was going to spend the weekend with some friends. She caught the lunch-time train."

"Did she leave an address?"

"I'm sorry. I don't think she did. I could try to er . . ."

"No. Don't bother."

"Can I take a message?"

"No. I'll get in touch with her when she comes back." Perhaps he could see Sue again . . . "When will she be back, by the way?"

"I don't really know. Sunday evening I should think."

"All right. Well, thank you."

"Sorry I couldn't be . . ."

"Not your fault." Morse put down the 'phone with less than average courtesy.

"One of our birds has flown, Lewis." He turned his attention to Bernard Crowther and decided to try the college first.

"Porter's Lodge."

"Can you put me through to Mr. Crowther's rooms, please?"

"Just a minute, sir." Morse drummed the table with the fingers of his left hand. Come on!

"Are you there, sir?"

"Yes. I'm still here."

"No reply, I'm afraid, sir."

"Is he in college this afternoon?"

"I saw him this morning, sir. Just a minute." Three minutes later Morse was wondering if the wretched porter had taken a gentle stroll around the quad.

"Are you there, sir?"

"Yes, I'm still here."

"He's away somewhere, sir, for the weekend. It's a conference of some sort."

"Do you know when he's due back?"

"Sorry, sir. Shall I put you through to the college office?"

"No, don't bother. I'll ring again later."

"Thank you, sir."

Morse held the 'phone in his hands for a few seconds and finally put it down with the greatest circumspection. "I wonder. I wonder . . ." He was lost in thought.

"It seems *both* of our birds have flown, sir."

"I wonder if the conference is being held in London."

"You don't think . . ."

"I don't know what to think," said Morse.

Nor was he sure what to think when half an hour later the findings of the laboratory were 'phoned through. Lewis watched the inspector's curious reactions.

"Are you sure . . .? You're quite sure . . .? Yes. Well, many thanks. You'll bring them over? Good. Thank you."

"Well, Lewis, you're in for a surprise."

"About the note?"

"Yes. About the note—the note someone wrote to the young lady who is now visiting 'some friends' in London. They say they know whose typewriter it was."

"And whose was it?"

"That's what's puzzling me. We've never heard of him before! He's a Mr. Peter Newlove."

"And who's Mr. Peter Newlove?"

"It's time we found out." He rang Lonsdale College for the second time that afternoon and found the same slow-motion porter presiding over the Lodge.

"Mr. Newlove, sir? No, I'm afraid he's not in college. Just let me check in the book . . . No, sir. He's away till Monday. Can I take a message? No? All right. Goodbye, sir."

"Well, that's that," said Morse. "*All* our birds have flown.

And I don't see much point in staying here, do you?" Lewis didn't.

"Let's just tidy up all this mess," said Morse.

Lewis gathered together the papers on his side of the table—the photographs of Sylvia Kaye and the carefully drawn diagrams of the yard at *The Black Prince*, annotated in thin, spidery writing with details of everything found therein. He looked again at the close-ups of the murdered girl lying there, and felt a paternally-protective urge to cover the harsh nakedness of her beautiful body.

"I'd like to get the bastard who did this," he muttered.

"What's that?" Morse took the photographs from him.

"He must be a sex maniac, don't you think, sir? Tearing off her clothes like that and leaving her for anyone and everyone to see. God, I wish I knew who he was!"

"Oh, I don't think there's much difficulty about that," said Morse.

Lewis looked at him incredulously. "You mean you *know*?"

Morse nodded slowly, and locked away the file on Sylvia Kaye.

3
Search for a Killer

22
Sunday, 17 October

Sue saw David off on the Birmingham train at 7:13 on Sunday evening. She told him what a marvellous weekend it had been—and so it had. On Saturday they had gone to the cinema, had a delicious Chinese meal and generally luxuriated in being together. Most of Sunday they had spent in Headington at the home of David's parents, pleasant, warm-hearted people, sensible enough to leave the two young love-birds alone for the greater part of the day. They hoped to marry some time next autumn, after David had finished his post-graduate year of research in metallurgy at the University of Warwick. He was hopeful (for he had taken a "first") of getting a lectureship somewhere, and Sue encouraged him: she would rather be married to a lecturer than to an industrial chemist, or whatever metallurgists became. She thought that was the only thing about David of which she couldn't wholeheartedly approve—his choice of metallurgy. It had something to do with her own schooldays and the distaste she'd always felt amid the smells and silver slivers of the metalwork shop. There was something, too, about the *hands* of people who worked with metal: a sort of ingrained griminess, however patiently they were scrubbed.

The train lingered at Oxford station for several minutes and Sue kissed David fully and freely as he leaned from the window of an empty carriage.

"It's been lovely seeing you again, darling," said David.

"Super."

"You enjoyed it, didn't you?"

"Of course I did." She laughed gaily. "Why on earth did you ask that?"

David smiled. "It's just nice to know, that's all." They kissed again, and Sue walked along with him for a few yards as the train pulled out.

"See you in a fortnight. Don't forget to write."

"I won't," said Sue. "Bye." She waved until the train had left the platform and she watched it curving its way towards the north, the red light on the rear coach bobbing and winking in the gathering darkness.

She walked slowly back down the platform, along the subway and up to the barrier on the other side. She gave in her platform-ticket and made her way to Carfax. Here she had to wait for half an hour before a number 2 bus came along, and it was eight o'clock before she got off in North Oxford. She crossed the road and with her head down walked along Charlton Road and thought about the last two days. She could never have told David about Wednesday night. There was nothing to tell anyway, was there? Just a minor peccadillo. She supposed most people had their foolish moments—even engaged people—and there were some things that just could not be told. Not that David would have been jealous; he wasn't that sort, at all—mild, equable, balanced David. Perhaps she wouldn't mind if he were a bit jealous. But she knew, or thought she knew, that he wasn't; she could spot jealousy a mile off. She thought of Morse. She really had been very naughty at *The Sheridan* with Doctor Eyres, and Morse had been jealous—rabidly, furiously jealous. She'd secretly enjoyed making him jealous until . . . Well, she wasn't going to think of him any more . . . But she'd never cried over David . . . She wondered if Morse believed her when she said she would be crying herself to sleep on Wednesday night. She hoped he had, for it was true. There she went again, starting with David and finishing with *him*. He'd probably not given her another thought . . . David! He was her man. Married to David she would be happy at last. Marriage. A big step, they all said. But she was twenty-three now . . . She hoped Morse *had* given her another thought . . . Forget him!

But she was not to be allowed to forget him. As she reached the house she saw the Lancia outside. Her heart pounded against her ribs and a wave of involuntary joy coursed through her blood. She let herself in and went straight to the living-room. There he was, sitting talking to Mary. He stood up as she came in.

"Hullo."

"Hullo," she said weakly.

"I really called to see Miss Coleby, but I gather she may not be back yet for a while. So I've been having a delightful little chat with Mary here."

Mary indeed! Dumpy, freckled, little man-eater! Why don't you go, Mary? Mary, why don't you leave us alone—just for a few minutes? Please! She felt viciously jealous. But Mary seemed very taken with the charming inspector and showed no signs of imminent surrender. Sue, still wearing her summer coat, sat on the arm of a chair, trying to resist the wave of desperation that threatened to engulf her.

She heard herself say: "She'll catch the 8:15 from Paddington, I should think. Probably get here about ten."

That was two hours. Two whole hours. If only Mary would go! He might ask her out for a drink and they could talk. But the wave swept her over, and she left the room and rushed upstairs. Morse got up as she left and thanked Mary for her hospitality. As he opened the front door he turned to Mary. Would she ask Sue to come down for a second? He would like to have a quick word with her. Mary, too, disappeared upstairs and blessedly faded from the scene. Morse stepped out into the concrete drive and Sue appeared, framed in the doorway. She stopped there.

"You wanted a word with me, inspector?"

"Which room do you sleep in, Sue?" She stepped out and stood next to him. Her arm brushed his as she pointed to the window immediately above the front door, and Morse felt a jagged ache between his temples. He wasn't a tall man and she was almost his own height in the very high wedge-heeled shoes she wore. She dropped her arm and their hands met in an accidental, beautiful way. Leave your hand there, Sue. Leave it there, my darling. He felt the electric thrill of the contact and gently, softly he ran his finger tips along her wrist.

"Why do you want to know that?" Her voice sounded hoarse and breathless.

"I don't know. I suppose if I drive past and see a light on in your window I shall know it's you in there."

Sue could bear it no longer. She took her hand from his and turned away. "You came to see Jennifer, then?"

"Yes."

"I'll tell her, of course—when she comes in." Morse nodded.

"You think she's got something to do with the Woodstock business, don't you?"

"Something, perhaps."

They stood in silence for a minute. Sue was wearing a sleeveless dress and she was trying not to shiver.

"Well, I'd better be off."

"Goodnight, then."

"Goodnight." He turned towards the gate and had almost reached it when he turned round. "Sue?" She stood in the doorway.

"Yes?"

He walked back. "Sue, would you like to come out with me for a little while?"

"Oh . . ." Sue got no further. She flung her arms around him and cried joyfully on his shoulder, and neither heard the front gate open.

"If you'll excuse me, please?" said a cool, well-spoken voice, and Jennifer Coleby edged past them into the house.

The other wanderers, too, were just returning. Bernard Crowther had returned from London on the same train as Jennifer Coleby; but they had travelled in separate parts of the train, and no-one watching them alight at platform number 2 could have formed the slightest suspicion that either was aware of the other's existence.

About this time, too, Peter Newlove was taking his leave of a red-headed, radiant girl in Church Street, Woodstock. They kissed again with eagerness and seeming insatiability.

"I'll be in touch, Gaye."

"Make sure you do—and thanks again."

It had been an expensive weekend; very expensive, in fact. But it was, in Peter's view, worth almost every penny.

On Monday morning, Morse decided that however embarrassing it would be he had his job to do. How he dreaded it, though! Here was the big moment, the dénouement of the case (of that he felt quite confident) and yet he felt as if he himself were the guilty party. Lewis collected Jennifer Coleby in his own car; Morse felt he could just about spare her the official trappings. Bernard Crowther said he would make his own way, if that was all right. It was. Morse had tried to think out the likeliest approaches, but his concentration had been lapsing sadly. He decided to let things take their course.

At 10:25 a.m. Crowther arrived, five minutes early, and Morse poured him coffee and asked him a few casual questions about the "conference."

"Oh. The usual thing, you know. One long yawn," said Crowther.

"What was it about exactly?"

"University admissions. Arguing the toss about A-level requirements. We're not very popular with the Schools Council, you know. They think Oxford is the last bastion of academic elitism. Still, I suppose it is really . . ." He had no chance to develop his theme. Lewis came in with Jennifer Coleby, and Crowther got to his feet.

"You two know each other?" asked Morse. There was not a hint of cynicism in his voice. Strangely, or so it seemed to Morse, Jennifer and Crowther shook hands. "Good mornings" were exchanged, and Morse, a trifle non-plussed, poured two more coffees.

"You *do* know each other?" He sounded rather unsure of himself.

"We live fairly near each other, don't we, Mr. Crowther?"

"We do, yes. I've often seen you on the bus. It's Miss Coleby, I think, isn't it? You come round for the SPCC."

Jennifer nodded.

Morse got up and passed the sugar-basin round. He felt he couldn't sit still.

During the next few minutes Lewis was forced to wonder if the inspector had lost his grip completely. He um'd and ah'd and said "to be honest with you" and "we have some reason to suppose" and finally managed to suggest to his pair of prime suspects, almost apologetically, that they might be having an affair with each other.

Jennifer laughed almost aloud and Bernard smiled shyly. It was Bernard who spoke first. "I'm sure I feel very flattered, inspector, and I very much wish perhaps that I *was* having some secret affair with Miss Coleby. But I'm afraid the answer's no. What else can I say?"

"Miss Coleby?"

"I think I have spoken to Mr. Crowther twice in my life —to ask him for a donation to the SPCC. I sometimes see him on the bus going into town—we get on and off at the same stops. But I think he always goes upstairs and I never do. I hate the smell of cigarettes."

Morse, who was smoking his third cigarette, felt once more that he was getting the worst of things with Jennifer Coleby. He turned to Crowther.

"I must ask you this, sir. Please think very carefully before you answer, and remember that you are here in connection with a murder, the murder of the girl who was travelling in your car." Morse saw a look of surprise on Jennifer's face. "Was Miss Coleby here the other passenger you picked up that night?"

Bernard replied with an immediacy and conviction that sorely troubled Morse. "No, inspector, she wasn't. Of that you can be completely assured."

"And you, Miss Coleby. Do you deny that you were the other passenger in Mr. Crowther's car?"

"Yes. I do deny it. Absolutely."

Morse drained his coffee.

"Do you want us to sign anything, inspector?" There was a deep cynicism in Jennifer's voice.

Morse shook his head. "No. Sergeant Lewis has made

notes on what you've both said. One more question though, Miss Coleby, if you don't mind. Can you give me the address of the friends you stayed with in London this weekend?"

Jennifer took a plain envelope from her handbag and wrote down an address in Lancaster Gardens. As an afterthought she added the telephone number, and handed the envelope to Morse.

"They're lying—both of 'em," said Morse when they had gone.

Crowther had to get to the centre of Oxford and had gallantly offered a lift to his fellow-suspect. Morse wondered what they would be talking about. Lewis had said nothing.

"Did you hear me?" Morse was angry.

"Yes, sir."

"I said they're a pair of prize liars. LIARS." Lewis remained silent. He thought the inspector was wrong, terribly wrong. He himself was no stranger to interviewing liars and he had the firm conviction that both Crowther and Coleby were telling the plain truth.

Morse looked hard at his sergeant. "Come on! Out with it!"

"What do you mean, sir?"

"What do I mean? You know what I mean. You think I'm up the bloody pole, don't you? You think I'm going bonkers. You're willing to believe what everyone else says, but you don't believe *me*. Come on. Tell me! I want to know."

Lewis looked at him and saw the bitter failure in the inspector's eyes. He wished he could put things right, but he couldn't. It had been the quality in him that from the start had endeared him to Morse. It was his basic honesty and integrity.

"I think you're wrong, sir." It took a lot of saying, but he said it, and he deserved better than Morse's cruel rejoinder.

"You think I'm wrong? Well let me tell you something, Lewis. If anyone's wrong here, it's not me—it's *you*. Do you understand that! YOU—not me. If you've not got the nous to see that these two slimy toads are *lying*, lying to save their own necks, you shouldn't be on this case. Do you hear me? *You shouldn't be on this case.*"

Lewis felt a deep hurt; but not for himself. "Perhaps you ought to have someone else with you, sir. On the case, I mean."

"You may be right." Morse was calming down a little and Lewis sensed it.

"There's this man Newlove, sir. Shouldn't we . . ."

"Newlove? Who the hell's he?" Lewis had said the wrong thing, and Morse's latent anger and frustration rose to fever pitch again. "Newlove? We've never heard of the bloody man before. All right—he's got a typewriter. That's not a sin, is it? He didn't write that letter. CROWTHER DID! And if you don't see that you must be blind as a bloody bat!"

"But don't you think . . ."

"Oh, bugger off, Lewis. You're boring me."

"Does that mean I'm off the case, sir?"

"I don't know. I don't care. Just bugger off and leave me alone." Lewis went out and left him alone.

The 'phone rang a few minutes later. Morse picked the receiver up and closed his mind to everything. "I'm not here," he snapped, "I've gone home." He slammed down the receiver and sat brooding savagely within himself. He even forgot Sue. The last castle had finally collapsed. Having stood the flood so long, it was now a flattened heap of formless sand. But even as it fell a curious clarification was dawning across his mind. He got up from his leather chair, opened the cabinet and took out the file on Sylvia Kaye. He opened it at the beginning and was still reading it late into the afternoon, when the shadows crept across the room and he found it difficult to read, and a new and horrifying thought was taking birth in the depths of his tortured mind.

The dramatic news broke at a quarter-past seven. Margaret Crowther had committed suicide.

Monday, 18 October

Bernard Crowther, after dropping Jennifer Coleby in the High, had been lucky in finding a parking space in Bear Lane. Not even the dons were permitted to park outside the college now. He had lunched in the Senior Common Room and spent the afternoon and early evening working. Both the children were away for a week on a school camping holiday in nearby Whitham Woods. On such ventures it was customary for the parents to visit their children on one evening during the week, but the young Crowthers had told their parents not to bother; and that was that. At least it would be a chance for Bernard and Margaret to have a few decent meals, instead of the inevitable chips and tomato sauce with everything.

Bernard left college at about twenty-past six. The roads were getting free again by now and he had an easy journey home. He let himself in with his Yale key and hung up his coat. Funny smell. Gas?

"Margaret?" He put his brief-case in the front room. "Margaret?" He walked to the kitchen and found the door locked. "Margaret!" He rattled the knob of the kitchen door, but it was firmly locked on the other side. He banged on the door. "Margaret! Margaret! Are you there?" He could smell the gas more strongly now. His mouth went completely dry and there was wild panic in his voice. "MARGARET!" He rushed back to the front door, through the side gate, and tried the back door. It was locked. He whimpered like a child. He looked into the kitchen through the large window above the sink. The electric light was on and for a fraction of a second a last ember of hope flared up, and glowed, and then was gone. The surrealistic sight that met his eyes was so strangely improbable that it registered itself blankly as a meaningless picture on the retina of his eyes—a sight without significance—a waxwork model, bright-eyed and brightly-hued, with a fixed, staring smile. What was she doing sitting on the floor like that? Cleaning the oven?

He picked up a house-brick lying by the side of the wall, smashed a pane in the window, and cut his fingers badly as he reached for the catch and opened the window from the inside. The nauseating smell of gas hit him with an almost physical impact, and it was some seconds before, holding his handkerchief to his face, he climbed awkwardly in through the window and turned off the gas. Margaret's head was just inside the oven, resting on a soft red cushion. In a numbed, irrational way he thought he should put the cushion back where it came from; it was from the settee in the lounge. He looked down with shocked, zombie-like eyes at the jagged cuts on his hand and mechanically dabbed them with his handkerchief. He saw the sticky brown paper lining the gaps by the door-jambs and the window, and noticed that Margaret had cut the ends as neatly as she always did when she wrapped the children's birthday-presents. The children! Thank God they were away! He saw the scissors on the formica top over the washing machine, and like an automaton he picked them up and put them in the drawer. The smell was infinitely sickly still, and he felt the vomit rising in his gorge. And now the horror of it all was gradually seeping into his mind, like a pool of ink into blotting paper. He knew that she was dead.

He unlocked the kitchen door, picked up the 'phone in the hall and in a dazed, uncomprehending voice he asked for the police. A letter addressed to him was lying beside the telephone directory. He picked it up and put it in his breast pocket and returned to the kitchen. Ten minutes later the police found him there, sitting on the floor beside his wife, his hand on her hair, his eyes bleak and glazed. He had been deaf to the strident ringing of the front door-bell.

Morse arrived only a few minutes after the police car and the ambulance. It was Inspector Bell of the Oxford City Police who had called Morse; Crowther had insisted on it. The two inspectors had met several times before and stood in the hallway talking together in muted voices. Bernard had been led unresistingly from the kitchen by a police doctor and was now sitting in the lounge, his head sunk into his hands. He appeared unaware of what was going on or what was being said, but when Morse came into the lounge he seemed to come to life again.

"Hello, inspector." Morse put his hand on Crowther's shoulder, but could think of nothing to say that might help. Nothing could help. "She left this, inspector." Bernard reached into his breast pocket and pulled out the sealed envelope.

"It's for you, you know, sir; it's addressed to you—not to me," said Morse quietly.

"I know. But you read it. I can't." He put his head in his hands again, and sobbed quietly.

Dear Bernard,
  When you read this I shall be dead. I know what this will mean to you and the children and it's only this that has kept me from doing it before—but I just can't cope with life any longer. I am finding it so difficult to know what to say—but I want you to know that it's not your fault. I have not been all that a wife should be to you and I have been a miserable failure with the children, and everything has built up and I long for rest and peace away from it all. I just can't go on any longer. I realise how selfish I am and I know that I'm just running away from everything. But I shall go mad if I don't run away. I must run away—I haven't the courage to stand up to things any longer.
  On your desk you will find all the accounts. All the bills are paid except Mr. Anderson's for pruning the apple trees. We owe him £5 but I couldn't find his address.
  I am thinking of the earlier times when we were so happy. Nothing can take them from us. Look after the children. It's my fault—not theirs. I pray that you won't think too badly of me and that you can forgive me.
  Margaret.

It wasn't going to be much comfort, but Crowther had got to face it some time.

"Please read it, sir."

Bernard read it, but he showed no emotion. His despair could plumb no lower depths. "What about the children?" he said at last.

"Don't worry yourself about that, sir. We'll look after everything." The police doctor's voice was brisk. He was no stranger to such situations, and he knew the procedure from this point on. It wasn't much that he could do—but it was something.

"Look, sir, I want you to take . . ."

"What about the children?" He was a shattered, broken man, and Morse left him to the ministrations of the doctor. He retired with Bell to the front room, and noticed the list of the accounts, insurances, mortgage repayments, and stock-exchange holdings which Margaret had left so neatly ordered under a paper-weight on the desk. But he didn't touch them. They were something between a husband and his wife, a wife who had been alive when he had interviewed Crowther earlier that day.

"You know him, then?" asked Bell.

"I saw him this morning," said Morse. "I saw him about the Woodstock murder."

"Really?" Bell looked surprised.

"He was the man who picked up the girls."

"You think he was involved?"

"I don't know," said Morse.

"Has this business got anything to do with it?"

"I don't know."

The ambulance was still waiting outside and curious eyes were peeping from all the curtains along the road. In the kitchen Morse looked down at Margaret Crowther. He had never seen her before, and he was surprised to realise how attractive she must have been. Fortyish? Hair greying a little, but a good, firm figure and a finely-featured face, twisted now and blue.

"No point in keeping her here," said Bell.

Morse shook his head. "No point at all."

"It takes a long time, you know, this North-Sea gas."

The two men talked in a desultory way for several minutes,

and Morse prepared to leave. But as he walked out to his car, he was called back by the police doctor.

"Can you come back a minute, inspector?" Morse re-entered the house.

"He says he must talk to you."

Crowther sat with his head against the back of the chair. He was breathing heavily and the sweat stood out upon his brow. He was in a state of deep shock, and was already under sedation.

"Inspector." He opened his eyes wearily. "Inspector, I've got to talk to you." He had great difficulty in getting this far, and Morse looked to the doctor, who slowly shook his head.

"Tomorrow, sir," said Morse. "I'll see you tomorrow."

"Inspector, I've got to talk to you."

"Yes, I know. But not now. We'll talk tomorrow. It'll be all right then." Morse put his hand to Crowther's forehead and felt the clammy wetness there.

"Inspector!" But the top corner of the walls where Crowther was trying to focus was slowly disintegrating before his eyes; the angles melted and spiralled and faded away.

Morse drove slowly out of Southdown Road and realised just how close Crowther lived to Jennifer Coleby. It was a black night and the moon was hidden away deep behind the lowering clouds. Rectangles of light, shaded by curtains, showed from most of the front-room windows, and in many Morse could see the light-blue phosphorescent glow of television screens. He looked at one house in particular and looked up at one window in it, the window directly above the door. But it was dark, and he drove on.

25
Tuesday, 19 October, a.m.

Morse had slept very badly and woke with a throbbing head. He hated suicides. Why had she done it? Was suicide just the coward's refuge from some black despair? Or was it in its way an act of courage that revealed a perverted sort of valour? Not that, though. So many other lives were intertwined; no burdens were shed—they were merely passed from the shoulders of one to those of another. Morse's mind would give itself no rest but twirled around on some interminable fun-fair ride.

It was past nine o'clock before he was sitting in his leather chair, and his sombre mood draped itself over his sagging shoulders. He summoned Lewis, who knocked apprehensively on the door before going in; but Morse had seemingly lost all recollection of the nasty little episode the day before. He told Lewis the facts of Margaret Crowther's suicide.

"Do you think he's got something important to tell us, sir?"

There was a knock on the door before Lewis could learn the answer to his question, and a young girl brought in the post, said a bright "Good morning" and was off. Morse fingered through the dozen or so letters and his eye fell on an unopened envelope marked "strictly private" and addressed to himself. The envelope was exactly similar to the one he had seen the previous evening.

"I don't know whether Crowther's got anything to tell us or not; but it looks as if his late wife has." He opened the envelope neatly with a letter-knife and read its type-written contents aloud to Lewis.

Dear Inspector,

I have never met you, but I have seen from the newspapers that you are in charge of the inquiry into the death of Sylvia Kaye. I should have told you this a long time ago, but I hope it's not too late even now. You see, inspector, I killed Sylvia Kaye. (The words were doubly underlined.)

I must try to explain myself. Please forgive me if I get a little muddled, but it all seems very long ago.

I have known for about six months—well, certainly for six months—perhaps I've known for much longer —that my husband has been having an affair with another woman. I had no proof and have none now. But it is so difficult for a man to hide this sort of thing from his wife. We have been married for fifteen years and I know him so well. It was written all over what he said and what he did and how he looked—he must have been terribly unhappy, I think.

On Wednesday, 22nd September, I left the house at 6:30 p.m. to go to my evening class at Headington— but I didn't go immediately. Instead, I waited in my car just off the Banbury Road. I seemed to wait such a long time and I didn't really know what I was going to do. Then at about a quarter to seven Bernard—my husband—drove up to the junction at Charlton Road and turned right towards the northern roundabout. I followed him as best I could—I say that because I'm not a good driver—and anyway it was getting darker all the time. There wasn't much traffic and I could see him clearly two or three cars ahead. At the Woodstock Road roundabout he turned along the A34. He was driving too fast for me, though, and I kept dropping further and further behind. I thought I had lost him—but there were road-works ahead and the traffic had to filter into single line for about a mile. There was a slow, heavy lorry in the front and I soon caught up again—Bernard was only about six or seven cars ahead of me. The lorry turned off towards Bladon at the next roundabout and I managed to keep Bernard in sight and saw him take the first turning on the left in Woodstock itself. I panicked a bit and didn't know what to do—I turned into the next street, and stopped the car and walked back. But it was hopeless. I drove back to Headington and was only twenty minutes late for my evening class.

The next Wednesday, the 29th September, I drove out to Woodstock again, leaving the house a good ten minutes earlier than usual, parked my car further along the village, and walked back to the street into which Bernard had turned the previous week. I didn't know where to wait and I felt silly and conspicuous, but I found a safe enough little spot on the left of the road —I was terrified that Bernard would see me—if he came that was—and I waited there and watched every car that came round the corner. It was child's play to see the cars turning in—and the occupants as well. He came at quarter-past seven and I felt myself trembling frantically. He was not alone—a young girl with long fair hair, in a white blouse, was sitting next to him in the front seat. I thought they must see me because the car turned—oh, only six or seven yards ahead of me— into the car park of *The Black Prince*. My legs were shaking and the blood was pounding in my ears, but something made me go through with it. I walked cautiously up to the yard and peered in. There were several cars there already and I couldn't see Bernard's for several minutes. I edged round the back of one car—just to the left of the yard—and then I saw them. The car was on the same side at the far end, with the boot towards the wall—he must have backed in. They were sitting in the front—talking for a while. I felt a cold anger inside me. Bernard and a blowzy blonde—about seventeen she looked! I saw them kissing. Then they got out of the front and into the back. I couldn't see any more—at least I was spared that.

I can't really explain what I felt. As I write now it all seems so flat—and so unimportant somehow. I felt more anger than jealousy—I know that. Burning anger that Bernard had shamed me so. It was about five minutes later when they got out. They said something—but I couldn't hear what it was. There was a lever—a long tyre-lever—I found it on the floor of the yard, and I picked it up. I don't know why. I felt so frightened and so angry. And suddenly the engine of the car was switched on and then the lights and the whole yard was lit up. The car moved off and out of the yard, and after it had gone the darkness seemed even blacker than before. The girl stood where he had left her, and I crept behind the three or four cars between us and came up behind her. I said nothing and I'm sure she didn't hear me. I hit her across the back of the head with an easy strength. It seemed like a dream. I felt nothing—no remorse—no fear—nothing. I left her where she was, against the far wall. It was still very

dark. I didn't know when or how she would be found
—and I didn't care.

Bernard knew all along that I had murdered Sylvia
Kaye—he passed me on my way back to Oxford. He
must have seen me because I saw him. He was right
behind me for some time and must have seen the number plate. I saw his car as clear as daylight when he
overtook me.

I know what you have suspected about Bernard. But
you have been wrong. I don't know what he's told
you—but I know you have spoken to him. If he has
told you lies, it has only been to shield me. But I need
no-one to shield me any longer. Look after Bernard and
don't let him suffer too much because of me. He did
what hundreds of men do, and for that I blame myself
and no-one else. I have neither been a good wife to him
nor a good mother to his children. I am just so tired—
so desperately tired of everything. For what I have done
I am now most bitterly sorry—but I realise that this is
no excuse. What else can I say—what else is there
to say?

Margaret Crowther.

Morse's voice trailed away and the room was very still. Lewis
felt very moved as he heard the letter read aloud, almost as
if Margaret Crowther were there. But she would never speak
again. He thought of his visit to her and guessed how cruelly
she must have suffered these last few months.

"You thought it was something like that, didn't you, sir?"

"No," said Morse.

"Comes as a bit of a shock, doesn't it? Out of the blue,
like."

"I don't think much of her English style," said Morse. He
handed the letter over to Lewis. "She uses far too many
dashes for my liking." The comment seemed heartless and
irrelevant. Lewis read the letter to himself.

"She's a good, clean typist anyway, sir."

"Bit odd, don't you think, that she typed her name at the
end instead of using her signature?"

Give Morse a letter and his imagination soared to the

realms of the bright-eyed Seraphim. Lewis groaned inwardly.

"You think she wrote it, don't you, sir?"

Morse reluctantly reined back the wild horses. "Yes. She wrote it."

Lewis thought he understood the inspector's feelings. There would have to be a bit of tidying up, of course, but the case was now substantially over. He'd enjoyed most of his time working with the irascible, volatile inspector, but now . . . The 'phone rang and Morse answered. He said "I see" a dozen times and replaced the receiver.

"Crowther's in the Radcliffe—he's had a mild heart attack. He's not allowed to see anyone for two days at least."

"Perhaps he couldn't tell us much more," suggested Lewis.

"Oh yes he could," said Morse. He leaned back, put his hands on his head like a naughty schoolboy, and stared vacantly at the farthest corner of the wall. Lewis thought it best to keep quiet, but he grew uncomfortably restless as the minutes ticked by.

"Would you like a coffee, sir?" Morse didn't seem to hear him. "Coffee? Would you like a coffee?" Morse reminded him of a very deaf person with his hearing-aid switched off. Minute after minute slipped by before the grey eyes refocused on the world around him.

"Well, that's cleared up one thing, Lewis. We can cross Mrs. Crowther off our list of suspects, can't we?"

26
Tuesday, 19 October, p.m.

At mid-day Peter Newlove was sitting in his rooms. He was expecting no-one. Normally Bernard might have dropped in about now for a gin, but the news had swept the college that morning: Margaret had killed herself and Bernard had suffered a heart attack. And the double-barrelled news hit no-one harder than Peter. He had known Margaret well and had liked her; and Bernard was his best friend in that academic, dilettante style of friendship which springs up in most collegiate universities. He had rung up the hospital, but there was no chance of visiting Bernard until Thursday at the earliest. He had sent some flowers: Bernard liked flowers and had no wife to send them now . . . He had inquired, too, about the children. They had gone to stay with an aunt in Hendon, though Peter couldn't imagine how such an arrangement could possibly help them very much.

There was a knock on the door. "It's open."

He had not met Inspector Morse before and was pleasantly surprised that his offer of a drink was accepted. Morse explained in blunt, unequivocal terms why he had called.

"And it was written on *that* one?" Newlove frowned at the open portable typewriter on the table.

"No doubt about it."

Newlove looked mildly perplexed, but said nothing.

"Do you know a young lady named Jennifer Coleby, Miss Jennifer Coleby?"

"I don't, I'm afraid." Newlove's frown grew deeper.

"She works in The High, not far from here. Town and Gown. Assurance place."

Newlove shook his head. "I might have seen her, of course. But I don't know her. I've not heard the name before."

"And you've never written to anyone of that name?"

"No. How could I? As I say, I've never heard of the woman."

Morse pursed his lips and continued. "Who else could have used your typewriter, sir?"

"Well, I don't know really. I suppose almost anyone in a way. I don't lock the place up very much unless there are question papers about."

"You mean you leave your doors open and let anybody just walk in and help himself to your booze or your books —or your typewriter?"

"No, it's not like that. But quite a few of the fellows do drop in."

"Who in particular, would you say?"

"Well, there's a new young don here this term, Melhuish, for example. He's been in quite a few times recently."

"And?"

"And a dozen others." He sounded a little uneasy.

"Have you ever seen any of these er friends of yours using your typewriter?"

"Well, no. I don't think I have."

"They'd use their own, wouldn't they?"

"Yes. I suppose they would."

"Not much 'suppose' about it, is there, sir?" said Morse.

"No."

"You've no idea then?"

"I'm not being very helpful, I know. But I've no idea at all."

Morse abruptly switched his questioning. "Did you know Mrs. Crowther?"

"Yes."

"You've heard about her?"

"Yes," said Newlove quietly.

"And Bernard Crowther?" Newlove nodded. "I understand he's one of your best friends?" Again Newlove nodded. "I've been to his room this morning, sir. If you want to put it crudely I've been snooping around. But you see, I often have to snoop around. I take no particular delight in it."

"I understand," said Newlove.

"I wonder if you do understand, sir." There was a clipped impatience in his voice now. "He often drops in to see you, is that right?"

"Quite often."

"And do you think he'd come to you if he wanted anything?"

"You mean rather than to somebody else?"

"Yes."

"He'd come to me."

"Did you know that his typewriter can't even cope with a comma?"

"No, I didn't," lied Newlove.

After dropping Morse at Lonsdale College, Lewis had his own duties to perform. For the life of him he couldn't understand the point of this particular errand, but Morse had said it was of vital importance. Something had galvanised the inspector into new life. But it wasn't the gay, rumbustious Morse of the early days of the case. Something grim had come over him and Lewis found him a little frightening sometimes. He only hoped they got no more letters upon which Morse could practise his misdirected ingenuity.

He pulled the official police car into the small yard of the Summertown Health Centre, situated on the corner of the Banbury Road and Marston Ferry Road. It was a finely built, large, red-stone structure with steps up to a white porch before the front door—one of the many beautiful large houses built by the well-to-do along the Banbury Road in the latter half of the nineteenth century. Lewis was expected and had only a minute or so to wait before being shown into the consulting room of the senior partner.

"That's the lot, sergeant." Dr. Green handed over a file to Lewis.

"Are you sure it's all here, sir? Inspector Morse was very anxious for me to get everything."

Dr. Green was silent for a moment. "The only thing that's not there is . . . is er any record that we had er may have had about any er conversation we er may have had with Miss Kaye about her er private sex-life. You understand, I know, sergeant, that there are er there is the ethical side of er the er confidential nature of the er doctor's relationship with the er patient."

"You mean she was on the pill, doctor." Lewis stepped boldly with his policeman's boots where the angelic Green had so delicately feared to tread.

"Er . . . I er didn't say that, did I, sergeant? I er said that we er it is er improper yes improper to er betray to betray the confidences that we er we er hear in the consulting room."

"Would you have told us if she *wasn't* on the pill?" asked Lewis innocently.

"Now that's er a very difficult er question. You er we er you er you are putting words into my er mouth a bit aren't you, sergeant? All I'm saying is er . . ."

Lewis wondered what the senior partner would say to a patient who had malignant cancer. It would be, he was sure, a most protracted er interview. He thanked the good doctor and left as quickly as he could, although he was halfway down the porch steps before he finally shook off the er persistent Green. He'd have to tell his wife about er Doctor Green.

As they had agreed, Lewis picked up Morse outside Lonsdale College at one o'clock. He told the inspector about the troubled state of Doctor Green's conscience on the problem of professional confidentiality, but Morse was cynically unimpressed.

"We know she was on the pill, remember?" Lewis should have remembered. He had read the reports; in fact Morse had specially asked him to get to know them as well as he could. It hadn't seemed very important at the time. Perhaps, even then, Morse had seen its relevance? But he doubted it, and his doubts, as it happened, were well justified.

As Lewis drove out of the city, Morse asked him to turn off to the motel at the Woodstock roundabout. "We'll have a pint and a sandwich, eh?"

They sat in the *Morris* Bar, Morse engrossed in the medical reports on Sylvia Kaye. They covered, at intermittent stages, the whole of her pathetically-brief little life, from the mild attack of jaundice at the age of two days to an awkward break of her arm in the August before she had died. Measles, warts on fingers, middle-ear infection, dysmenorrhoea, headaches (myopia?). A fairly uneventful medical history. Most of the notes were reasonably legible, and oddly enough the arch-apostle of indecision, the conscientious Green, had a beautifully clear and rounded hand. His only direct contacts with Sylvia had been over the last two afflictions, the headaches and the broken arm. Morse passed the file over to Lewis, and went to refill the glasses. Some of the details had appeared in the post-mortem report anyway, but his memory wasn't Lewis's strongest asset.

"Have you ever broken your arm?" asked Morse.

"No."

"They say it's very painful. Something to do with the neurological endings or something. Like when you hurt your foot, Lewis. Very, very painful."

"You should know, sir."

"Ah, but if you've got a basically-strong constitution like

me, you soon recover." Lewis let it go. "Did you notice," continued Morse, "that Green saw her on the day before she died?"

Lewis opened the file again. He had read the entry, but without noticing the date. He looked again and saw that Morse was right. Sylvia had visited the Summertown Health Centre on Tuesday, 28 September, with a letter from the orthopedic surgeon at the Radcliffe Infirmary. It read: "Arm still very stiff and rather painful. Further treatment necessary. Continuation of physiotherapy treatment recommended as before—Tuesday and Thursday a.m."

Lewis could imagine the consultation. And suddenly a thought flashed into his mind. It was being with Morse that did it. His fanciful suspicions were getting as wild as the inspector's. "You don't think, surely that er . . ." He was getting as bad as Green.

"That what?" said Morse, his face strangely grave.

"That Green was having an affair with Sylvia?"

Morse smiled wanly and drained his glass. "We could find out, I suppose."

"But you said this medical stuff was very important."

"That was an understatement."

"Have you found what you wanted, sir?"

"Yes. You could say that. Let's say I just wanted a bit of confirmation. I spoke to Green on the telephone yesterday."

"Did he er did he er er," mimicked Lewis. It was an isolated moment of levity in the last grim days of the case.

Sue had Tuesday afternoon off, and she was glad of it. Working in the casualty department was tiring, especially on her feet. The other girls were out and she made herself some toast and sat in the little kitchen staring with her beautiful, doleful eyes at the white floor-tiles. She'd promised to write to David and she really must get down to it this afternoon. She wondered what to say. She could tell him about work and she could tell him how lovely it had been to see him last weekend and she could tell him how much she looked forward to seeing him again. Yet all seemed empty of delight. She blamed herself bitterly for her own selfishness; but even as she did so, she knew that she was more concerned with her own wishes and her own desires than with anyone else's. With David's—particularly David's. It was futile, it was quite impossible, it was utterly foolish, it was even dangerous to think of him—to think about Morse, that is. But she wanted him so badly. She longed for him to call—she longed just to see him. Anything . . .And as she sat there in the little kitchen staring at the white tiles still, she felt an overwhelming sense of self-reproach and loneliness and misery.

Jennifer was busy on Tuesday afternoon. Palmer had sent her a draft letter and wanted her to look it through. Premiums on virtually everything were to be increased by 10% after Christmas and all the company's clients had to be informed. The dear man, thought Jennifer; he's not so very bright really. The first paragraph of his letter was reminiscent of the tortuous exercises she'd been set in Latin prose. "Which" followed "which," which followed yet another "which." A coven of whiches, she thought, and smiled at the conceit. She amended the paragraph with a bold confidence; a full stop here, a new paragraph there, a better word here—much clearer. Palmer knew she was by far the brightest girl in the office, and over important drafts he always consulted her. She wouldn't be staying there much longer, though. She had applied for two jobs in the last week. But she wouldn't dream of telling anybody, not even Mr. Palmer. Not that it was unpleasant working where she was—far from it. And she earned almost as much as Mary and Sue put together . . .Sue! She thought of Sunday evening when she had returned from London. How glad she had felt to find them like that! She visualised the scene again and a cruel smile played over her lips.

She took the amended drafts to Mr. Palmer's office, where Judith was trying to keep pace with the very moderate speed at which her employer was dictating a letter. She handed the draft to him. "I've made a few suggestions."

"Oh, thank you very much. I just rushed it off, you know. Put down the first things that came into my head. I realised it was, you know, a bit er a bit rough. Thanks very much. Jolly good."

Jennifer said no more. She left, and as she walked up the

corridor to the typists' room, the same nasty smile was playing about her pretty mouth.

The third of the triad, the undaunted, dumpy, freckled little Mary, worked for Radio Oxon. In the BBC she might have been accorded the distinguished title of "continuity girl"; but she was in a dead-end job with the local radio station. Like Jennifer she had been thinking of a change, although unlike Jennifer she had few qualifications behind her. Jennifer had some A levels and all her shorthand and typing certificates; she must have been clever at school, thought Mary. Cool, sort of *knowing* all the time . . .It worked well enough, the three of them living together; but she wouldn't mind a move. Sue was all right, she quite liked Sue really, although she'd been a bit moody and broody just recently. Men trouble. Had she fallen for that inspector chap? She wouldn't blame her, though. At least Sue was human. She wasn't quite so sure about Jennifer.

After lunch on Tuesday one of the assistants came in to chat with her. He had a beard, a light-hearted manner, five young children and a roving eye for the ladies. Mary did not positively strive to discourage his attentions.

27
Thursday, Friday; 21,22 October

Bernard Crowther was, in the words of the ward sister, "satisfactory," and on Thursday afternoon he was sitting up in bed to receive his first visitor. Strangely, Morse had not seemed anxious to press his claims, and had waived his rights at the head of the queue.

Peter Newlove was glad to see his old friend looking so lively. They talked naturally and quietly for a few minutes. Some things just had to be said, but when Peter had said them, he turned to other matters and he knew that Bernard understood. It was almost time to go. But Bernard put his hand on his friend's arm and Peter sat down again beside the bed. An oxygen tube hung over the metal frame behind Bernard's head and a multi-dialled machine stood guard on the other side of the bed.

"I want to tell you something, Peter."

Peter leaned forward slightly to hear him. Bernard was speaking more labouredly now and taking a deep breath before each group of words. "We can talk again tomorrow. Don't upset yourself now."

"Please stay." Bernard's voice was strained and urgent as he went on. "I've got to tell you. You know all about that murder at Woodstock?" Peter nodded. "I picked up the two girls." He breathed heavily again and a light smile came to his lips. "Funny really. I was going to meet one of them anyway. But they missed the bus and I picked them up. It ruined everything, of course. They knew each other and—well, it scared me off." He rested a while, and Peter looked hard at his old friend and tried to keep the look of incredulity out of his eyes.

"To cut a long story short, I finished up with the other one. Think of it, Peter! I finished up with the other one! She was hot stuff, good Lord she was. Peter, can you hear me?" He leaned back, shook his head sadly, and took another deep breath.

"I had her—in the back of the car. She made me feel as randy as an old goat. And then—and then I left her. That's the funny thing about it. I left her. I drove back home. That's all."

"You left her, you mean, at *The Black Prince*?"

Bernard nodded. "Yes. That's where they found her. I'm glad I've told you."

"Are you going to tell the police?"

"That's what I want to ask you, Peter. You see I . . ." he stopped. "I don't know whether I should tell you, and you must promise me never to breathe it to a living soul"—he looked anxiously at Peter, but seemed confident of his trust—"but I'm pretty sure that I saw someone else in the yard that night. I didn't know who it was, of course." He was becoming progressively more exhausted each time he spoke, and Peter rose to his feet anxiously.

"Don't go." The uphill climb was nearly done. "I didn't know—it was so dark. It worried me though. I had a double whisky at a pub nearby and I drove home." The words were coming very slowly. "I passed her. What a stupid fool I was. She saw me."

"Who do you mean? Who did you pass, Bernard?"

Bernard's eyes were closed, and he appeared not to hear. "I checked up. She didn't go to her night class." He opened his heavy eyes; he was glad he'd told somebody, and glad it was Peter. But Peter looked dazed and puzzled. He stood up and bent over and spoke as quietly but as clearly as he could into Bernard's ear.

"You mean you think it was—it was *Margaret* who killed her?" Bernard nodded.

"And that was why she . . ." Bernard nodded his weary head once more.

"I'll call in again tomorrow. Try to rest." Peter prepared to go and was already on his way when he heard his name called again.

Bernard's eyes were open and he held up his right hand with a fragile authority. Peter retraced his steps.

"Not now, Bernard. Get some sleep."

"I want to apologise."

"Apologise?"

"They've found out about the typewriter, haven't they?"

"Yes. It was mine."

"I used it, Peter. I ought to have told you."

"Forget it. What does it matter?"

But it did matter. Bernard knew that; but he was too tired and could think no more. Margaret was dead. That was the overwhelming reality. He was only now beginning to grasp the utter devastation caused by that one terrible reality: *Margaret was dead.*

He lay back and dozed into a wakeful dream. The cast of the scene was assembled and he saw it all again, yet in a detached, impersonal way, as if he were standing quite outside himself.

When he saw them he had known immediately it was her, but he couldn't understand why she was hitch-hiking.

They exchanged no words and she sat in the back. She must have felt, as he had, how dangerous it had suddenly become; she obviously knew the other girl. It was almost a relief to him when she said she was getting off at Begbroke. He made an excuse—getting cigarettes—and they had whispered anxiously together. It was better to forget it for that night. He was worried. He couldn't afford the risk. But surely he could pick her up later, couldn't he? She had asked it with a growing anger. He'd sensed, as they were driving along, the jealousy she must have felt as the girl in the front had chatted him up. Not that he had given her any encouragement. Not then, anyway. But he felt genuinely worried, and he told her so. They could meet again next week: he would be writing in the usual way. It was half a minute of agitated whispering—no longer; just inside the door of *The Golden Rose*. There had been exasperation and a glint of blind fury in her eyes. But he understood how she felt. He wanted her again, too—just as badly as ever.

He got back into the car and drove on to Woodstock. Now that she had the field to herself, the blonde girl seemed even freer from any inhibitions. She leaned back with a relaxed and open sensuality. The top button of her thin, white blouse was unfastened, and the blouse itself seemed like a silken seed-pod ready to burst open, her breasts swelling like two sun-ripened seeds beneath it.

"What do you do?"

"I'm at the University."

"Lecturer?"

"Yes." Their eyes met. It had gone on like that until they reached Woodstock. "Well, where shall I drop you?"

"Oh, anywhere really."

"You going to see the boy friend?"

"Not for half an hour or so. I've got plenty of time."

"Where are you meeting him?"

"*The Black Prince*. Know it?"

"Would you like to come for a drink with me first?" He felt very nervous and excited.

"Why not?"

There was a space in the yard and he backed in, up against the far left-hand wall.

"Perhaps it's not such a good idea to have a drink here," she said.

"No, perhaps not."

She lay back again in the seat, her skirt rising up around her thighs. Her legs were stretched out, long, inviting, slightly parted.

"You married?" she asked. He nodded. Her right hand played idly and irregularly with a gear lever, her fingers caressing the knob. The windows were gradually misting over with their breath and he leaned over to the compartment on the near side of the dashboard. His arm brushed her as he did so and he felt a gentle forward pressure from her body. He found the duster and half-heartedly cleaned her side window. He felt the pressure of her right hand against his leg as he moved slightly across her, but she made no effort to remove it. He put his left arm around the back of her seat and she turned towards him. Her lips were full and open and tantalisingly she licked her tongue along them. He could resist her no longer and kissed her with an abrupt and passionate abandon. Her tongue snaked into his mouth and her body turned towards him, her breasts thrusting forward against him. He caressed her legs with his right hand, revelling in sheer animal joy as she swayed slightly and parted them with wider invitation. She broke off the long and frenzied kissing and licked the lobe of his ear and whispered, "Undo the buttons on my blouse, I'm not wearing a bra."

"Let's get in the back," he said hoarsely. His erection was enormous.

It was over all too soon, and he felt guilty of his own reactions. He wanted to get away from her. She seemed quite different now—metamorphosed in a single minute.

"I'd better go."

"So soon?" She was slowly fastening her blouse but the spell was broken now.

"Yes. I'm afraid so."

"You enjoyed it, didn't you?"

"Of course. You know I did."

"You'd like to do it again some time?"

"You know I would." He was getting more and more anxious to get away. Had he imagined someone out there? A peeping Tom, perhaps?

"You've not told me your name."

"You've not told me yours."

"Sylvia. Sylvia Kaye."

"Look Sylvia." He tried to sound as loving towards her as he could. "Don't you think it would be better if we, you know, just thought of this as something beautiful that happened to us. Just the once. Here tonight."

She turned nasty and sour then. "You don't want to see me again, do you? You're just like the rest. Bi' of sex and a blow out and you're off." She spoke differently, too. She sounded like a common slut, a cheap, hard pick-up from a Soho side-street. But she was right, of course—absolutely right. He'd got what he wanted. But hadn't she? Was she a prostitute? He thought of his days in the army and the men who'd caught a dose of the pox. He must get out of here; out of this claustrophobic car and this dark and miserable yard. He put his hand in his pocket and found a £1 note. But for some loose silver, he had no more money on him.

"A pound no'! One bloody pound no'! Chris'—you must think I'm a cheap bi' of goods. You 'ave a bi' of money on you nex' time mate—or else keep your bloody 'ands off."

He felt a deep sense of shame and corruption. She got out of the car and he followed her.

"I'll find ou' who you bloody are, mister. I will—you see!"

What had happened then he didn't know. He remembered saying something and he vaguely remembered that she had said something back. He remembered his headlights swathing the yard and he remembered waiting for a gap in the traffic as he reached the main road. He remembered stopping to buy a double whisky and he remembered driving fast down the dual carriageway; and he remembered coming up behind a car and then swerving past it and flying through the night, his mind reeling. And on Thursday afternoon he had read in *The Oxford Mail* of the murder of Sylvia Kaye.

It had been foolish to write that letter, of course, but at least Peter would be out of trouble now. It was always asking

for trouble—putting anything down on paper; but it had
been a neat little arrangement until then. It was her sug-
gestion anyway, and it seemed necessary. The post in North
Oxford was really dreadful—10:00 a.m. or later now—and
no-one seemed to mind the girls at the office getting letters.
And so often he couldn't be quite sure until the last minute.
Sometimes things got into a complex tangle, but more often
the arrangement had worked very smoothly. They had worked
out a good system between them. Quite clever really. No-
one even looked at the date anyway. Sometimes he had
incorporated a brief message, too—like that last time. That
last time . . .Morse must have had his wits about him, but
he hadn't deliberately meant to mislead him. A bit, certainly.
That height business, for example . . .He'd like to see Morse.
Perhaps under other circumstances they could have got to
know each other, become friends . . .

He dozed off completely and it was dark when he awoke.
The lights were dim. The silent, white figure of a nurse sat
behind a small table at the far end of the ward, and he saw
that most of the other patients were lying asleep. The real
world rushed back at him, and Margaret was dead. Why?
Why? Was it as she said in the letter? He wondered how
he could ever face life again, and he thought of the children.
What had they been told?

Sharp spasms of agonising pain leaped across his chest
and he knew suddenly and with certitude that he was going
to die. The nurse was with him, and now the doctor. He
was drenched with sweat. Margaret! Had she killed Sylvia
or had he? What did it matter? The pains were dying away
and he felt a strange serenity.

"Doctor," he whispered.

"Take it gently, Mr. Crowther. You'll feel better now." But
Crowther had suffered a massive coronary thrombosis and
his chances of living on were tilted against him in the bal-
ances.

"Doctor. Will you write something for me?"

"Yes. Of course."

"To Inspector Morse. Write it down." The doctor took his
note-book out and wrote down the brief message. He looked

at Crowther with worried eyes: the pulse was weakening rapidly. The machine was working, its black dials turned up to their maximum readings. Bernard felt the oxygen mask over his face and saw in a strangely lucid way the minutest details of all around him. Dying was going to be much easier than he had ever hoped. Easier than living. He knocked away the mask with surprising vigour, and spoke his last words.

"Doctor. Tell my children that I loved them."

His eyes closed and he seemed to fall into a deep sleep. It was 2:35 a.m. He died at 6:30 the same morning before the sun had risen in the straggly grey of the eastern sky and before the early-morning porters came clattering along the corridors with their hospital trolleys.

Morse looked down at him. It was eight-thirty a.m. and the last mortal remains of Bernard Crowther had been unobtrusively wheeled into the hospital mortuary almost two hours ago. Morse had liked Crowther. Intelligent face; good-looking man really. He thought that Margaret must have loved him dearly once; probably always had, deep down. And not only Margaret. There had been someone else, too, hadn't there, Bernard? Morse looked down at the sheet of notepaper in his hand, and read it again. "To Inspector Morse. I'm so sorry. I've told you so many lies. Please leave *her* alone. She had nothing to do with it. How could she? I killed Sylvia Kaye."

The pronouns were puzzling, or so they had seemed to the doctor as he wrote the brief message. But Morse understood them and he knew that Bernard Crowther had guessed the truth before he died. He looked at the dead man again: the feet were as cold as stone and he would babble no more o' green fields.

Morse turned slowly on his heel and left.

28
Friday, 22 October, a.m.

Later that same Friday morning Morse sat in his office bringing Lewis up to date with the morning's developments. "You see, all along the trouble with this case has been not so much that they've told us downright lies but that they've told us such a tricky combination of lies and the truth. But we're nearly at the end of the road, thank God."

"We're not finished yet, sir?"

"Well, what do you think? It's not a very tidy way of leaving things, is it? It's always nice to have a confession, I know, but what do you do with *two* of 'em?"

"Perhaps we shall never know, sir. I think that they were just trying to cover up for each other, you know—taking the blame for what the other had done."

"Who do you think did it, sergeant?"

Lewis had his choice ready. "I think she did it, sir."

"Pshaw!" Well, it had been a 50-50 chance, and he'd guessed wrong. Or at least Morse thought he was wrong. But *he* hadn't been on very good form recently, had he? "Come on," said Morse. "Tell me. What makes you pick on poor Mrs. Crowther?"

"Well, I think she found out about Crowther going with this other woman and I believe what she said about following him and seeing him at Woodstock. She couldn't have known some of the things she mentioned if she hadn't been there, could she?"

"Go on," said Morse.

"I mean, for instance, about where the car was parked in the yard. About them getting in the back of the car—*we* didn't know that; but it seems to fit in with the evidence we got when one of Sylvia's hairs was found on the back seat. I just feel she couldn't have made it up. She couldn't have got those things from the newspapers because they were never printed."

Morse nodded his agreement. "And I'll tell you something else, Lewis. She wasn't at her Headington class on that Wednesday night. There's no tick for her on the register anyway. I've looked."

Lewis was grateful for the corroborative evidence. "But you don't believe it was her, sir?"

"I know it wasn't," said Morse simply. "You see, Lewis, I think that if Margaret Crowther had been in murderous mood that night, it would have been Bernard's skull on the other end of a tyre-lever—not a nonentity like Sylvia's."

Lewis seemed far from convinced. "I think you're wrong, sir. I know what you mean, but all women are different. You can't just say a woman would do this and wouldn't do that. Some women would do anything. She must have felt terribly jealous of this other girl taking her husband from her like that."

"She doesn't say she was jealous, though; she says she felt 'burning anger,' remember?"

Lewis didn't but he saw his opening. "But why are you all of a sudden so anxious to believe what she says, sir? I thought you said you *didn't* believe her."

Morse nodded his approval. "That's exactly what I mean. It's all such a mixture of truth and falsehood. Our job is to sift the wheat from the chaff."

"And how do we do that?"

"Well, we need a bit of psychological insight, for one thing. And I think she was telling the truth when she said she was angry. To me, it's got the right sort of ring about it. I'm pretty sure if she was making it up she'd have said she was jealous, rather than angry. And if she was angry, I think the object of her anger would be her husband, not Sylvia Kaye."

To Lewis it all seemed thin and wishy-washy. "I've never cared much for psychology, sir."

"You're not convinced?"

"Not with that, sir. No."

"I don't blame you," said Morse. "I'm not very convinced myself. But you'll be glad to know that we don't have to

depend on my abilities as a psychologist. Just think a minute,
Lewis. She said she entered the yard, keeping close in—
that is, to her left—and edged her way behind the cars. She
saw Crowther at the far end of the yard, also on the left.
Agreed?"

"Agreed."

"But the tyre-lever, if we can believe the evidence, and I
can see no possible reason for *not* doing so, was either in,
or beside, the tool-box at the farthest right-hand corner of
the yard. The weapon with which Mrs. Crowther claims she
killed Sylvia Kaye was at least twenty yards away from where
she stood. She mentions in her statement that she was not
only angry but frightened, too. And I can well believe her.
Who wouldn't be frightened? Frightened of what was going
on, frightened of the dark perhaps; but above all *frightened
of being seen.* And yet you ask me to believe that she crossed
the yard and picked up a tyre-lever that was almost certainly
no more than four or five yards from where Bernard stood
with his bottled blonde? Rubbish! She read about the tyre-
lever in the papers."

"Someone could have moved it, sir."

"Yes. Someone could, certainly. Who do you suggest?"

Lewis felt that his arguing with Morse in this mood was
almost as sacrilegious as Moses arguing with the Lord on
Sinai. Anyway, he ought to have spotted that business about
the spanner from the start. Very bad, really. But something
else had bothered him about Margaret's statement. It had
seemed so obvious from the start that this was a man's crime,
not a woman's. He had himself looked down on Sylvia that
first night and he had known perfectly well, without any
pathologist's report, that she had been raped. Her clothes
were torn and quite obviously someone had not been able
to wait to get his hands on her body. It had been no surprise
to him, or to Morse surely, that the report had mentioned
the semen dribbling down her legs, and the bruising round
her breasts. But all that didn't square with Margaret Crowther's evidence. She'd seen them in the back of the car, she
said. But had she been right? The hair was found in the
back of the car, but that didn't prove very much, did it? It
could have got there in a hundred different ways. No. Things

didn't add up either way. It beat him. He put his thoughts into words and Morse listened carefully.

"You're right. It's a problem that caused me a great deal of anxiety."

"But it's not a problem now, sir?"

"Oh no. If that were our only problem we'd have some plain sailing ahead of us."

"And you don't think we have?"

"I'm afraid we've got some very stormy seas to face." Morse's face was drawn and grey, and his voice was strained as he continued. "There's one more thing I should have told you, Lewis. After I left the Radcliffe this morning, I called to see Newlove. He'd been to see Bernard yesterday afternoon and was quite willing to talk about him."

"Anything new, sir?"

"Yes, I suppose you can say there is, in a way. Newlove didn't want to talk about the personal side of things, but he told me that Crowther had spoken to him about the night of the murder. Very much what we already knew or what we've pieced together. Except one thing, Lewis. Crowther said he thought *there was someone else in the yard* that night."

"Well we knew that, didn't we, sir?"

"Just a minute, Lewis. Let's just picture the scene, if we can. Crowther gets out of the front seat and into the back, right? Sylvia Kaye does the same. Now there was precious little room where the car was, and this was certainly not the place or the occasion for old-world gallantry; and I reckon it's odds-on that she got out the front nearside and into the back nearside and that he did the same on his side. In other words they sat on the same sides in the back of the car as they did in the front—he on the right, she on the left. Now whatever peculiar posture Crowther got himself into, I think that for most of the time he had his back to where his wife was standing—in other words she was almost directly behind him. But Bernard hadn't got eyes in the back of his head, and Margaret, as we've said, was probably scared stiff of being seen. And it tends to lead to one conclusion, as I see it, and one conclusion only: Crowther did not see his wife that night. I'm sure she was there, but I don't think he saw her. But he did see somebody else. In other words *there was yet another person in the yard that night*, another person much nearer to him than Margaret ever got; someone standing very near to the tool-kit, and someone Crowther caught a shadowy glimpse of, as he sat in the back of his car. And I think it may have been that person, Lewis, who murdered Sylvia Kaye."

"You don't think it was Bernard either, then?"

For the first time Morse seemed oddly hesitant. "He could have done it, of course."

"But I just don't see a motive, do you sir?"

"No," said Morse flatly, "I don't." He looked around the room dejectedly.

"Did you get anything else from Mr. Newlove, sir?"

"Yes. Crowther told him he'd used his typewriter."

"Newlove's typewriter, you mean?"

"You sound surprised."

"You mean Crowther *did* write that letter after all?"

Morse gave him a look of pained disappointment. "You've never doubted that, surely?"

He opened a drawer in his desk and took out a sealed white envelope which he handed across to Lewis. It was addressed to Jennifer Coleby. "I want you to go to see her, Lewis, and give her this, and stay with her while she opens it. Inside there's one sheet of paper and a return envelope addressed to me. Tell her to answer the question I've asked and then to seal up her answer in the return envelope. Is that clear?"

"Wouldn't it be easier to ring her up, sir?"

Morse's eyes suddenly blazed with anger, although when he spoke his words were quiet and controlled. "As I was saying, Lewis, you will stay with her and when she has written her answer you will make sure that the envelope is sealed tight. You see, I don't want you to see the question I've asked, nor the answer that she gives." The voice was icy now, and Lewis quickly nodded his understanding. He had never realised quite how frightening the inspector could be, and he was glad to get away.

After Lewis had gone, Morse sat and thought of Sue. So much had happened since Monday, but Sue had remained uppermost in his thoughts for almost all the time. He had to see her again. He looked at his watch. Mid-day. He wondered what she was doing, and suddenly spurred himself into action.

"Is that the Radcliffe?"

"Yes."

"Accident department, please."

"I'm putting you through, sir."

"Hello. Accident department." It wasn't Sue.

"I want to have a quick word with Miss Widdowson, please."

"You mean Staff Nurse Widdowson." He hadn't known that.

"Susan, I think her Christian name is."

"I'm sorry, sir. We're not allowed to take outside telephone calls except . . ."

"It might be an emergency," interrupted Morse hopefully.

"Is it an emergency, sir?"

"Not really, no."

"I'm sorry, sir."

"Look, this is the police."

"I'm sorry, sir." Obviously she had heard that one before. Slowly Morse was getting angry again. "Is the Matron there?"

"You want me to put you through to Matron?"

"Yes, I do."

He had to wait a good two minutes. "Hello. Matron here."

"Matron, I'm speaking from Thames Valley Police Station. Chief Inspector Morse. I want to speak to Staff Nurse Widdowson. I understand you have your rules about this, and of course I wouldn't in the normal way wish to break them . . ."

"Is it urgent?" *Vox auctoritatis.*

"Well, let's say it's important."

For the next few minutes Matron coolly and lucidly explained the regulations governing the delivery of personal mail to, and the acceptance of incoming telephone calls by, members of "my" nursing staff. She spelled out the rules and the reasons for the rules, and Morse fidgeted at his table, the fingers of his left hand drumming the top of his desk in characteristic fashion.

"You see, you have no idea of the volume of official letters and telephone calls that all my departments receive every day. And if we had the additional complication of all personal letters and calls, where would it all end? I have tried and I think I have succeeded . . ."

Morse heard her out. As she had been talking a wildly improbable thought had taken root in his mind. He almost wanted to hear her repeat the tedious catalogue of constraints. "I'm most grateful to you, Matron. I do want to apologise . . ."

"Oh, not at all. I've enjoyed talking to you. Now, please let me help in any way I can." She would do anything for him now, he knew that. But the situation had changed. There was just the wildest, slimmest chance now, where before there had been none at all. He rang off as soon as he could, the Matron almost begging for the chance of doing him some favour. But he wanted none: his course was now clear.

Sue was having lunch while Morse was finishing his lengthy call to her immediate superior. She was thinking of him, too. Would she had known him earlier! She knew with a passionate certainty that he could have changed her life. Was it too late even now? Dr. Eyres sat next to her, taking every opportunity he decently could of effecting the closest physical contact with the lovely staff nurse; but Sue loathed his proximity and his insinuations and, not worrying about a sweet, she left the table as quickly as she could. Oh Morse! Why didn't I meet you before? She walked back to the out-patients' room at the casualty clinic and sat down on one of the hard benches. Absently she picked up a long-outdated copy of *Punch* and flicked mechanically through the faded pages . . . What was she to do? He hadn't been anywhere near since that wretched night when Jennifer had come home. Jennifer! And she had been fool enough to confide in Jennifer. David? She would have to write to David. He would be so upset; but to live with someone, to sleep with someone, forty, even fifty years—someone you didn't really and truly love . . .

Then she saw him. He stood there, an anxious, vulnerable look in his grey eyes. The tears started in her eyes and she felt an incredible joy. He came and sat beside her. He didn't even try to hold her hand—there was no need of that. They talked, she didn't know what about. It didn't matter.

"I shall have to go," she said. "Try to see me soon, won't you?" It was after half-past one.

Morse felt desperately sick at heart. He looked at Sue long and hard, and he knew that he loved her so dearly.

"Sue?"

"Yes?"

"Have you got a photograph of yourself?"

Sue rummaged in her handbag and found something. "Not all that good, is it, really?"

Morse looked at the photograph. She was right. It didn't really do her justice, but it was his Sue all right. He put it carefully into his wallet, and got up to go. Patients were already waiting: patients with bulky plasters over legs and arms; patients with bandages round their heads and wrists; a road casualty with blood around the mouth, the face an ashen white. It was time to go. He touched her hand lightly and their fingers met in a tender, sweet farewell. Sue watched him go, limping slightly, through the flappy, celluloid doors.

It was almost a quarter to two as Morse walked down from the Radcliffe Infirmary to the broad, tree-lined avenue of St. Giles. He thought of postponing his next task; but it had to be done some time, and he was on the spot now anyway.

Keeping to the right-hand side of St. Giles as he made his way in the general direction of the Martyrs' Memorial, Morse stopped at the first snack-bar he came to, the Wimpy Grill, and walked inside. On his own admission the small, swarthy Italian, turning beefburgers on a hotplate, "no speake, signor, the English so good," and promptly summoned his slatternly young waitress into the consultation. Morse left amid a general shaking of heads and a flurry of gesticulation; it wasn't going to be easy. A few yards further down he stopped and entered *The Bird and Baby*, where he ordered a pint of bitter and engaged in earnest, quiet conversation for several minutes with the barman, who also as it happened was the landlord and who always stood lunch-time duty behind his bar. Sorry, no. Oh yes, he'd have noticed; but no. Sorry. It was going to be a long, dispiriting business, but one which only Morse himself could do.

He worked his way methodically along the dozen likely places in the Cornmarket below the ABC Cinema, crossed the road at Carfax, and started up the other side. It was at a little ("snacks served") cake shop nestling alongside the giant pile of Marks and Spencer that he found the person he was searching for. She was a grey-haired, plumpish woman, with a kindly face and a friendly manner. Morse spoke to her for several minutes, and this time too there was much nodding of the head and pointing. But pointing not vaguely outside, up alleys or down side-streets; this time the pointing was towards a little room, beyond the shop, wherein the establishment's snacks were served. To be precise, the pointing was towards one particular small table standing in the far corner of the room, with one chair on each side of it, both now empty, and a cruet, a dirty ashtray and a bottle of tomato sauce upon its red-and-white striped tablecloth.

It was 3:45 p.m. Morse went over to the table and sat down. He knew that the case was nearly over now, but he could feel no elation. His feet ached, especially the right one, and he was badly in need of something to cheer him up. Again he took out the picture of Sue from his wallet and looked at the face of the girl he loved so hopelessly. The grey-haired waitress came up to him.

"Can I get you anything, sir? I'm sorry I didn't realise you might . . ."

"I'll have a cup of tea, luv," said Morse. It was better than nothing.

* * *

He was not back in his office until 4:45 p.m. A note from Lewis lay on his desk. His sergeant hoped it would be all right going off a bit early. Please to ring him if he was needed. His wife had a touch of 'flu and the kids were a bit of a handful.

Morse screwed up the note and tossed it into the waste-paper basket. Underneath the note lay the letter that Lewis had brought from Jennifer Coleby. Making certain that it was carefully sealed, Morse placed it unopened into the bottom left-hand drawer of his desk and turned the key in the lock.

He looked up a number in the directory and heard the drumming "purr purr, purr purr." He looked at his watch: almost 5:00 p.m. It wouldn't matter of course if he had gone, but he wanted to get things over straightaway. "Purr purr, purr purr." He was on the point of giving up when the call was answered.

"Hello?" It was Palmer.

"Ah. Glad to catch you, sir. Morse here."

"Oh." The little manager sounded none too overjoyed. "You're lucky. I was just locking up, but I thought I'd better get back and answer it. You never know in this job. Could be important."

"It is important."

"Oh."

Palmer lived in the fashionable Observatory Street at the bottom of the Woodstock Road. Yes. He could meet Morse —of course, he could—if it was important. They arranged a meeting at *The Bull and Stirrup* in nearby Walton Street at 8:30 p.m. that evening.

It was a mean-looking, ill-lighted, spit-and-sawdust type of pub; a dispiriting sort of place, with gee-gees, darts and football-pools the overriding claims upon the shabby clientele. Morse wanted to get things over and get out as quickly as he could. It was a struggle for a start, and Palmer was cagey and reluctant; but Morse knew too much for him. Grudgingly, but with apparent honesty, Palmer told his pitiable little tale.

"I suppose you think I should have told you this before?"

"I don't know. I'm not married myself." Morse sounded utterly indifferent. It was 9:00 p.m. and he took his leave.

He drove up the Woodstock Road at rather more than 30 m.p.h.; but spotting a police car up ahead he slackened off to the statutory speed limit. He swung round the Woodstock roundabout, the starting point of all this sorry mess, and headed for Woodstock. At the village of Yarnton he turned off and parked the Lancia outside the home of Mrs. Mabel Jarman, where he stayed for no more than a couple of minutes.

On his way home he called at police HQ. The corridors were darkened, but he didn't bother to turn on the lights. In his office he unlocked the bottom left-hand drawer and took out the envelope. His hand shook slightly as he reached for his paper-knife and neatly slit open the top. He felt like a cricketer who has made a duck, checking the score-book just in case an odd run made by the other batsman had been fortuitously misattributed to his own name. But Morse had no faith in miracles, and he knew what the note had to say before he opened it. He saw the note; he did not read it. He saw it synoptically, not as the sum of its individual words and letters. Miracles do not happen. He turned off the light, locked his office door, and walked back along the darkened corridor. The last piece had clicked into place. The jigsaw was complete.

30
Saturday, 23 October

Since breakfast Sue had been trying to write to David. Once or twice she had written half a page before screwing up the paper and starting a fresh sheet; but mostly the elusive phraseology had failed her after nothing more than a miserably brief sentence. She tried again.

My dear David,

    You've been so kind and so loving to me that I know
this letter will come as a terrible shock to you. But I
feel I must tell you—it's not fair to keep anything from
you. The truth is that I've fallen in love with someone
else and I . . .

What else could she say? She couldn't just leave it at
that . . . She screwed up the latest draft and added it to the
growing collection of tight paper-balls upon the table.

A sombre-looking Morse sat in his black, leather chair that
same morning. Another restless, fitful night. He must have
some holiday.

    "You look tired, sir," said Lewis.

    Morse nodded. "Yes, but we've come to the end of the
road, now."

    "We have, sir?"

    Morse seemed to buoy himself up. He took a deep breath:
"I've taken one or two wrong turnings, as you know, Lewis;
but by some fluke I was always heading in the right
direction—even on the night of the murder. Do you remember when we stood in that yard? I remember staring up at
the stars and thinking how many secrets they must know,
looking down on everything. I remember trying even then
to see the pattern, not just the bits that form the pattern.
There was something very odd, you know Lewis, about that
night. It looked like a sex murder right enough. But things
are not always what they seem, are they?"

    He seemed to be speaking in a dazed, sing-song sort of
way, almost as if he were on drugs. "Now you can *make*
things look a bit odd, but I've not met any of these clever
killers yet. Or things just *happen* like that, eh? It was odd
if Sylvia had been raped where she was found, wasn't it? I
know it was very dark in the yard that night, but cars with
full headlights were coming in and out all the time. It's
surely stretching the imagination a bit to think that anyone
would be crazy enough to rape a girl in the full blaze of
motorists' headlights." He seemed to Lewis to be relaxing

a little and his eyes had lost their dull stare. "Well?" That was more like the chief.

"I suppose you're right, sir."

"But it looked odd. A young, leggy blonde murdered and raped or raped and murdered. Whichever way round it was, it all pointed in the same way. We've got a sex-killer to find. But I wasn't sure. Raping isn't easy they tell me if the young lady isn't too willing, and, as I say, I discounted the likelihood of Sylvia being raped in the yard. She could have screamed and yelled—unless of course she was dead already. But I'm a bit squeamish about that sort of thing, and I thought the chances of us having to deal with a Christie-like necrophiliac were a bit remote. Where does that leave us, then?" Lewis hoped it was a rhetorical question, and so it was. "Well, let us concentrate our attention separately upon each of the two components—rape and murder. Let us assume two distinct actions—not one. Let us assume that she has intercourse with a man—after all, there was no doubt about the fact of intercourse. Let us assume further that this took place entirely with her consent. Now there was one shred of evidence to support this. Sylvia wasn't a member of women's lib, but she wasn't wearing a bra, and it seemed to me, if not unusual, well—a little suggestive. We discovered that Sylvia had several white blouses, but no white bras. Why not? No-one as conscious of her figure and her appearance as Sylvia Kaye is going to wear a black bra under a thin, white blouse, is she? I could draw only one conclusion—that Sylvia not infrequently went out without a bra; and if she did wear a bra, it would be a black one, because all the girls believe that black underwear is terribly sexy. Now all this suggested that perhaps she was a young lady of somewhat easy virtue, and I think it's pretty clear she was."

"She wasn't wearing pants either, sir."

"No. But the pathologist's report suggests that she had been—there were the marks of elastic round her waist. Yes, I'm pretty sure that she had been wearing pants and that they got stuck in someone's pocket and later got thrown away or burned. Anyway, it's not important. To get back to the separate components of the crime. First, a man had

intercourse with Sylvia—pretty certainly without too much
opposition. Second, someone murdered her. It could have
been the same man, but it's not easy to see the motive. The
evidence we got at a very early stage seemed to suggest that
this was a completely casual acquaintanceship, a chance
pick-up on the road to Woodstock. All right. But since it was
established that Bernard Crowther was the man who had
stopped at the Woodstock roundabout, certain aspects of the
case seemed to get more puzzling rather than less. I could
well imagine that Crowther was the sort of man who might
now and then be unfaithful to his wife; from what we now
know, his relationship with his wife seems to have drifted
over the last few years from idyllic bliss to idiotic bickering.
But if we were looking for a sex-crazed maniac, I felt fairly
sure Crowther wasn't the man we were looking for. He seemed
to me an essentially civilised man. You remember when you
looked at those photographs of Sylvia, Lewis? You remember
you said you'd like to get the bastard who did it? But you
had a composite picture of the crime in your mind, I think:
you were putting together the rape and the murder and
something else—*the obvious interference with Sylvia's scanty
clothing*. Now I couldn't fit Crowther into that picture; and
if Mrs. Crowther's evidence was right in any respect, it was
surely right at the point where she described what she saw
in the car. You made that point yourself, Lewis. What have
we got then? First, he makes love to the girl in the back of
the car. Second, he may have had a quarrel with her about
something. Let's say she's a mercenary young tart and she
agreed to make love with him on the sort of terms a common
prostitute would ask. Let's say he couldn't or wouldn't pay
her. Let's say they quarrel and he kills her. It's a possibility.
But I just couldn't believe that if this had been the sequence
of events that we should have found Sylvia in the condition
we did—with her blouse torn and ripped away from her. Or
at least not if we were right in thinking of Crowther as the
guilty party."

Lewis interrupted him quietly. "You said that you knew
who did that."

"I think you do, too," replied Morse. "As the case progressed there seemed to be only one person who had a mind sufficiently warped and perverted to interfere with the body of a murdered girl. A man who had been waiting to see her anyway; a man we know who perpetually tantalised and tortured himself by thoughts of sex; a man who feasted on a weekly diet of blue films and pornography. You know all about him, Lewis. And I went to see him a week ago. His bedroom is cluttered with the whole paraphernalia of dirty postcards, Danish magazines, hard pornography and all the rest. He's sick, Lewis, and he knows he's sick, and his mother knows he's sick. But he's not a vicious type of chap. In fact he's not unlikeable in a nasty sort of way. He told me that he'd often had a dream about undressing the body of a dead girl."

"My God!" said Lewis.

"You shouldn't feel too surprised about it, you know," said Morse. "I'm told that Freud mentions that sort of dream as being quite a common form of sexual fantasy among frustrated voyeurs." Lewis remembered the film. He'd found it a bit erotic himself, hadn't he? But he hadn't wanted to admit it—even to himself.

"He'd met Sylvia several times before. They usually met in the cocktail lounge of *The Black Prince*, had some booze and then went back to his house—to his bedroom. He paid for it. He told me so."

"He had quite a lot of expense one way or another, sir."

"He did indeed. Anyway, on the night when Sylvia was murdered he'd been waiting since about a quarter to eight. He drank more and more and felt more and more desperate as the time ticked by and Sylvia didn't appear. He went out several times to look for her. But he saw nothing. When he did find her he was sick in mind and body: sick from pent-up sexual frustration and sick from too much drink. He found her quite by chance—so he says—and I believe him."

"And then . . . you mean he . . . he fiddled about with her?" Morse nodded. "Yes. He did."

"He needs treatment, sir."

"He's promised me to see a psychiatrist—but I'm not very optimistic about that. I only ever knew one psychiatrist.

Funny chap. If ever a man was in need of psychiatric treatment it was him." Morse smiled ruefully, and Lewis felt his chief was becoming more like his normal self.

"So that's cleared that bit up, sir."

"Yes. But it didn't help all that much, did it? I was as sure as I could be that Sylvia Kaye was not murdered by Mr. John Sanders. She was murdered, so the pathology report says, between seven and eight p.m. or thereabouts. Now we know all that stuff about the murderer going back to the scene of the crime, but I just couldn't believe that Sanders had stood for about two and a half to three hours drinking whisky no more than fifty odd yards away from where his victim lay murdered. He'd have hopped it, that's for sure. What seemed so odd to me was why she wasn't found earlier. But you cleared that up."

Lewis was glad to know that he had been of value somewhere along the line, and he knew what Morse was referring to, for he had himself interviewed all the drivers of vehicles parked in the yard that night. The driver of the car beside which Sylvia had been found had earlier parked in an awkward position just outside the yard of *The Black Prince*; but he had been anxious about blocking other cars and he had immediately taken the opportunity, on seeing a car drive out from the yard, of backing his own car into the space left vacant. His light of course could not possibly have picked up Sylvia's body, and when he got out of the driving seat the body was against the wall on the other side of the car.

"Well," continued Morse, "by this time, for one reason or another we managed to get on to Crowther. Or rather the Crowthers. Perhaps we shall never know the exact part each of them played that night. But one thing I think we can confidently suggest—that as a result of what happened *Margaret thought that Bernard had murdered Sylvia*. Whether she killed herself just because of what she suspected, I don't know, though it was surely one of the factors that drove her to it. But that's only half the matter. I think, too, that *Bernard thought that Margaret had murdered Sylvia*. If I'm right about this, it seems to me to explain a lot of things. Bernard had two overwhelming reasons for keeping quiet. First, his love affair would almost certainly be brought out into the open, with all the consequences that would entail. But second, and even more important, his evidence might well help us find the murderer who, as Bernard saw things, was probably his own wife, Margaret. Oh dear, Lewis, if only they had spoken to each other about it! You don't suspect someone else of a crime if you've done it yourself. And I think each of them was quite genuine in suspecting the other. So we can say with every confidence that *neither of them did it*. And if Bernard had shown any intelligence he would have known how improbable it was that Margaret was actually involved in the murder. He passed his wife on the way back to Oxford! Now we know from Margaret's evidence that she's a slowish driver and perhaps most cars would pass her anyway. But if he left for Oxford *before* her, it is a physical impossibility for him to have overtaken her. Agreed?"

"Unless he called for a drink or something, sir."

"I hadn't thought of that," said Morse slowly. "But it isn't a vital point. Let's go on. Now the key person in the case from the beginning has been Miss X—the Miss X who was with Sylvia in Bernard Crowther's car. What did we learn about her? The most vital fact we learned was something Mrs. Jarman heard; and she's utterly convinced that she *did* hear it—I saw her again last night. She heard Sylvia say, 'We'll have a giggle about it in the morning.' So. We find the field narrowed very considerably, do we not? We investigate the Town and Gown Assurance Co. and we discover some interesting facts. And the most interesting fact of all is that someone tells Miss Jennifer Coleby to keep her mouth shut." Lewis opened his own mouth, but got no further. "I know you think I've been anti that young lady from the beginning, but I am now convinced—more than ever convinced—that the letter we found addressed to Jennifer Coleby was written to her by Bernard Crowther. If you want chapter and verse, it was written on the afternoon of Friday, 1 October in the rooms of Mr. Peter Newlove in Lonsdale College on the same Mr. Peter Newlove's typewriter. That, Lewis, is a *fact*."

Again Lewis made an effort to protest, and again Morse waved the protest aside. "Hear me out, Lewis. Jennifer Coleby lied from the word 'go.' In fact of all the people in this case, it's Jennifer Coleby who had the monopoly of the lies. Lies, lies and more lies. But why *should* she lie? Why should anyone be so anxious to mislead us to the extent that she did? I felt sure, fairly early on, that the reason was pretty simple really. The young lady who sat in the back of Bernard's car was his mistress, and everything we learned from Margaret confirmed the truth of his own admission that he did in fact have a mistress. Now I needn't go over all the lies we got from Jennifer; but there was some truth amid the tangled web of all the lies. And the one thing she told us that seemed the biggest whopper of the lot was just about the one thing that was true. *She said she'd got a car.*"

Lewis could restrain himself no longer. "But she had a puncture, sir. We know all about that."

"Oh, I don't doubt she had a puncture. We know she did. She rang up the Battery and Tyre people. But if they couldn't mend it, someone else could, eh? If you remember, Jennifer didn't ask the tyre man to call some other time; and she didn't have it done at Barkers. But somebody mended her puncture, Lewis. Perhaps she did it herself? She's not a fool, is she? Perhaps she asked the man next door? I don't know. But you can repair a puncture in five minutes without much trouble, and *Jennifer Coleby is a practical girl and she had to have a car that night.*"

"I don't follow that at all," said the mystified Lewis.

"You will, have no fear." Morse looked at his watch. "I want you to go and pick her up, Lewis."

"You mean Miss Coleby?"

"Who the hell else?"

Morse followed Lewis out, knocked at the office of Chief Superintendent Strange and went in.

Some half an hour later the door was opened, and Strange stood on the threshold with Morse. Both men looked stern-faced, and Strange nodded his head gravely as the Chief Inspector said a few final words.

"You look tired, you know, Morse. I think you ought to put in for a fortnight's furlough now this is over."

"Well, not quite over, sir."

Morse walked slowly back to his office.

When Jennifer Coleby arrived Morse asked her to sit down

and then walked over to Lewis. "I want this to be private, Lewis. You understand, I know."

Lewis didn't understand and he felt hurt. But he left them together, and walked along to the canteen.

"Look inspector. I really thought that after your sergeant saw me yesterday that you'd finished . . ."

Morse interrupted her sharply. "*I've* asked you here and *I'll* do the talking. You just sit back and shut up for a few minutes." There was thinly-veiled menace in his voice, and Jennifer Coleby, looking very much on her guard, did as Morse had bidden her.

"Let me tell you what I suspected, long ago in this case, Miss Coleby. You can interrupt me if I go wrong, but I want no more of your miserable lies." She glanced viciously into his hard eyes, but said nothing. "Let me tell you what I think. I think that two girls were picked up by a man one night and that one of the girls was the man's mistress. I think that this mistress usually travelled by car to see her lover, but on that particular night she couldn't get there by car, and that was why she either had to catch a bus or hitch-hike. Unfortunately, and by sheer chance, she was picked up *by the very man she was going to see*. Unfortunately, too, there were two girls, and he had to pick them both up, and *these two girls knew each other*. Now the whole thing suddenly seemed too dangerous—this is what I think, Miss Coleby, you understand—and somehow they decided to forget their date and wait until the next opportunity arose. I think that this girl, the mistress, asked to be dropped off somewhere on the way. She probably made some perfectly natural excuse—she was a good liar—and she asked him to drop her off. But she knew where the other girl was going—no doubt the other girl had told her—and she felt uncontrollably jealous that night. She'd perhaps sensed something as they'd all driven along together. You see, the girl who was sitting in the front was very attractive to men. And perhaps? Who knows? The man, the man she knew so well, had been unfaithful to his wife. He had been unfaithful with her! Why not with some other girl? So I think this is what happened. She got out of the car, but she didn't return home. No. She waited for a bus and one came almost immediately. How she must have cursed her luck. If only she'd not hitched a lift! Anyway, she caught the bus and found her way to the place where she knew she might find them. And she did find them. It was dark there and she couldn't see very much, but she saw enough. And she felt a murderous jealousy welling up inside her, not so much against her lover, but against that cheap slut of a girl, a girl she'd got to know but never liked, a girl she now hated with unspeakable fury. I think perhaps they may have spoken to each other when the man had gone—but I can only guess, and I may be wrong. I think that the girl who had just got out of the car could sense the deadly fury in the other girl's face, and I think she tried to run away. But as she did a vicious blow crashed across her skull and she lay dead in a heap upon a cobbled yard. I think the dead girl was dragged by the arms into the darkest corner of the yard and I think the girl who murdered her walked out into the night and caught a bus that took her home."

Morse stopped, and there was utter silence in the room. "Do you think that's how it happened, Miss Coleby?"

She nodded her head.

"We both know who murdered Sylvia, don't we?" Morse spoke so very softly that she could only just catch his words. Again she nodded.

Morse rang Lewis and told him to come in. "Take a few notes, sergeant. Now, Miss Coleby. A few more questions, please. Who mended your puncture for you?"

"The man across the road. Mr. Thorogood."

"How long did it take him?"

"Five, ten minutes. Not long. I helped him."

"How long have you been the mistress of your employer, Mr. Palmer?" Lewis lifted his eyes in amazement.

"Nearly a year."

"Didn't you think it a bit dangerous—telling someone else?"

"I suppose it was. But it meant we could have a room once a week."

"Palmer told you this morning that I knew?"

"Yes." She had answered mildly enough thus far. But the old flash blazed in her eyes once more. "How did you know?"

"I had to guess. But there had to be some reason. It was accidental, really. I checked the night-school register for Wednesday, 29 September, to see whether Mrs. Crowther had been present. She wasn't. But I noticed another name on the list, and she *had* been present, a Mrs. Josephine Palmer. Well . . ."

"You've got a suspicious mind, inspector."

"And when did this business of the letters start?"

"In the summer. Stupid really. But it worked all right—so they said."

"Can you give me your solemn word, Miss Coleby, that you will say nothing of this to anyone?"

"Yes, inspector. I think I owe you that at least."

Morse got up. "Well, get someone to take her back to work, Lewis. We've taken up enough of Miss Coleby's time." A flabbergasted Lewis gaped at them like a fish out of water, and Jennifer looked round and gave him a wan, sad smile.

"You're not being very fair to me are you, sir?" Lewis seemed downcast and annoyed.

"What do you mean?" asked Morse.

"You said the case was nearly over."

"It is over," said Morse.

"You know who murdered her?"

"A person has already been arrested and charged with the murder of Sylvia Kaye."

"When was this?"

"This morning. Here!" Morse took out the letter which Lewis himself had brought from Jennifer Coleby, and passed it over. Lewis took out the sheet of paper and read with blind, blank, uncomprehending disbelief the one line answer that Miss Coleby had written to Morse's question.

"Yes," said Morse softly. "It's true."

Lewis was full of questions, but he received no answers. "Look, Lewis, I want to be alone. You go home and look after your wife for a change. I'll talk to you on Monday."

The two men left the office. Lewis got his coat and was soon away. But Morse walked slowly to the cells at the far end of the north wing.

"Want to go in, sir?" said the sergeant on duty.

Morse nodded. "Leave us alone, will you?"

"Anything you say, sir. Cell number 1."

Morse took the keys, unbolted the main door to the cells and walked along to cell number 1. He put his hands on the bars and stood staring sadly through.

"Hello, Sue," he said.

31
Monday, 25 October

The day had broken bright and clear, but by mid-morning a melancholy army of heavy-grey cloud had massed overhead; and flurries of light rain were already sprinkling the window panes of Morse's office as, for the last time on the case of Sylvia Kaye, the two detectives faced each other across the desk.

"What did we know about Miss X?" asked Morse, and proceeded to answer the question himself. "We knew roughly what she looked like, we knew roughly what she was wearing, and we knew roughly what age she was. It was a start, but it could never have got us very far. But we also knew that the two girls waiting at the bus stop not only knew each other but that *they would be seeing each other again the following morning*. Now this, without a doubt, was by far the most important single piece of evidence we ever got, and we acted upon it immediately. Naturally we assumed that we could narrow down the field of our inquiries, and quite properly we concentrated our attentions on the office girls who worked with Sylvia Kaye. Of course, it could have been a friend of Sylvia's, someone she would be meeting at lunch-time perhaps, or someone she would be meeting on the bus. It could have been a hundred and one things. But we didn't think so. And we didn't think so because our suspicions were very soon aroused, and with every justification, by the peculiar behaviour of one of the girls who worked in the same office as Sylvia—Miss Jennifer Coleby. But although we didn't know it at the time, there was someone else Sylvia would be meeting that next morning, and if we'd been a fraction brighter earlier on, Lewis, we might have got on to it more quickly. Sylvia was undergoing physiotherapy treatment at the Radcliffe Infirmary for her broken arm, and she was going for this treatment regularly on Tuesday and Thursday mornings. That is, she would be reporting for physiotherapy to the staff nurse in charge of the Accident Outpatients' Department *on the morning of Thursday, 30 September.* In other words, she would be reporting to Staff Nurse Widdowson." Lewis got up to close the windows upon which the rain was splattering more heavily now. "This, of course," continued Morse, "meant nothing very much by itself. But we learned that Sylvia didn't have many close girl friends, didn't we? It was interesting. Yes, at the very least it was interesting." Morse's attention wandered momentarily, and he stared as Lewis had done through the windows to the concrete yard outside, now gleaming under the lowering sky. "But let's return to Jennifer Coleby. Crowther wrote to her—that's established now beyond any question of doubt. But Crowther didn't write the note *for* Jennifer: she was merely the messenger boy. She's admitted that, and she had no option really. When I wrote to her I didn't ask her to accuse anyone of murder; but I did ask her if the letter was meant for Sue Widdowson, and she confirmed that it was. You'll never know, Lewis, how much I dreaded the truth of all this . . ."

The rain plashed across the yard, and the room was sombre and dark. Electric lights flashed on in several adjoining rooms, but not in Morse's office. "Just consider a minute, Lewis. *Jennifer had a car.* That was a central fact in the case. And in spite of the temporary trouble she had with a puncture, *she used her car on the night of the 29th.* She said she did, remember? And she did. I didn't believe her at the time, but I was wrong. She met someone that night who saw her car and saw Jennifer Coleby in it. Someone who had nothing whatsoever to do with Sylvia's murder. And that was someone with whom Jennifer was having an affair—her employer, Mr. Palmer. So, although the evidence had pointed at almost every stage to Jennifer Coleby, she suddenly acquired for herself a wholly incontrovertible alibi. Up to that point I had felt utterly convinced that the other girl in this affair was Jennifer; but I now had to face the undoubted, unchallengeable fact that whoever it was who sat behind Sylvia Kaye that night in Bernard Crowther's car, it was not, quite definitely *not*, Jennifer Coleby. Who was it then? Although I was forced to abandon Jennifer as suspect number one—indeed, forced to abandon her as a suspect at all—I stuck stubbornly to my original idea that whoever the girl was, she was Crowther's mistress, and that it was to her that Crowther had sent his message. So let us look at things from Crowther's angle for a few minutes. I think that without a shadow of doubt he must have been a very frightened man. Just put yourself in his shoes, Lewis. He had left Sylvia Kaye alive and well—he knew that—on the Wednesday night. And the next day—what does he discover? He reads in the press that this same girl has been found murdered. But not murdered *anywhere*. Murdered on the very spot where he had last seen her—in the courtyard of *The Black Prince*. Who *knew* that he'd been there? Just himself and Sylvia— and she could never again say anything to anyone. But Sue Widdowson would have *guessed*, because Sylvia would have told her where she was going. He must have been worried out of his wits, and certainly for an intelligent man he doesn't seem to have been very sensible in what he did. Again and again the thought must have flashed across his mind: would Sue realise how dangerous it would be to say one single word to a living soul? He must have thought she would surely realise this. But still the doubts must have nagged away at his mind. She was the one person who could upset the whole apple-cart—not only bring him under suspicion for Sylvia's murder but throw the whole of his family-life into a turmoil he felt he couldn't face. He just had to make sure, or at least he had to do *something*. He daren't see her. So he wrote." Lewis showed the familiar signs of unease and Morse nodded his understanding, "I know, Lewis. Why does he write to *Jennifer*?"

"Why did he write at all, sir? Why not just ring?"

"Yes. I'm coming to that. But first let's be absolutely certain about the *fact* of the matter—and the fact is that Crowther *did* write to Jennifer Coleby. For if we fully recognise the significance of that, we can begin to answer the perfectly valid question you raise. Why not ring her? Why not? The answer is fairly straightforward, I think. *Who* was he to ring, and *where*? Let's assume for the minute that he wants to ring up Jennifer—the faithful messenger girl. At work? No. It was too dangerous. All the girls in the office knew Palmer's views on using his company's 'phones, and they played it fair because he turned a blind eye to personal correspondence coming in. But more than that. It was also far too dangerous, because all incoming telephone calls—except to the private 'phone in Palmer's office, which his personal secretary handled—came through the switchboard; as you well know anyone on the switchboard can listen in with complete impunity to whatever's being said. No. That was out. Well? Why not ring Sue Widdowson herself? Why not ring his mistress and speak to her direct, either at her home or at the hospital? Again it's not difficult to see why he didn't. If he rang Sue up at home, he could never be sure that the other two weren't there, could he? He could risk Jennifer, but not Mary. He must have felt pretty certain—and I'm sure he was right—that listening in, even to a one-sided telephone call, is a temptingly easy and interesting pastime."

After politely knocking on Morse's door, the young girl with the office correspondence entered brightly and placed the inspector's morning mail into his in-tray.

"Not a very nice day, sir."

"No," said Morse.

"It'll probably clear up later." She gave him a warm and pleasant smile as she left, and Morse nodded in a kindly way. It was some vague consolation to know that life was still going on around him. He stared absently out of the window and noticed that the rain had slackened. Perhaps she was right. It would probably clear up later . . .

"But why couldn't he ring her at work, sir?"

"Ah yes. I'm sorry, Lewis. Why couldn't he ring her at work, you say? I found the answer to that only last Friday. It is virtually impossible for any outsider, even for the police, to get into direct contact with any of the nursing staff at the Radcliffe. I tried it myself, and you might as well ask direc-

tory inquiries for a number if you haven't got the address.
There's an old battle-axe of a matron there . . ."

"Couldn't Crowther have written to her, though? Surely . . ."

"He could, yes. And I don't know why he didn't really,
except . . . You see, Lewis, he'd got into this routine with
Sue Widdowson. Let me try to explain how it must have
started. As you know, the post gets worse and worse everywhere. But in North Oxford it seems it's particularly bad. It
seldom arrives before ten in the morning—far too late for
anyone to receive a letter before setting off for work. And
even if it arrived early, say at eight, it would still not be in
time. Why not write to her at the hospital, then? The answer
is that our dear Matron puts her foot down there as well;
she postitively forbids all private mail being accepted in the
hospital."

"But if Crowther had posted a letter to her home address,
she would have got it as soon as she came back from work,
wouldn't she?"

"Yes, you're right. But you put your finger right on the
central difficulty, and this is why I should think Jennifer
Coleby was brought into the picture in the first place. Bernard Crowther, you see, like most of these University fellows, didn't work any regular hours at Lonsdale College.
Something would always be cropping up at odd times—
disciplinary matters, unexpected visitors, unscheduled
meetings—and he could never plan his extra-marital es-
capades with any more than the hopeful anticipation that
he might be free at any particular time in the days ahead.
But much more important than this, he had to keep a very
careful eye on the day-to-day comings and goings of his own
family. Margaret might arrange something, the children might
get a half-day holiday out of the blue, or be ill or—well, here,
too, there was plenty that could go wrong and mess up the
best-laid plans completely. So it seems to me that Crowther
often didn't know for certain until the day itself, even perhaps until a few hours beforehand, if and when and where
he was going to be free to meet his mistress. But, Lewis,
Lonsdale College is no more than a hundred yards or so
from the premises of the Town and Gown Assurance office
in The High."

"You mean Crowther just walked along and dropped a note in?"

"He did just that."

"But Jennifer wouldn't be able to contact Sue during the day either, would she? You just said . . ."

"I know what you're going to say. He might just as well have written to Sue's home address. She wouldn't get the message any earlier, because the letter would be lying on the door-mat when she got in. In fact she'd almost certainly get it later. But all this is assuming that Crowther could write *the day before* to arrange a meeting, and as I say I suspect that he very often couldn't. But there's another much more important point, Lewis. You say that Jennifer couldn't contact Sue during the day. *But she could, and she often did.* The two of them met fairly regularly for a snack at lunch-time. They met in a little café next to M and S. I know that, Lewis. I've been there." Morse intoned the last words in a melancholy, mechanical way, and Lewis looked at him curiously. There was something that Morse had said a few minutes ago. It was almost as if . . .

"Jennifer Coleby must have known all about it then, sir."

"I don't know about *all*. She knew enough, though. Too much. I suppose . . ." He lapsed into silence for a few moments, but when he resumed there was more spring and spirit in his voice. "I don't know how it started, but at some stage they must have told each other about themselves. They tell me that women, and men, too, for that matter, enjoy talking to someone else about their conquests; and some chance remark probably brought the two of them together, and a bond of conspiracy was soon forged. I think there can be no doubt about that. I suspect it was Crowther, perhaps after a couple of misunderstandings and disappointments over meetings with Sue, who suggested the idea of dropping some harmless-looking note addressed to Jennifer Coleby into the letter-box of Town and Gown. I'm pretty sure he had the sort of mind that enjoyed the idea of cryptic messages, and the practice grew and this became their normal channel of communication. He would stroll past and put a letter or a postcard through the front door of the office. Simple—not even out of his way. It probably only happened

at first when an unexpected opportunity arose, but as time
went on it became the normal practice, so normal that he
even followed it for his last and crucial message to her. And
quite apart from being a neat and extremely useful device,
it must have seemed a god-send to Crowther not to have to
write any actual letters as such to Sue. Like most people in
such illicit affairs he must have had a dread of a letter going
astray, being opened by the wrong person, or being found
somewhere. No-one could learn very much this way, could
he, even if he did find the letters?"

"When did you first think it was Miss Widdowson, sir?"
Lewis asked his question with an unwonted gentleness, for
at last he had begun to understand.

Morse stared wearily and sadly at the desk in front of him,
the fingers of the left hand drumming nervously on the
surface. "I suppose there were the vaguest hints—oh, I don't
know. But I wasn't certain until last Friday. Perhaps the
first time I began to suspect the truth was when I checked
the evening-class register for Margaret Crowther's attend-
ance record. I happened to notice, purely by accident really,
that by some divine mischance Palmer's wife was a member
of the same class. And it made me wonder; it made me
wonder a lot. I thought it most improbable that Jennifer
Coleby was the sort of person to grant a lot of favours without
getting some in return; and I pondered on the bond that
must exist between her and the other girl. In a roundabout
way I considered the possibility of both girls being in similar
circumstances, in the same sort of relationship with other
people. With men. And so I did a lot of guessing, and I
thought of Crowther with somebody and Jennifer with somebody; and then Palmer fitting in somewhere perhaps? And
then . . . Well, and then I thought of Sue Widdowson, and
suddenly the pieces began to click together. Could Jennifer
be having an affair with Palmer? So often in this sort of
situation it's someone you meet at work; and who was there
at Town and Gown but Palmer? He was the only man on
the premises. I kept wondering what it was that Jennifer
was getting out of the bargain. And it suddenly struck me
that there was one thing that she would want above all. Do
you know what that was, Lewis?"

"I'm afraid I've no experience in that sort of thing, sir."

"Nor have I," said Morse.

"Well, I suppose you'd want a place where you could be alone together . . . Oh, I see. You mean . . ."

"Yes, Lewis. Someone could offer Jennifer a room where she could be alone with Palmer. Mary wasn't out all that much. But whenever she was, the coast was clear, because the other member of the trio could also arrange to be conveniently absent at the same time. And that's what she did."

"Just a minute, sir." Some worry was nagging away at the back of Lewis's mind. He was thinking back to the night of Wednesday, 29 September . . . Then he had it. "But the house would have been free, wouldn't it, on that Wednesday night? I thought you said that Mary had gone to the pictures or something."

"We'll make a detective of you yet, Lewis." Morse got up from his leather chair, clapped his hand on his sergeant's shoulder, and stood watching the threatening clouds roll slowly westward. It had stopped raining now and the shallow puddles in the yard lay undisturbed. "That was another of Jennifer's lies, I'm afraid. Mary was at home that night— she told me so. But even if Mary had been out, I don't think it would have made any difference. I'm pretty sure that Jennifer's job was to drive Sue to meet Crowther. That was her part of the bargain. And on Wednesday, 29 September, they both had their dates—as we know."

"But why didn't they . . ." Lewis appeared reluctant to continue the sentence, and Morse did it for him.

"Why didn't the four of them take the opportunity of using the house whenever Mary was out? Is that what you mean?"

"Yes."

"Well, it was a pretty safe bet for Palmer, of course. He lives a good way off and very few people would be likely to know him in North Oxford. Anyway it was a reasonable risk. In fact I know he's been there. I had the house watched all last week, and on Wednesday night Palmer's car was parked in the next road. McPherson found it—I'd put him on special duty." A slightly pained expression crossed Lewis's face, but Morse ignored it. "He didn't actually see Palmer go in, but he saw him come out, and I saw Palmer myself on Friday night when I had it all out with him."

"But it was too risky for Crowther?"

"What do you think? He lived only a stone's throw from the place. No, it would be the stupidest thing imaginable for him to do. He'd lived there for years. Virtually everyone knew him, and he walked along the same street almost every night when he went for a drink at *The Fletcher's Arms*. People would have started talking immediately. No, no. That was not on from the start."

"So when they both had dates . . ."

"It was Jennifer's job to give Sue a lift, yes."

"So if Jennifer hadn't suddenly found a puncture in her tyre that night, Sylvia might never have been murdered."

"No, she wouldn't." Morse crossed the room and sat down again in his chair. He had almost finished. "On the night of the murder, Sue Widdowson was impatient and probably a bit annoyed with Jennifer. I don't know. Anyway she felt she couldn't wait while Jennifer was ringing up about the puncture, and finally finding some decent old boy across the way who might take ages. She thought she'd be late and so she decided to catch a bus. She walked over to the Woodstock Road and she stood at Fare Stage 5 and . . . well you know the rest. She found someone else waiting. She found Miss Sylvia Kaye."

"If only she'd waited."

Morse nodded. "If only she'd waited, yes. Jennifer got the puncture mended in no more than five or ten minutes, so she says. She'd arranged to meet Palmer at *The Golden Rose* that night. You see she always took Sue to Woodstock and it was convenient for her and Palmer to meet at some pub nearby—Begbroke, Bladon, or Woodstock itself. And they met that night, we know that. In fact, in spite of all her troubles, Jennifer was there before Palmer. She bought herself a lager and lime and went out to sit in the garden to watch out for him coming."

"Funny, isn't it, sir. If Sue Widdowson . . ."

"You're full of 'ifs,' Lewis."

"Life *is* full of 'ifs,' sir."

"Yes, that's true."

"But you were still guessing, weren't you? I mean, you had no solid evidence to go on."

"Perhaps not then. But everything was adding up. Sue and Jennifer were about the same height, same sort of colouring, except . . ."

"Except what, sir?"

"It doesn't matter. Forget it. Dress? I saw the coat that Mrs. Jarman described; I saw the same sort of slacks; and Sue Widdowson was wearing them. On Friday night I showed Mrs. Jarman a photograph of Sue and she recognised her immediately. No wonder the poor woman couldn't pick anybody out at the identity parade. The girl she had seen at the bus-stop just wasn't there."

"People do make mistakes, sir."

"If only they did, Lewis. If only they did!"

"But it's still not *proof*."

"No, I suppose it isn't. But I found something else. When I called at the Radcliffe to see Crowther's body, I got his keys from the ward-sister—they'd been in his trouser pocket. I asked her if anyone from the nursing staff had been along to see him, and she said that no-one had. But she said that Staff Nurse Widdowson had asked her how he was getting along and that she had stood at the top of the ward and looked for a long time at the bed where Crowther lay."

Morse's voice was growing agitated, but he pulled himself together as quickly as he could. Once more he walked over to the window and saw the sun beginning to filter through the thinning cloud. "I went to Lonsdale College and I looked through Crowther's room. I found only one drawer locked up in the whole place, one of the drawers in his table desk—the bottom drawer on the left, if you're interested." He turned round and glared at Lewis, and his voice sounded harsh and fierce. "I opened the drawer, and I found . . . I found a photograph of Sue." His voice had suddenly become very quiet and he turned again to look out of the window. "A copy of the same photograph she gave to me." But he spoke these last words so softly that Lewis was unable to catch them.

Epilogue

It was done.

Lewis drove home for his lunch, hoping that his wife was feeling better. He passed a newspaper placard with bold, large headlines: WOODSTOCK MURDER—WOMAN HELPING POLICE. He didn't stop to buy a copy.

Morse went along once more to the cell block, and spent a few minutes with Sue. "Anything you want?"

There were tears in her eyes as she shook her head, and he stood by her in the cell, awkward and lost. "Inspector?"

"Yes."

"Perhaps you can't believe me, and it doesn't matter anyway. But . . . I loved you."

Morse said nothing. He felt his eyes prickling and he rubbed his left hand across them, and prayed that she would notice nothing. For a while he could not trust himself to speak, and when he did he looked down at his darling girl and said only, "Goodbye, Sue."

He walked outside and locked the door of the cell behind him. He could say no more. He tore himself away and walked along the corridor, and he heard her voice for the last time.

"Inspector?"

He turned. She stood by the bars of the cell, her face streaming with tears of anguish and despair. "Inspector, you never did tell me your Christian name."

It was getting dark when Morse finally left his office. He climbed into his Lancia, drove out of the yard on which the puddles now had almost dried, and turned left into the main stream of the city-bound traffic. As he passed the ring-road roundabout, he saw two people standing on the grass verge thumbing a lift. One was a girl, a pretty girl by the look of her. Perhaps the other was a girl, too. It was difficult to tell. He drove on to his home in Oxford.

ABOUT THE AUTHOR

After leaving Cambridge in 1954, COLIN DEXTER was Classics Master at Loughborough Grammar School before taking up his present position as Assistant Secretary to the Oxford Delegacy of Local Examinations. Mr. Dexter lists his hobbies as "reading poetry, drinking good beer, playing bad bridge and listening to *The Archers*." But his consuming hobby is crossword puzzles and he was for three years the national champion in the Ximenes clue-writing competitions.

He lives in Oxford with his wife and two children.

THE MYSTERIOUS WORLD OF AGATHA CHRISTIE

Acknowledged as the world's most popular mystery writer of all time, Dame Agatha Christie's books have thrilled millions of readers for generations. With her care and attention to characters, the intriguing situations and the breathtaking final deduction, it's no wonder that Agatha Christie is the world's best-selling mystery writer.